Prologue

We had the past; we have the present, but what about the future? There had been a rash of murders occurring throughout the spring and early summer in the state of Maryland.

These murders were not your typical garden-variety type, like most others that usually occurred throughout the state. They were wreaking havoc on a state treasure.

That state's treasure happens to be the Baltimore Orioles baseball club. The people of Baltimore and all the surrounding counties fell deeply in love with their O's from the time of their arrival from St. Louis in 1954, where they'd been known as the St. Louis Browns.

The city and the state embraced them immediately from their humble beginnings. With a home run from the Orioles opening day starting catcher Clint Courtney, the Orioles were off and running with a win over the Chicago White Sox. It was the first major league game played in old Memorial Stadium. Then came the arrival of the human vacuum cleaner that played third base named Brooks Robinson.

The Orioles won their first Word Series with a stunning upset over the heavily favored Los Angeles Dodgers led by Sandy Koufax in 1966. Leading the Orioles was their new arrival and Triple Crown winner Frank Robinson who was backed by Brooks Robinson, Boog Powell, and a very young pitching staff that was anchored by a 19-year-old named Jim Palmer. The O's swept the series and de-throned defending World Series champs and hall of famer Sandy Koufax four games to none.

They continued their winning ways with another World Series appearance in 1969, only to lose to the upstart and underdog New York Mets led by future hall of fame pitcher Tom Seaver four games to one. But the Orioles returned the following year and defeated the high-powered Cincinnati Reds four games to one.

In a three-year span, they won over a hundred games each year. Their excellence continued and the Orioles never finished below second place under a fiery little manager named Earl Weaver. They won another American League pennant in 1979, although they lost to the "We are Family" Pittsburgh Pirates four games to three.

With the retirement of Weaver, the 'Earl of Baltimore', in 1982, things looked as if they would keep rolling along. They won the World Series again in 1983 beating the Phillies four games to one. The Orioles were now led by a new star named Cal Ripken and longtime standout Eddie Murray, both future Hall of Famers.

From 1966 to 1983 the Orioles produced six Hall of Famers: manager Earl Weaver, Brooks Robinson, Frank Robinson, Jim Palmer, Eddie Murray and Cal Ripken. They won three World Championships, five American League Pennants and seven American League East crowns.

The team also enjoyed a ton of individual success- four M.V.P. awards, three Rookies of the year awards, and six CY Young awards. There were many twenty game winners among the pitching staff, including four in one year in 1971; something that many believe will never happen again. It was perhaps the greatest pitching staff of all time. They had enough Gold Glove Award winners to fill the vaults at Fort Knox, totaling 58 in all - eighteen alone by Brooks Robinson. On top of it all, they had a Hall of Fame announcer named Chuck Thompson whose catch phrase was "ain't the beer cold?" It was a great time to be an Orioles fan.

Unfortunately, the wheels started falling off the cart after the '83 season. The Orioles started the '85 season by losing their first twenty-one games, setting an unfortunate major league record. Yes, the Orioles were setting records again, but they were records in futility. About the only good thing to happen during that time was the opening of their new state-of-the-art stadium, Oriole Park at Camden yards in 1992. It became the crown jewel of the Major

Leagues and the bench mark for all future stadiums to this day.

They had a brief run of success in the late 90's led by their former second baseman, a multiple Gold Glove winner, Manager Dave Johnson. But mostly it was failure; failure that had to stop and stop soon. The Orioles upper management was determined to turn it around.

When they first opened the stadium, they had sell outs for years, even though they were losing. Sadly, attendance had fallen off through the years, and fallen off badly, to the point Yankee and Red Sox fans out numbered their own at the yard.

Something had to be done, so ownership made a complete overhaul. They hired all new front office people, including a new General Manager who knew how to build a team from the ground up. Ownership and fans alike felt that the team was finally headed in the right direction; there was a light at the end of the dark tunnel.

But now, the unthinkable was happening; someone was killing some of the best prospects in the organization. In small towns scattered throughout the state, where the Organization had many of their minor league teams, someone was killing the building blocks of the Orioles future.

If the killings did not stop, the organization would start to crumble. Many minor league teams and towns rely on the revenue generated from the games, the Orioles and the city of Baltimore included. The state of Maryland could not stand to lose millions of dollars in tax revenue or their beloved Birds.

I knew the task of solving these murders would fall on me, along with my longtime friend and partner, Roger "Guinea" Ginavan, and a team of some of the most qualified officers assembled from around the state of Maryland. Our task force typically is called upon to handle the toughest cases.

From Aberdeen, to Ocean City, to Fredrick, Maryland and beyond to the neighboring states of Virginia and West Virginia, we'll follow the leads wherever they may take us and for however long it takes us. We will not stop in our quest to end this madness, before the madness cripples the state's economy and destroys our beloved state treasure.

It will become a battle of will and determination to win, to see who will outlast, out think, and outmaneuver the other.

Chapter 1

Born and raised by his grandparents in Front Royal, a small town about fifty miles west of Washington DC., located in the beautiful Shenandoah Valley of picturesque Warren County, Virginia, Mark Newman was a 6'4", 245 lb. piece of granite, a five-tool baseball player in every sense of the word.

In the opinion of many locals, he was the most gifted athlete in the county, or perhaps even in the state. Warren County had already produced two former major leaguers: Darryl Whitmore and Dana Allison, both staying only long enough for a cup of coffee with their big league clubs.

Mark, though, would be different. On a baseball diamond, he would beat you with his arm or his glove, not to mention his speed. But it was his bat that did the real damage; his bat did his talking.

In football, it was the same thing. Mark ran like a deer, darting in and out of defenders arms with cat-like moves, or he just mowed them over like a raging bull.

On the basketball court, what he lacked in skills and ability he made it up with hustle and determination. Whoever said white men couldn't jump, never saw Mark play. He was their go to guy.

Baseball was his true passion though; he ate, drank, and slept it. He was a twice-named baseball player of the year by both the Winchester Star and the Northern Virginia Daily. Both papers predicted he would be a first round pick in the upcoming draft.

Baseball was going to get him out of Front Royal. Mark was certain of it. Fame and fortune awaited. It was all there for the taking. No one or nothing was going to stop him. It was his destiny.

The only two people who thought Mark was wasting his talents were his grandmother and grandfather. His grandparents had become his legal guardians after the terrorist attacks of 9-11 on the pentagon which killed both of his parents.

They both had taught Mark, along with his childhood buddies, at an early age that the areas true sport and passion was hunting! It's a well-known fact that in the Shenandoah Valley and surrounding counties the only things that really matter are hunting and tracking. It's a lifestyle that's been handed down from generation to generation and it's been woven into the fabric of the community

Just about everyone in Warren County is a hunter. Few, if any however, had been trained to hunt and shoot the way Mark had. No one could shoot or track quite as well as he could.

Mark had learned to be as quiet as a church mouse when he moved through the woods. His maw-maw taught him how to blend into his surroundings, to be "stealth," never to be seen or heard. She also taught him how to be skilled with a knife, how to kill up close and personal if need be.

Mark's pa-paw taught him how to shoot; shoot from all kinds of angles and distances, with small caliber hand guns to assault rifles. He would become a marksman with them all, even mastering a compound bow.

His grandparents thought Tracking and Killing was his true talent. He could have been a highly paid tracker out west or perhaps an agent for the A.T.F. or the F.B.I. or an operative for the C.I.A; they could have all been possibilities. Now, four years after graduating from high school, with his baseball career floundering, they were sure of his future.

They had to somehow help their only daughter's son in any way they could, using all the resources they had available to them. By using all the wisdom, the years had given them, at all cost and risk, they would help their boy before it was too late.

Chapter 2

Mark had been assigned to the Orioles minor league extended spring training facility in Florida. He had re-injured his hand by tearing ligaments in his right thumb and index finger, the same injury he had suffered two years before. He expected to hear from Oriole officials any day as to where he would be assigned next.

"I hope to be going to either the class AA Fredrick Keys or AAA Norfolk Tides pa-paw," Mark said into his cell phone, "but they could send me anywhere from Bowie to play with the Bay Sox, or maybe to the Delmarva Shorebirds in Salisbury. In fact, that wouldn't be too bad, you know. It is only 32 miles from Salisbury to Ocean City pa-paw. I could mix a little play with my work."

"When will you know?" His grandfather asked.

"A day or two tops, and if I go to Prince William you and maw-maw can come see me play. It's close to home, right down route 66 in Woodbridge, Virginia. They're called the Cannons. You know you never taught me to shoot one of those," he said laughing in the phone. "But I'll tell you this pa-paw, I'm on the bubble here. If I don't soon figure out what I'm doing wrong, the front office may decide to release me. But I swear I'm going to do whatever it takes pa-paw. I'll do whatever I have to do. I'm not, I repeat, I am not going to let anything or anybody stand in my way. Nobody is taking my dream away, nobody!!!"

"Calm down, just calm down boy. You've never had any self-doubt. Didn't you once tell me that doubt is a death sentence to a ballplayer? You need to relax. Why don't you go out to the local shooting range and unload some stress and think about what you need to do."

"Thanks pa-paw, you're right as usual. "That's what I'll do, I just need to go chill out a while and relax. Do me a favor, give maw-maw a kiss for me and tell her I send my love."

"I will son, and you keep your head up and remember we love you and are very proud of you." Mark's grandfather put down the receiver and turned to his wife. "Honey, Mark sends his love."

"How's he doing?" she asked.

"Not well. We've got to find some way to help that boy out. I'm worried about his state of mind… he's not thinking right."

As Mark hung up the phone, he went to the closet and pulled out his old black Nike batting bag. His mind was racing now. *I know what it takes to win, always did. I've never accepted failure or defeat. I refuse to lose. I've always overcome my shortfalls. I was once a local hero. They called me a man beast. I'm a friggin' stud. The scouts where wrong. I should have been a first round pick, not a fifteenth,* he thought as he grabbed a green military bag and sat down with it. He dumped out various boxes with small caliber guns in them and different types of boxed ammo. He reached in, pulled out a large black case, and sat it on his lap.

Clicking the latches, he slowly opened it up. He proceeded to pull out his graduation present - a Cheytac M 200 sniper rifle along with a 9 mm glock that he got for being drafted. Getting two boxes of shells, he decided that his fate was sealed. *I just have to keep practicing,* he thought, as he loaded the weapons into the black Nike bag. *Just keep practicing,* he thought as he zipped the black bag back up.

Grabbing the keys to his Chevy Tahoe off his coffee table, Mark's mind continued to race to the point of paranoia. It only got worse as he closed and locked the front door behind him.

Looking around as he headed toward his truck only added to his anxiety. Mark lived in one of the least desirable areas of Front Royal, affectionately known as "The Village." It was an area with some good people, but a fair share of problems. Like so many other towns across America, there were drugs, drunks, and crime that lower income communities unfortunately must deal with.

It was all Mark could afford on his paltry minor league salary. Walking toward his pride and joy, he couldn't help but to crack a small smile as he approached his big black beautiful Chevy Tahoe, with all its chrome and big Mickey Thompson tires. The truck always put a smile on his face. It was all he had to show for the fifty thousand dollars signing bonus he received four years ago.

It was time to put up or shut up, he thought as he drove his truck out of town toward the old drive-in on Strasburg Road. Mark had gotten permission to shoot there years ago. The owner of the old property on route 55 was a friend of his grandparents. As his mind kept racing, he thought, *I might as well practice both of my skill sets. After I'm done at the old abandoned drive in, I'll head up to Stephen City, take some swings in the batting cages, and hone both of my skills. I may need them soon if I am going to succeed.*

Chapter 3

The following day Mark got the call from the General Manager of the Aberdeen Iron Birds, located in northern Maryland between Baltimore and Philadelphia. In fact, it's almost dead center in between both cities.

This was one place he didn't expect to be. He knew he had a bad spring and a pretty lousy year before that. But to start at what was essentially the beginning again was a major setback. And to start in a short season league? The outlook was not good.

It was now gut check time. Mark was in the final year of a four-year contract that gave him the 50k signing bonus and a monthly salary that started at $1600.00, with a $500.00 a month raise every year. He had figured he would be in the major leagues in two years, making the league minimum of $263,000.00 a month until he signed a long-term mega deal. Mark had been happy to make the deal, but he knew now that it was a huge mistake.

He had driven all the way home from the Sarasota Florida site of the Orioles spring training facility. It had taken him three days and $185.00 in gas, not to mention a ton of 99-cent double cheeseburgers. Aberdeen was a two-hour walk in the park compared to that.

As much as he hated to admit it, self-doubt was creeping into his mind. *I was here two years ago; could I still be that bad?* Mark knew the club had its doubts about him, or he wouldn't be here in the first place. *I just have to get my head right. When a ballplayer has self-doubts, he's done,* he thought.

Mark knew what his problem was, hell everyone knew. *I do so much right, why can't I make the adjustments? I've had great hitting coaches in my three years working to help me fix this, and I never had this or any other problems in high school.*

Upon arriving at Cal Ripken Sr. stadium, he parked his black Tahoe in the player's parking lot and took a deep breath. He turned off the truck and made his way out, closing and locking the door behind him. Mark proceeded toward the stadium and spotted Billy Ripken, a former major leaguer and the younger brother of Hall of Famer Cal Ripken Jr.

Billy shouted "Mark, Mark Newman?"

"Yea Billy, it's me"

"Hey pal, you know you've got some serious competition at first base this year. The kid they brought in is a real beast. I hope you've gotten that hole in your swing fixed."

"I'm still working on it." Mark mumbled as he looked down to the ground and kept walking his voice trailing off.

Everyone knows major league prospects don't have holes in their swings. You might not be able to hit a curve ball or a back-door slider or may even have lousy plate coverage, but you can make adjustments and learn. A hole in your swing means you're not getting the bat head through the hitting zone fast enough, which meant slow hands, and you can't teach bat speed. God gives you that ability, either you have it or you don't, period.

Mark new he hadn't lost his bat speed. He was still young, not even close to reaching his full potential. *You don't lose bat speed at my age, you just don't. Maybe it would happen in your mid to late thirties. But not now - it has to be something else. I'll figure this out. I have no other choice. I just need some time to fix this, I just need a little more time. I have to figure out a way to buy some time, just a little more time...*

The Orioles' front office would surely be running out of patience with him, and he knew that. Maybe it was time to use his other skill sets to accomplish his goals. *Mark needed to solve his problems, and he had to make sure the Orioles' brass wanted him, needed him, and had to keep him around.* Mark knew he had no choice. He had to master his skill sets to succeed.

Chapter 4

... Accident

Man, I should be getting promoted pretty soon, Albert Griffin thought as he headed out of the player's tunnel after an impressive day at the plate. Albert went three for four with two homers and a double, and five runs batted in. Going over his future in his mind, he was thinking, *not bad for a kid who wasn't even drafted. I'm so glad I went to that tryout with the guys last year or I'd probably still be flipping burgers at Mickey D's. Sometimes it's better to be lucky than good.*

Albert was a kid who was in the right place at the right time. A high school dropout, he was persuaded by a couple of his friends to go to a local try out the Orioles were holding at Friendly High School in Fort Washington, Maryland. He had played baseball all his life and excelled at it. But as good as he was at baseball, that's how bad he was in the classroom. It's not like he wasn't smart, he just had no interest in school. After his tryout, the Orioles immediately signed him to the minor league minimum and made him study and get his G.E.D. His life was going in the right direction.

"Good game, Albert," a fan shouted as Albert walked across the stadium parking lot feeling all full of himself after he led the Aberdeen Iron Birds to a seven to two win.

"Thanks, man. I appreciate it," Albert responded.

"You keep that up, you won't be here long," the fan continued.

"That's the plan man, that's the plan," Albert said, smiling broadly.

Albert continued his walk across the lot toward the grounds where all the fields were located. The Ripkens had modeled all the ball fields after famous major league stadiums. The replicas used by various baseball youth groups, camps, and the clinics the Ripkens and their staff put on. Albert couldn't help but admire the various ball parks that he hoped one day to be playing in. Passing the replica of Camden yards, he saw some boys hanging out the windows of the warehouse replica that housed the boys and waved.

Albert noticed a truck that seemed to be following him. He figured it must be someone wanting an autograph. As he turned to look again, he realized the truck was picking up some speed. *That's odd,* he thought as the truck came at him faster.

Just then, the truck went screaming by at a very high rate of speed. It was going so fast, in fact, that it nearly scared the shit out of him.

"Watch where the hell you're going, you stupid son of a bitch," Albert yelled in anger. The truck made the next left, squealing its tires as it went out of sight. He took mental note of the make and model of the black truck, thinking he'd give the driver a piece of his mind if he ever saw him hanging around again. *That asshole nearly hit me, and here I thought it was a good idea to walk home after the games and get my head right. I never expected mental decompression to be so life threatening.* A small smile crept across his face as he continued walking.

Heading toward his apartment, Albert started thinking to himself again. The type of year he was having, plus the fact that the organization had just brought in another power hitting first baseman, must mean that he was about to get promoted to a higher class soon. Just then, he thought he caught sight of something out of the corner of his eye. He looked again and it was gone. *Man, it must be the light; they say your eyes play tricks on you at dusk; but that sure as hell looked like that black truck,* he thought.

As he crossed the street, he looked over to his apartment complex. Many of the ballplayers lived there or in the same neighborhood. It was cheap and clean, and on their salaries, that made it the perfect place to live.

Stepping off the curb, Albert was thinking that if he just kept his head clear and stayed focused he'd be moving up. He was in the zone. The game was 80% mental and he was firing on all cylinders. His dream now seemed attainable, and soon he'd be moving to a new town and better digs.

Just then, the black truck appeared out of nowhere and it was barreling down on him. Albert thought, *what's this guy doing, he's going to hit me.* He didn't have time to react, because within seconds, the truck was upon him. The bright lights of the truck froze him. He then felt a burst of pain and then felt nothing as the truck veered sharply away. The last thought he had was, *Is this it? Was it all over?*

For Albert, his life and his dream had ended in a white flash. A youthful dream was gone in just a fraction of a heartbeat.

Chapter 5

Good afternoon ladies and gentleman and welcome to another broadcast coming to you from Oriole Park at Camden Yards, in beautiful Baltimore Maryland, came the voice of the announcer.

As the pre-game broadcast blared out of my truck's radio, I thought the announcer was right. It was a great day for a ballgame with my sons.

Highs in the mid-eighties, with a slight breeze blowing out to the short porch in left field. If we're lucky maybe one of the boys will be able to catch a ball.

Driving down Washington Boulevard toward the ballpark with my two sons, Josh and Shane, we passed Cross Street in a section of the city known as Pig Town where I had once worked for my parents as a teenager bar tending at their place called the "Office Bar."

I have fond memories of that place, so named to throw the wives off when their husbands would call them after work. The best line used was, "Honey, I'll be late getting home, I'm still at the office." That way the husbands weren't lying, technically speaking. They were at the Office, just not the office the wives thought.

"Dad, why do you call this part of town Pig Town?" Shane asked.

"Well, a long time ago, the farmers use to lead the pigs through the streets here, on the way to the slaughter houses."

"By the way it looks; the pigs may still be running through the streets," my oldest son, Josh said as we sat at the red light at the corner of Scott Street and Washington Boulevard.

"It was never the best of neighborhoods in the city to begin with, but it really has gone downhill since the drug dealers and users took over the streets. Do you see all those white steps on those row homes over there? They're all white marble. When I was working down here in the seventies and eighties, women would come out and scrub those steps every morning to keep them gleaming white. Guys, they did it for generations, all through the city. In fact, back then there was a thing called civic pride! Some families even had the screens on their screen doors painted with beautiful scenes. People cared about the looks of their homes and their neighborhoods back then."

"I guess with the end of civic pride, it was also the end of the Orioles winning tradition?" Josh asked.

"You know Josh, I never gave it much thought, but thinking about it, it did seem to coincide with the Orioles losing."

21

"Dad, when was the last time the Orioles won a World Series?" Shane asked as he was staring out the window at the trash blowing about in the street.

Josh spoke up before I had a chance to answer. "1983, Shane. Rick Dempsey was the World Series M.V.P. and Cal Ripken narrowly beat out his teammate Eddie Murray for the league M.V.P."

"Who was Rick Dempsey?" asked the inquisitive Shane with a look of puzzlement on his face.

"He was their funny catcher," Josh responded, and then continued, "He used to entertain the crowd whenever there was rain delay. He'd go out on the field and pretend to be Babe Ruth, swinging an imaginary bat at imaginary balls. It was great." Shane's facial expression did not change but I just smiled, remembering the rain delay antics of the playful catcher.

As we made the left onto Emory Street to avoid paying for parking, the boys saw the sign for the Babe Ruth Museum. A very rare silence fell over the F-250 Ford King Cab as we passed the shrine of the first god of baseball.

After finding a place to park midway between the Railroad Round House Museum and the Babe's, I thought that maybe I should take the boys there one day. They seemed to think the old trains were amusing.

After admiring the big locomotives, we continued the discussion of our beloved O's as we started walking towards the ball park. "Guys, when I was growing up we were always in the middle of a pennant race. It seemed that it was a birth right if you were an O's fan. We won the series in 1966 and never finished lower then second from 1968 to 1983. The O's even had a brief run of success in 1996 and 1997. Unfortunately, Josh, you were too young to remember, and Shane, you weren't even born yet. You guys have yet to experience the thrill of a pennant race."

"You think they'll ever be contenders again? I'm already fifteen. How much longer will I have to wait?" Josh asked.

"Well, they've got some great kids in the system, plus you'll be eligible for the draft in five years. So yeah, I figure five years tops. That's really not that far away guys". Josh smiled broadly with the answer.

No sooner had we reached Martin Luther King Boulevard and made the right, we could see both Oriole Park and M&T Bank Stadium, home of the Baltimore Ravens, along the beautiful Baltimore skyline.

Shane asked, "Dad, can we get some Oriole Eskay hot dogs with ketchup, mustard and onions please?"

"I was hoping to get some of Boog's Barbecue, little man; I had my mind set on a big roast beef sandwich with horseradish and mayonnaise. What about you Josh?"

"I vote for Boog's, too," chimed in Josh. "We all know he was your favorite growing up. Maybe you can get an autograph, Dad."

"That's not fair," Shane complained.

"How about we get them both," I said reluctantly.

"Dad we're going to need some nachos with cheese, something to drink, and what about some souvenirs, and programs? And who knows what other kind of cool stuff we're going to need to have?" Shane sermonized.

As we continued walking toward the stadium, we could see all the vendors lined up on both sides of the street leading up to the ballpark. Josh looked at his wide-eyed brother and then said with a sly smile, "Dad, I hope you brought your plastic. This could really become an expensive day."

Chapter 6

Mark had an appointment at Royal Auto Body on Luray Avenue in Front Royal. He had to get some body work done on the right front fender of his 2003 black Chevy Tahoe.

His cherished the big, black beauty. He knew he had to pay a huge deductible, but his truck was his pride and joy. It was also all he had to show for his less than stellar four-year career.

As he stepped out of his truck, his grandparent's neighbor and old high school acquaintance approached Mark. For some reason he couldn't place his name. Then Mark noticed the knife hanging off his belt.

Buck, that's his name. No, that's his nickname; damn I should remember his real name. Jesus, he lives beside maw-maw and pa-paw, hell he even went hunting with all of us. As Buck reached out his hand to Mark's, all Mark could think was, *what's his name?*

"Hey, Mark, I never expected to see you around here again. Thought you'd be a rich superstar and have left Front Royal in your rear view mirror by now."

"Well things don't always go as planned," he answered, while thinking to himself, *what do you know asshole? It's a hell of a career choice you got here, you toothless bastard.* Instead of voicing those comments, he simply asked, "How long is the estimate going to take?"

"It should only take a half hour, forty-five minutes to check out all the damage, and then all I have to do is write it up," Buck said, thinking, *you arrogant bastard, you think you're a big shot superstar stud but you will never amount to squat; If I thought I could get away with it I'd charge you double.*

"Well I'm going to head over to the Knotty Pine and grab some breakfast. I'll be back when I'm finished, Buck." As Mark stepped off the sidewalk onto Luray Avenue, he noticed Bing Crosby Stadium and the little league fields in the background. *This is where it all began; one of the few pleasures of this town was playing ball, Skyline Drive, hunting and the Knotty Pine, where you can always get a home cooked breakfast morning, noon, and night* Mark thought, smelling the aroma of bacon frying as he crossed the street.

The Knotty Pine is a typical restaurant you will find in any small town throughout the country, with its 1950 style counter and stools, and its pine-varnished walls, complete with stained wooden booths. The Knotty Pine still has the old-style record player selectors at the booths. Here a woman or a man can come in for breakfast with a newspaper and cigarette in hand, and enjoy it with a never-ending cup of brew.

26

In the back room, there is a bar and lounge, which features a dartboard and a shuffleboard table. The Knotty Pine is, without a doubt, a true American classic.

But that's how Front Royal is, it has it good and bad parts, just like every other town in America. It just seems that if you're under forty, the minute you cross the bridges entering town, you enter a time warp. The only thing missing is bobby socks, poodle skirts, leather jackets, greased back hair, John Travolta and Olivia Newton-John.

I really need to get out of this town, I need to get my swing right, I need to get my head right, I need to stop obsessing about this damn town. All this shit is going to drive me fucking nuts...

Chapter 7

As Mark opened the door, the bell above it announced his arrival. All heads turned toward him. A mixture of different smells immediately assaulted Mark. The bacon he had smelled when crossing the street was now accented with the smell of fresh brewed coffee and the stench of cigarettes. *I wonder when they will move into the twenty first century and go non-smoking?* he thought as he walked through the door.

Mark exchanged pleasantries with those who either knew or recognized him, a smile here, a handshake there, but he couldn't help but read some of their minds which he figured all said the same thing. *There's the ballplayer, the ballplayer that failed not only himself but all of us. The ballplayer that let himself, and our community down.*

As he passed an older, balding man smoking a non-filtered cigarette, Mark saw an empty stool at the end of the counter and sat down. He turned and looked again at the dining area, noticing a lot of familiar faces of days gone by. In Front Royal, it seems everybody knows everyone else and everyone's business. *Small town America at its best and worst,* he mumbled to himself.

Out of the corner of his eye he caught a glimpse of someone he definitely did not mind seeing. Radiating out of the kitchen was Julie, Julie Wines.

Julie and Mark were friends, confidants, and part time lovers. At one time, were brief high school sweethearts. She was without a doubt a friend with benefits for Mark. As of late though, Mark had been thinking more and more about her. She was one of his few bright spots lately.

"Hey stranger, what brings Mister Baseball to this fine establishment today?"

"I had to get some work done on my truck. So I thought I'd come in and get some breakfast and look at your fine ass, how about you Jules?"

"You know Mark, same old shit, different day. Not much ever changes around here, including your smart remarks. So what's wrong with your truck?"

"Somebody hit it in the parking lot at Ripken Stadium in Aberdeen. I came out and it had a huge dent in the front fender."

"Sure, I believe that Mark."

"Seriously that's what happened, Jules."

"So, you came all the way back here just to get your truck fixed?"

"No, the Organization canceled the games this weekend and gave us off because of a death on the team."

"Who was it, did you know him?" Julie asked.

"Not well, I just met him a few days ago, In fact, I was either his back up or the skipper would put me in as the designated hitter."

"So now you'll get more playing time?"

"Yeah, I suppose so Jules."

"Well good for you then," she added, "do you want some coffee to go with that lucky horse shoe you seem to have?"

"Very funny, Jules. You have a sick sense of humor. But, on second thought, I will have some scrapple and eggs on toast with extra mustard. Could I also get a side of fried potatoes with onions with a large milk and orange juice please?"

"Will there be anything else?"

"Yeah Jules, there is - you and me tonight?" Mark asked with a sheepish grin on his face.

Julie responded and said, "Like I said earlier, same old shit different day. Mark asks girl out, girl gets giddy and says yes. Some things never change, do they?"

While eating, Mark decided to do some things a little different. Instead of just taking her back to his house he thought, *Maybe I should take Julie out to a nice dinner at the new T.G.I. Fridays that just opened outside of town and then to a movie. Then hopefully, we'll end up back at my house, in bed with any luck.*

But as he watched Julie walking away from the counter, Mark found himself really looking at her. It was almost as if he was looking through her. *She is stunning, isn't she,* he thought; long, beautiful, wavy blond hair, the perfect butt, well rounded and tight, small waist and large ample breasts. Above all else, he found himself thinking she was genuine, sincere and really a joy to be with. He also realized those big beautiful blue eyes always seem to suck him right in.

The more he thought about her, the more intrigued he became. They had been seeing each other on and off ever since high school, and never once had she hinted about a more meaningful commitment. But, she was always willing to be there when he called.

As far as Mark knew, and by what his few friends who remained here had told him, Julie had never been seen with other guys, and no one had ever heard of her dating.

She had, on numerous occasions, said to Mark that she wouldn't care if he pumped gas at Bo's Belly Barn or made millions playing ball, she would always love him unconditionally. He felt himself now starting to hope so.

Mark had never given her any hope, or reason to think that they would ever have a serious relationship. But she never once tried to put any kind of boundaries on him or what they had going on.

It was at that moment sitting there in the Knotty Pine sipping his coffee and waiting for his scrambled egg sandwich that Mark realized what he had. A person like Julie who would give him such unconditional love, so much respect, honesty, integrity, passion, commitment, and total support, deserved nothing but the same from him. A blind man could see it - why hadn't he?

At that moment in time, he realized what only a cherished few ever do. Not all the fame and wealth in the world, all the security that money can buy, can buy the security of true love. A love that can carry you through the best and worst of times, a love that says it's us against the world, a love that can and will conquer all, and won't be conquered.

That is when Mark decided Julie would always be first, whatever else happened was icing on the cake. He would love her as she had always loved him, unconditionally.

Chapter 8

As the truck started, the radio came to life with the post-game broadcast. The boys and I settled in for the ride home to Edgewater, a small town located south of the state capitol of Annapolis, and, of course, we talked baseball.

The discussion on the post-game radio broadcast, and in the F-250, centered on the big Indians' rookie left-hander, and Cumberland, Maryland native, Aaron Laffey. The Allegheny high alumni came in and shut the Orioles down pitching two no hit innings, including five strikeouts, to preserve the Indians 5-3 win.

"Well, dad, what did you think?" Josh asked.

"Well the food was good, the beer was cold, and the souvenirs were expensive."

Josh sighed and said, "Come on dad."

"Seriously? I thought the kid was lights out. He had excellent movement on his fastball, nice slider, he located his pitches well, plus he mixed it up. I think striking out five batters out of six says it all."

"He definitely got inside their heads! Striking out Roberts, Jones, and then Markakis was impressive," Shane said. "Heck, for all we know he may be just a 'flash in the pan,' as dad would say, but I doubt it. He really had us off balance; chasing bad pitches, keeping the ball down, and throwing some serious heat. The big dude can really pitch."

This kind of talk made me smile; both boys were right on point and it made me proud that my sons, at twelve and fifteen, understood the 'ins and outs' of the game, the game within the game. This attention to detail would one day serve them well in the real world.

As we were exiting the Harbor Tunnel, the local radio affiliate broke in with a special news bulletin. *"Please excuse this interruption of the Oriole post game broadcast, but 105.7 the fan has just learned that the Orioles free agent signee, 18-year-old Albert Griffin, of Chesapeake, Virginia, was found dead of an apparent hit and run near his apartment in Aberdeen, Maryland. Again, 18 year old, free agent signee Albert Griffin has been found dead of an apparent hit and run not far from his residence. No further details available at this time. We will continue to follow this story as it develops and will bring you further details as they become available to us. We will now return you to your regular broadcast."*

As the broadcast went back to the post game show, it was as if the game had never been played. All the talk now was centered on the death of Albert Griffin, and rightfully so.

The hairs on the back of my neck stood straight up. 'Hit-and-run' just didn't sound right to me. If it was determined to be a homicide, I knew this was the type of case that would be thrown right into my lap. This case was right in my team's wheelhouse. We handle high profile cases and you really couldn't get much more high profile than this, especially considering it involved the Baltimore Orioles organization. I knew my time with the boys would once again become tight; the juggling act would again begin. Always a part of the job, this had become more challenging since their mother had died in the 9/11 attacks.

I love my job. I've always felt I made a difference, but the time with my boys is priceless and everyday lost is irreplaceable. They both are at the age where they need guidance and are very impressionable. In my job, I have seen it a million times. From ten to eighteen, young men and woman are vulnerable and need strong support systems. They need role models and somehow, I had to be there for my boys.

I couldn't and wouldn't let them become statistics. I do love my job, but I have always preached family first to my boys, and I am determined to practice what I preach. After all, when it's all said and done, all you really have, all you can really count on, is the love and support of family. Sure, some family members can be self-serving and self-centered. Call me old fashioned, but I believe in the love and commitment of family.

I had no idea where this case was going to take me or even if it would hit my desk, but I knew the boys would end up on the short end if it did. Driving home, I told the boys this case could end up on my desk.

They responded as they always have, by saying lines that they must have practiced and patented through the years.

"Dad we know what you do and that you do it for us, to make the world a safer place."

Another favorite of theirs was, "Dad we know you work hard to put a roof over our heads, food on the table, and to buy us nice things." If nothing else, I knew the boys could have a bright future in politics always telling me what they thought I wanted to hear, *just singing to the choir.*

As I turned on to route 50, for the last leg home, I looked to my right and Josh had just fallen asleep. I checked my rear view mirror and there were no signs of Shane. He was undoubtedly stretched out across the back seat asleep.

Cracking the window to feel the cool night breeze, I gazed out to the road ahead. Soon I started to wonder what windy road this case would lead me and my team down.

Chapter 9

... *Execution*

Taking out the big first baseman in Aberdeen had been a walk in the park. The idea was to make it look as if it was an accident, which, as it turned out, was very easy to do.

All that I had needed to do really was scout around for a couple days, get to know my target, find the perfect kill zone, then execute the plan. I had been taught to do exactly that a zillion times in the woods back home. To me, it was still just hunting. The only difference was the weapon of choice.

Unexpectedly the schedule had suddenly been moved up. So, I had less time to stalk my prey. Time was no longer on my side and things had suddenly changed. I had to act, and act now with a sense of purpose. I had to make a statement, not only for myself, but also for my love.

I knew the Keys had a three-game series in Frederick, Maryland, about an hour and twenty-minute drive from Front Royal, if I went the same way I did when I was on my way back home from Aberdeen. I go through Berryville, Virginia, via 522, meandering between route 7 and I-270 all the way to Frederick.

I found this to be very important when I stopped to scout the area on my way back home. I had to get up there before dusk and set up my shot, so the route had to be flawless. The place I found was almost perfect. I knew I'd be exposed to people for a brief period, but it was the perfect place for the kill shot. Plus, I doubted anyone would notice or pay attention to me.

I would have the advantage of a fast exit from the kill nest. I also would have altitude for the shot, which was critical because of the distance of the shot. Plus, it had a natural sound barrier to help conceal the sound of the shot.

I already had Bobby's schedule. The Fredrick Keys played at two pm on Sunday, and I knew the game would last two and a half to three hours. I also knew Bobby liked to go out after the games and try his luck at finding female companionship. He'd head right back home to change and get ready to go out. The timing will be perfect. I'll be sitting in my nest waiting for Bobby to arrive at his townhouse, knowing full well he will be leaving in a body bag.

I arrived in Frederick at six thirty and was surprised to hear the game was still on the local radio station. The game had gone into extra innings, so I decided to ride around until it was over.

The game went fourteen innings. By the time, I had pulled up to the killing nest that I had picked out, it was already 8 pm. Bobby should have been arriving at his townhouse at about the same time. There was an hour, tops, until it got dark. The sun was already beginning to set. It was going to be tight. Nerves were beginning to become an issue. I didn't like the fact that I would be rushed and fighting against the clock, and I didn't like the idea of leaving my truck exposed for any length of time. But, that couldn't be helped. It was extremely important that I could get out of there in a hurry.

As I climbed the 18-foot grassy embankment, for some reason I started to think about the Kennedy assassination that I heard and read about so many times. I was on the verge of my very own Kennedy shot.

I reached the top of the embankment and sat my black bag down, checking my watch. It now read 8:15 pm. I unzipped the bag and pulled out my binoculars, immediately looking toward Bobby's townhouse, focusing in on his windows. The light was on, but I didn't see Bobby. I knew he was home, so it was a go. I pulled out my Cheytac-408 sniper rifle and attached the scope to it. I mashed down the four-foot-high grass to form the nest.

Once again, I checked my watch. It was now 8:27 pm. Again, I looked down at my truck as numerous cars and other trucks sped by. A few thoughts ran through my mind. *About a million people will see my truck and about half that many saw me climb this hill. Hopefully, they'll think that I'm climbing the hill to steal some apples from the orchard behind me. It will only take me five minutes to get down to my truck and be gone.*

But most of all, this shot will be life-changing, not only for me, but also for Julie and others. Yes, it will end one life, but it's a necessary loss. Call it a casualty of war, if you will. He and many others standing in my way and I am at war, a war of survival.

It was all running through my head so fast. I could feel myself starting to obsess. I had to steady myself, clear my head, and focus.

I went back to work and set up the tripod and attached the Cheytac to it, then leveled it out. I checked the bubble on the tripod to make sure it was level and true, and then I peered through the scope and looked at the killing zone.

Getting my binoculars, I checked the wind direction. It was near perfect, two miles an hour and at my back. That negated the humidity, which would have created a slight down force on the shot.

The range was simple; as I put down my binoculars and again picked up the rifle and dialed in, I peered through the scope. It was a near perfect killing scenario. The temperature will soon be changing as the sun goes down. If it dropped 5 degrees then I'd have to recalculate. *I need to take the shot and take the shot now. The longer I wait, the greater chance of something going wrong. It has to be one shot, one kill.*

I had done this dozens of times in the woods when the deer would come out of their bedding at dusk to feed or frolic. But this was a bigger trophy, the biggest ever, in fact. It would be a 'shot heard around the world', or at least all over Maryland and the surrounding area.

Finally, I was ready. As I put the scope up to my eye, I could hear the tractor-trailers screaming down I-70, heading toward Baltimore, below me. With that kind of noise, I knew the shot would not be heard. I could feel a small smile forming on my face as I started to block out all outside distractions

Focus now; zero in. I looked through the scope, peering at the window of my prey some 2200 yards away. While I was waiting for Bobby to appear, I quickly checked my watch again. It was now 8:39 pm. Light was beginning to become a major factor; I only had seven to ten minutes of daylight left.

Show yourself my friend, just show yourself for a couple seconds. That's all I need. You will become famous, and I will be a step closer to accomplishing my goals. Just show yourself to me my friend.

Stay relaxed and focus. Take a deep breath and exhale slowly, lower your heart rate, and breathe. That's it, nice and easy, exhale, lower your heart rate, breathe,

41

that's it. Where are you my friend? Oh, there you are, in the bedroom window. Just breathe slowly. That's it my friend, keep moving toward your right. That's it, keep moving into the living room.

Good man, stand right there and keep staring at yourself on the TV. Just keep admiring yourself, you self-centered prick. You'll be the last thing you see. Breathe slow breath. I have you now, at the base of the brain. One shot, one kill. Exhale slowly and squeeze. Right then, the birds nesting nearby sprang into flight.

I peered through the scope until I saw the back of Bobby's head explode against the wall. He was dead before he hit the floor. I quickly, but methodically, removed my scope and disassembled the rifle, along with the tripod, and quickly put it in my bag. I peered at the apartment complex and thought to myself, *scratch one playboy ballplayer.*

After zipping up my bag, I put my sunglasses on and turned the bill of my Oriole's cap around to shield my face as best I could from the traffic below.

Running with a purpose, I descended the hill with my bag in one hand and my keys in the other. I made my way to the black beauty, hitting the door locks, and climbing in while I put the black bag in the back, covering it with a blanket. I started the truck, hitting the shoulder, and was gone. Glancing again at my watch, it read 9:03 pm. Nightfall had arrived.

Chapter 10

Every Oriole fan was in mourning. Bobby Brannon was to be the corner-stone of the future. The whole state of Maryland and parts of Virginia were abuzz about his death, an apparent homicide, as both Washington papers and the Baltimore Sun were now reporting.

The Orioles drafted Bobby #1 overall in the first round out of Indian River High School in Chesapeake, Virginia. The area in recent times had become a hotbed of first and second round picks which included current Major League stars David Wright (Mets), B.J. Upton (Rays), his brother Justin (Diamondbacks), Brandon Inge (Tigers), and a little to the northwest, Justin Verlander (Tigers), among others.

The Orioles obviously thought he was the real deal, when they inked him to a 13 million dollar signing bonus. The largest ever for a draft pick. Several sources in the Oriole front office thought so highly of Bobby that they compared him to the second coming of either Eddie Murray or Mickey Mantle.

First base had been a major weakness for the Birds ever since the sad departure of Rafael Palmeiro, due to the steroid allegations many years ago.

If the comparisons to Eddie or the Mick had panned out, it would have been a gold strike for the Birds. Brannon had it all, per Baseball America. The kid could hit for average and power, from both sides of the plate. He had great speed, and cannon for an arm. Baseball America projected him to be a 40/40 man, 40 home runs to go along with 40 steals a year. Couple that with projected batting averages of 300 or better to go along with more than 100 R.B.I. They were some lofty expectations for such a young man, but the O's thought so highly of him it justified the 13 million dollars signing bonus in their minds.

Now it was all gone in an instant. This apparent murder was going to cripple the Orioles for years to come. The Baltimore Sun was reporting there was a major insurance policy in place to recoup the money, but it had yet to be confirmed.

Insurance or not, this was going to hurt the team on the field and at the gate. This was going to have a domino effect on the whole organization. It was apparent the team and the fans could not catch a break. You just couldn't replace a player with such a high ceiling. They only come along once every few decades, if you're lucky. And the Birds and their fans apparently weren't lucky.

Just three days ago, Albert Griffin, another first base prospect playing for the Iron Birds in Aberdeen, had been killed in an apparent accidental hit-and-run after walking home from his ballgame.

Bobby's death, though, would be felt immediately. Attendance would drop where he would have played; fans had been coming out in droves to catch a glimpse of the young phenomenon. This would mean that much needed revenue would be lost for the team, the farm system, and the local towns that supported them. Those local economies counted on fans showing up and spending their hard-earned dollars in local restaurants and shops.

But most importantly, it would hurt the morale in the organization and in the state itself. There would be no more light at the end of the tunnel; it seemed the Orioles were destined for continued failure.

Chapter 11

We read the stories in all the local papers, while the boys and I ate our usual Sunday breakfast of two eggs over easy with bacon and toast and locally made apple butter. We sat enjoying the view on our back deck overlooking the South River.

Like most single parents, money was always an issue and I was mindful of finances. I tried to eliminate unneeded expenses whenever possible. I was trying to lessen the need of my neighbor and part time baby sitter Juanita, so it was time the boys learned to fend for themselves. I had been trying to teach both boys how to cook. Josh was at the age where he could begin to take on more responsibility, like watching his brother and doing things around the house.

"Guys, we've got some work to do on this cooking thing. These eggs aren't exactly what I would call over easy."

"Yeah, but the bacon is perfect," Shane said, while taking another bite and scanning the sport section of The Capital.

I looked at the boys and wondered if my late wife, Shannon, would have approved of the way I was raising them. It was easy for me to envision her cooking breakfast for 'her men,' as she liked to say. How she had loved cooking and taking care of us. The years since we lost her in the 9/11 tragedy at the pentagon had been difficult. Memories of Shannon were always right there, waiting to intervene at all times.

"Hey boys, let's get this mess cleaned up. I have to stop by the office. Me and your uncle Guinea have the lead on this Bobby Brannon thing."

"You mean, 'your uncle Guinea and I'," Shane said, obviously happy to correct my grammar.

"Whatever Mr. English major. Let's just get it together. I don't want to get stuck at the office all day," I said, grinning at my smart little comeback.

"Dad, can you drop Shane and I off at the seafood festival? It's this weekend, and we've never missed it."

"Now, you know I would never forget that. How could I? It's plastered up on every billboard in town. Besides, your mother and I went every year since before both of you were born. I would never break that family tradition. Why do you think I want you guys to hustle up and get this mess cleaned up? I want to get to the office and get down to the docks as soon as possible. Shane, take the breadcrumbs down to the pier for the seagulls and change that shirt. You've had it on for two days. I'm jumping in the shower. Josh, call your uncle Guinea. Tell him to meet us at the State House in 45 minutes, and

48

remind him to bring some cash, because afterward we're going to the festival."

"Bring on some good old fashion Maryland seafood; I'm getting a boatload of shrimp, raw oysters, a bucket of steamers, and of course a crab cake," Shane hollered from the pier below.

Josh looked at me with that look again and said, "Dad, don't forget your wallet."

Chapter 12

As the boys and I were heading out of Edgewater on Route 2 toward Annapolis, I started to reflect on how the boys were growing up.

Both were turning into handsome, bright young man. Both had sandy blond hair and blue eyes, from my side of the family I thought. Both were very athletic, and that came from both Shannon and me. We had been athletes at Towson State. Shannon played volleyball for the Tigers, while I played baseball.

Shane had my mischievous and quick-witted side. Josh was blessed with common sense and a strong passion to succeed, which he definitely got from his mother. Both had a short fuse, courtesy of me, and an Irish temper that they got from both their mother and me.

I found myself thinking, *Honey, I hope you're not missing any of this. You did well. We did well. I know you must be as proud of them as I am.* Then, looking at Shane, I had to wonder where he got his fashion sense. That was one of the world's mysteries.

Just then, a beautiful blond who looked to be about 35 passed us on the Route 2 Bridge in a black 325 I convertible that all three of us immediately noticed. I looked in the rear-view mirror and saw my reflection thinking, *I'm not that bad at 45. I'm still in decent shape, 6 ft. tall, buck 85. I still have blond hair with a touch of gray around the temples, but it is thinning. Like the boys often have said, I still have it going on for an old man.*

As I caught up to the BMW for another peek at the blond, she must had sensed us looking because she turned her head and gave us a warm, inviting smile.

"Dad, look! No wedding band."

"I didn't notice," I said.

"And you call yourself a detective," Shane said sarcastically.

Soon afterwards, we began to enter Annapolis. I got on my cell phone to call my partner, Roger 'Guinea' Ginavan. He was also my best friend and brother-in-law. He, too, had attended Towson. I had met him in a behavioral science class where we became fast friends. He's the one who had introduced me to Shannon, his sister.

Guinea and I had a lot in common. We both came from Irish heritage, and like most Irish men, we loved a good cold beer, sports, and competition. Back then, besides woman, that was all we figured we needed. Well, throw in a pizza and some red meat. And we weren't too sure we really needed the woman, except for sex. Not real bright, looking back on it. But at the time we thought we were ten feet tall and full of piss and vinegar.

Guinea is a large man in a small man's body. At 5' 9", 255 pounds, he's not in the best of shape, but is still as strong as an ox. He could and would start and finish a barroom brawl and enjoy it with a shit-eating grin on his face. I think that is what made Guinea such a good cop; he just doesn't give a rat's ass about his own safety. Problem is, being his partner, my safety is also always in jeopardy.

Guinea also enjoys playing the role of the bad cop, and he plays it to perfection. His heart, on the other hand, is that of a big teddy bear. The guy has a soft spot for anyone in need of help, loves animals and has a strong affection for old ladies and children. But there is a special place in his heart for his nephews and the boys adore him.

"Hey Guinea, where are you?"

"I'm pulling into the State Building right now, Mike."

"Okay, wait there. I'm at the city dock dropping of the boys. This place is bumping, but I'll be there in a couple minutes."

"You leaving the boys down there by themselves Mike?"

"Yeah, I've got to cut the apron strings sometime. Josh is fifteen; he's getting his license next year. In addition, he's got more common sense then most grown men I know. Besides Guinea, he has a cell phone."

"I don't know Mike."

"I trust them Guinea. They are bright boys."

Josh, while eavesdropping on the conversation, was grinning from ear to ear. I turned and said "Josh, do me a favor and make sure your phone is on, and don't get separated from your brother".

"Dad, we're going to need some money," Shane said.

"How much," I asked, knowing the minute I said it that it was definitely the wrong response.

Their replies were, "How much you got?"

I should have known better, but I did my best to back pedal. "I think twenty bucks a piece should hold you until your Uncle Guinea and I get back."

"Dad, you better hurry back because I'll have that spent before you put the truck in gear," Shane said sarcastically.

"Shane, have you forgotten? Dad sometimes suffers from short-term memory loss. He still thinks you can buy a burger and fries with a soda for five dollars," Josh countered as both boys shoved the twenties in their pockets. Continuing, Josh said, "Dad, we'll wait for you before we eat any seafood," knowing that appetizers and finger foods would cost them more than twenty a piece.

53

"I figured you guys would, because I'm so much fun to be around," and we all laughed.

As the boys headed to the festival, they both turned to wave good-bye. My little guys weren't so little anymore; they were both becoming young men.

Chapter 13

I met Guinea at the State Building. We both had been assigned there four years ago by the States Attorney General's office to work on a permanent task force that handles high profile cases.

The H.P.C.D. was designed to work in unison and pull resources from every police department in the state putting all of the resources it had under one umbrella. This was all in an effort to solve crimes the A. G's office deemed high profile or detrimental to the state and well-being of its citizens.

Michael Samuel 'Smitty' Smith had been a twenty-year veteran with the Baltimore City Police Department. He was now the M.R.R., our departments' media relations representative. Our unit was unique in that it was set up in a round table format. Unfortunately, I was the appointed the liaison to deal with the politicians and their requests or demands. More often than not it turned out to be the latter.

As luck, or lack thereof, would have it, Smitty was on vacation with his family in Mexico. That thought hit me head-on as I pulled into the state building and saw all the news vans with their satellite dishes flying sky high. *Great, guess whose responsibility this circus just became?*

"Hey Mike, this isn't going to take, long is it? I really don't feel like spending my whole day off here with all those good eats just seven blocks away."

"No bro, the Attorney General called and wanted a little meet-and-greet to go over some of the high points of the case. You know how this works. The big dogs call in us pups to go over the ground rules. Then they tell us how they want this to look in the press and publics' eye. Which reminds me, did you see all the press in the lot, Guinea?"

"Yeah I feel for you."

Attorney General Dewayne Wilson was waiting for us in the lobby as we entered the state building. He is a man of large stature - 6'6", 340 pounds. Wilson is a former pitcher at James Madison University where, in fact, we played against each other in the C.A.A (Colonial Athletic Association). He looks like he could still be playing today.

"Hey guys, thanks for coming by on your days off," Dewayne said as we came through the door.

"Dewayne every time I see you I can't help but think of that C.C. Sabathia guy for the Yankees," I said.

"Yeah, the only difference between us is he throws 95 mph heat and can control it. That and he has a lot more zeros at the end of his paycheck." We laughed.

"Well Dee, I haven't seen you for a while. Congratulations on making it to the big leagues, first African American States Attorney and all that."

"In Maryland, Mike, in Maryland," responded Dewayne.

"Still not too bad for an ex-jock," Guinea said, while embarrassing his buddy with a big bear hug. "I guess this means you'll be too busy to go fishing now."

"Your days just got a whole lot busier too my old friend and I'll tell you why," was Dewayne's reply.

Dewayne proceeded to lay it all out for us as we sat down on some old wooden benches in the lobby of the state building.

"Look guys, the Lieutenant Governor and State Controller both are bent out of shape about this. Hell, everybody in the State Building is getting in on this. I think this just might be the straw that breaks the camel's back."

"What do you mean," I asked.

"There's been some grumbling for years now that the O's might be on the market. That all quieted down when they signed this Brannon kid. Especially with all the fanfare of him being the corner stone and all that, but now," .... Dewayne's voice trailed off.

We looked at Dewayne in disbelief. "I never heard anything about them being for sale", Guinea said.

"You won't, either. The radio talk shows and our lovely friends in the press have been lobbying long and hard for ownership to sell. We haven't had a winner here since '97, and then Cal retired. Attendance started falling...." Dewayne's voice trailed off again.

"Yeah, but," Guinea started to say before he was cut off by Dewayne.

"Look, guys, ownership made some really bad decision for years and they have taken a lot of heat for it. Finally, they do something right and hire a new G.M., and draft this Brannon kid. They start to get some other young talent. Things start to look up and it buys ownership a little bit of time, gets the press off their backs, and most of all, gives the fans some hope," Dewayne said. "Then some asshole kills the cornerstone of the dream. Now ownership is back to square one. Sure, they'll be given a grace period, but the wolves will come back again and be calling for ownerships' heads. You guys remember the Colts leaving town? What we remember in State politics is how the press backed the Colts and us into a corner, knowing the city and the state didn't have the money to finance a new stadium. They always reported on Irsay's drinking, always saying he didn't know what he was doing, and trashing him personally. They made him into a mockery. But when you want a piece of ass from a girl do you call her a whore, even if she is one? Hell no - you keep your mouth shut and get laid." Dewayne was on a roll now and there was no stopping him. "The press and the fans seem to think the city or the state control these teams. Well, they don't. Rich, powerful men with even bigger egos than their wallets do. These men who have walked over many people to get what they have. But even these men have feelings and pride, and when these people get bitten, they bite back. By no means am I giving Irsay a pass. He was pure asshole and the press was right. He didn't have a clue. My Uncle Carl could have run the team better. Still, you don't put it in the man's face 24/7."

"Yeah, but Irsay wanted out, he was shopping around. I remember."

"Mike, he was shopping around and using the threat of moving as leverage. At least that's what Mayor Shaffer and the powers that be in Annapolis thought. Then Indy comes in with a sweetheart deal. He flies out there; the fans treat him as if he's the best thing that's come along since sliced bread. The press out there hangs on his every word like he's the second coming. He returns here, the local press meets him at the airport, notices that he's been partying, and both papers call him a drunk. A week later, our Colts where gone. Irsay follows the cash cow to Indy." Dewayne explained.

Guinea looked at me and shrugged. "I'd have moved the team, too," he said.

Then I countered, "I remember how the press ran Eddie Murray out of town. They dogged him, saying he never played hard, that he didn't hustle, and all he did was play his way into the Hall of Fame. So much for the press knowing what they're talking about."

"Well, politicians remember history well, and the powers that be don't want to repeat it. They're not going to be so naive this time around. They will be very proactive in doing whatever it takes to keep the O's here," Dewayne said before continuing. "This is a 100-million-dollar cash cow in tax revenue guys, the Orioles and all their minor-league affiliates throughout the state. Think about that, not to mention the civic pride throughout the state. Politicians like their jobs.

"What about someone local buying the team?" Guinea asked.

"How many people do you know that have 700 million, pal? Plus, the whole idea is to keep ownership in place so the economic damage is kept to a minimum."

"So how does solving this keep the O's from being sold?" Guinea asked Dewayne.

"Well, the O's have insurance on all of their ballplayers, so they'll get the signing bonus back. And with any luck, the league may even give them some extra picks in the draft. We know it's a reach, but the league may feel compelled to do something under the circumstances. That, in turn, will spark interest in all the towns with Orioles affiliates. As bad as it sounds, it will put more fans in the seats. That fifteen-million-dollar investment that just seemed lost now has the potential of turning into a forty five million dollar windfall. How do you spell free agents fellas?"

"So, to answer your question, Guinea, empathy and hope will put fans in the seats for now. And when the murder is solved, insurance will pay off, giving ownership much needed funds and more time to put a better product on the field," I said.

Guinea looked at me and as I stared back he said what we both where thinking. "Mike, we've got a lot of suspects who could profit from this. Everyone associated with the O's, including ownership, has motive; jealous players, coaches, front office people on all levels, even rival organizations could possibly be involved.

"Fellas, one more thing - everyone involved with this case has to keep a tight lid on it. The press could create nightmares for us and the future of baseball in Maryland. So, to keep the wolves at bay and barking at the door, I'll be handling all the press releases out of my office till Smitty gets back. I can't stress enough how negative press could affect the Orioles and everyone involved. You both know how shit runs." Dewayne needed to say no more. Guinea and I were both well versed in the downhill slope.

Chapter 14

Monday had started uncommonly rough; it wasn't the traffic or the impending workload, though. The hangover from all the beers at the festival and the ones that followed later at the house with Guinea was what hurt.

After the festival, Guinea followed us home. We both proceeded to drink more beers than we knew we should, while burning the midnight oil discussing the new case. And now, at least, I was paying for it, but hoping I wasn't alone. You know the old saying misery loves company? Well, I didn't want to be alone. Minutes later I got my answer. In strolled Guinea, sporting sunglasses and looking like hell.

On the way to Frederick, the home of the Orioles minor league affiliate the Keys and the sight of the Brannon murder, we rode in total silence all along I-95 and up I-70. Guinea read up on Brannon's back ground, something I had done earlier in the morning while downing umpteen cups of coffee.

Bobby's parents had done an outstanding job in raising their children. Besides Bobby, they had two older daughters, both enrolled in Virginia Tech in Blacksburg, VA. Bobby himself had a 4.0 G.P.A his senior year in high school. He had received over forty nine scholarship offers from all over the country. He had worked as hard on his education as he did on the ball field. It's a trait I have tried to instill in my boys. "As hard as you work between those white lines, you have to work twice as hard in the classroom to achieve your goals. It's called a backup plan," I've often told them. I found myself admiring Bobby's parents for instilling the importance of education in such a gifted athlete.

As we pulled into the parking lot of Brannon's apartment, you'd have thought the circus was in town. We came upon all the local news outlets as well as C.N.N and E.S.P.N. I couldn't help but think of what Dewayne had said to us at the State House.

As I lifted up the yellow crime scene tape, I noticed the manicured lawns and the professional landscaping with its wide variety of mountain laurels, rhododendrons and pink, white and red azaleas. Then, as I looked to my left in the parking lot, I saw a B.M.W., a Lexus, a Cadillac, and a brand-new Toyota Four Runner. These were all high dollar vehicles, and I thought, *this is where the rich and famous of Frederick must live.*

Guinea and I made our way through the horde of uniformed police, entered the apartment building, and headed up to the crime scene. Detective Fred Hunt met us there. Freddie was a thirteen-year veteran of the Frederick County Police Department. I had worked with him on a joint task force to bust a drug ring several years ago. I found Freddie to be very thorough and detail oriented, an

63

all-around good guy both professionally and in private. Freddie stands about six foot two and two hundred pounds and always looks to be in good shape. Without a doubt, he is one of the nicest guys you'll ever want to meet.

Freddie is a 'cop's cop.' He knows his job, the people in his district and the lay of the land. He would definitely be an asset to the investigation. As soon as Freddie saw us he extended his hand and greeted us with a broad smile.

"I knew the big wigs in Annapolis would be sending the cavalry. I just didn't know the cavalry kept banker's hours," Freddie said with a grin.

"Traffic was bad," was my immediate response, though honestly I was still feeling the effects of the previous night.

"Judging by the looks of Guinea, I'd say more than the traffic was bad," Freddie said, laughing.

"Very funny Fred, very funny,' Guinea said. "So, what do you have for us funny man?"

"Guys, it's pretty cut and dry. Follow me in here and I'll show you how we think it all went down," Freddie replied

We followed Freddie from the foyer into the living room. Guinea and I both noticed splatters of blood throughout the room as Freddie led us toward the window.

"The bullet came through here," Freddie said as he pointed toward the upper left of the large window. "Had to have been a very high powered rifle; I'm guessing some type of fifty Cal, we'll know more when ballistics comes back. Anyway, it strikes our boy here," he said, pointing to his left ear. "It blows the back of his head completely off and sprays it across the room," Freddie explained as he walked across the room, following the bullets path and then the path of the impact. Standing beside a dried pool of blood that must have been at least a 6x6 square Freddie continued, "The kid drops right here. If you look carefully, you'll see brain matter here, there, and over on the lamp shade there, some thirteen feet away from the point of impact," Freddie said.

"We get the picture," Guinea interrupted the grim detailed report, as he stared at the pool of blood at his feet. "What else you got Fred?"

"Just that I figure he came into the living room to channel surf or turn up the TV. He had a towel wrapped around his waist and the remote was laying less than a foot from his hand, over there," he said, pointing a few inches from the coffee table.

As the three of us walked toward the door Freddie asked, "Have you guys noticed the furnishings in here? It's some high dollar stuff - crushed leather sofa and chairs, Ethan Allen coffee and end tables. Not bad for a minor leaguer."

65

"Freddie, this was not your average minor leaguer, he was the next great one, the savior of the franchise. That's why they sent us up here. I was told that he was a state asset!"

"Damn, Mike, I knew when they told me you guys were coming something big was up."

"Read the papers, pal. They'll fill you in," Guinea deadpanned as we reached the hallway.

"Fred, have you found the spot where the shooter took the shot?" I asked.

"Yeah, we have, and you both may find it very interesting."

As we got outside, I noticed immediately that the parking lot was still full of reporters milling around. I also noticed that it was at least two hundred twenty to two hundred and fifty yards from the highway. Beyond that was a hay field about twice that size that ended at I-70, which we couldn't see. It seemed to be at least thirteen to fifteen feet below the field, judging from the noise of the tractor-trailer we could hear, but not see.

Guinea and I stepped off the sidewalk and started across the parking lot toward the field, trying to avoid the large group of reporters.

Fred then hollered, "Where are you guys going?"

"To the field, to see where the shot was fired"

"Mike, the shooter didn't take the shot from there."

Guinea and I looked at each other with bewilderment, and Guinea said, "You've got to be kidding me."

Meanwhile, the press was shouting questions at us as the uniforms tried to keep them at bay. I figured I'd play it close to the vest again, remembering what Dewayne had said, and hollered as we continued walking, "We have no comment at this time. When we get something, we'll be sure to let you know. We thank you for your patience." At the same time, Fred opened the door to his crown Vic, and Guinea and I hurried in.

As Fred drove us to the shot sight, he explained to us how C.S.I. figured the kill shot.

"The crime scene guys thought the kill shot came from someplace high, due to the hole in the glass, the trajectory, the downward angle into the skull and the blood splatter. So, with all that in mind, they looked for high ground from out the window and they spotted a high embankment on the east bound side of I-70."

While Fred was explaining the thought process of the crime scene crew, we took the ramp onto I-70 going west. We drove about an eighth of a mile and made the left into a service road in the median, then made a left again, heading back east. Fred drove about six hundred yards and pulled over on the shoulder behind three patrol cars parked on the shoulder of I-70.

As we parked, Fred finished explaining how the shot went down.

"The guys found a partial tire print about five yards ahead. They figure the shooter gets out of his truck and climbs up the embankment, finds a place on top of it in the high grass backed by the apple orchard, setting him up perfectly in a killing nest. He just waits, and then takes the fatal shot."

Looking at the embankment, I noticed how steep it actually was.

"Fred, about what time did he take the shot?" I asked.

"It was around dusk, somewhere between eight and nine pm. Again, we'll know more when the autopsy and ballistics are done. The coroner said she'll be done today."

"How do they know it was a truck?" Guinea asked.

"The tire print is some type of balloon tire that is only used on four-wheel drive trucks."

As we climbed the hill, I noticed Guinea was having a hard time getting up it. I also couldn't help but notice all the traffic on the interstate behind him. I thought to myself,

68

this guy must have some big balls; no fear of all the onlookers going by. He also must be in good shape to hump a high-powered rifle up here, no doubt in some sort of bag to conceal it. There must have been a hundred people who saw him, or at least his truck. But he climbs up here without a care in the world, sets up, takes his shot, and climbs back down. Real big balls.

We finally got to the top of the hill to the shooters nest and I only had four questions.

"Fred, how do they know he waited here for a while?"

"The grasses were still mashed down pretty well when they got up here, probably twelve hours after the kill. Plus, they found a few cloth fibers."

"How long do you think this shot is?" I asked as I looked out toward the apartment building that appeared to be no larger than my thumbnail from this distance.

"About 2200 yards, the crime scene boys figure," was Freddie's reply. I gave a puzzled look to Guinea, and he read my expression.

"That's a mile and a quarter, Mike. That is one hell of a shot," Guinea said, still trying to catch his breath from the climb.

"Did we retrieve any shell casings?" I asked.

"No, the shooter policed the area," Freddie replied.

"Last question - do you think we're dealing with a pro?"

Guinea was quick to respond, "Without a doubt. The distance of the shot, total disregard of all the possible witnesses and cleaning of the area makes him a smart individual. Not to mention that this appears to be a one shot kill.

"I'm assuming we're dealing with someone with a military back ground, ex sniper or mercenary," I replied.

"Not so fast, Mike. I thought the same thing until I saw the tire tracks. There is another possibility." Fred stopped and just looked at us.

"Well, spit it out pal," Guinea demanded.

"As I said earlier, the tire track is that of a big balloon tire, which is very popular around here and further west around Virginia and West Virginia. Most of the people who own that type of truck, outdoor enthusiasts. They're avid hunters, guys."

"You mean to tell me you think a hunter could have taken that shot Freddie?" Guinea asked.

"Guys, I know this area and the people in it. I've lived here all my life. I'm telling you, hunting is like a religion. Kids learn to shoot before some of them hit first grade. If you go further west into Virginia and West Virginia, it's definitely a way of life. It's how you're raised."

"C'mon, you really believe that Freddie?" pressed Guinea.

"Well, If we run up on this guy and you don't believe my theory, I hope your willing to bet your life on him missing you just because he's a hunter," Freddie countered with conviction.

Chapter 15

Mark had been back in Aberdeen for a week and since his return he had been hitting the cover off the ball. He went fifteen for twenty, with three home runs, four doubles and nine runs batted in. But he had also struck out five times, all on high and tight fastballs. The time in Front Royal had done him some good. Mark got some personal problems solved and his head was clear. He still had that mysterious hole in his swing, but at least the pitchers here weren't good enough to hit that spot on a regular basis. It still worried him a little though because he used to hit that pitch all the time.

Things were getting better; the skipper had taken him out of the designated hitters spot and put him back at first base since Albert's accident. There were still some issues rattling around in Mark's brain that he was stressing about on occasion, but as long as he kept in the hitting zone, it was easier to block it out.

There was one thing he couldn't block out though, and that was Jules. Mark had found himself thinking a lot about her lately. He'd known her since their freshman year in high school.

They'd been going out since their junior year. Well, not exactly going out - more like whenever Mark got horny they'd get together. He'd been hitting it off and on since eleventh grade. She'd always just been something to do. Mark always found that he enjoyed Julie's company. Hell, she even seemed to enjoy herself, too, and liked his sense of humor.

He had to admit that the last couple of days he'd spent with her were a blast. They had fun the whole time, just hanging out and doing simple things, like walking down Main Street, going into all the antique shops and eateries. Then Sunday night at her house, she fixed homemade meatloaf with mashed potatoes, green beans with bacon that was to die for, and a banging salad with homemade blue cheese dressing. Mark had had no idea Jules was such a good cook.

Maybe it was the time spent with her or the homemade meals that got my blood flowing. Maybe that's what made my hitting come around. Whatever it was I don't want to change it. Maybe I should invite her down to watch me play and to take care of me.

Then again, it could be this place, Mark thought as he pulled into the complex. It's a great atmosphere - all baseball, all the time. Home of the Oriole's first family, the Ripkens. You look around and all you see are baseball diamonds, replicas of some of the most hallowed stadiums in all of baseball. Kids of all ages playing, getting taught by some of the best instructors in the business. Little kids dreaming the same dream that Mark, and millions more just like him, dreams every day. The dream to make it to the show, to make it to the major leagues.

Yeah, a lot was going good for Mark right now. *I'm just hoping I can continue to ride it out.* He walked through the players entrance and saw the Iron Bird's G.M., Mr. Dennis Cook, at the 'players only' entrance to the locker rooms. His experience told Mark that, nine times out of ten, this was not a good sign for the player that he was waiting for.

"Mark, you got a minute? I'd like to talk to you." Dennis Cook is a short man in stature, but if you played for the Iron Birds he was like a god. Mark's heart stopped beating and raced to his throat.

"Mark, I got a call from the front office in Baltimore. It seems they want to make some changes in the organization. Mark, I'm afraid we're going to have to let you..." *he paused, that can't be good. Oh God this is it, they're letting me go. I'm gonna be sick,* "You're going to the shorebirds in Salisbury."

"What?" Mark blurted out.

"You've been promoted to the Delmarva Shorebirds in Salisbury, Maryland Mark".

Mark was in shock. In the span of a few seconds, he had roller-coastered from thinking his life was finally headed in the right direction, to thinking his career was over, to a feeling of relief that he wasn't being released. In fact, he was being promoted to a class Low A. Well, not exactly a promotion but at least another rung up the ladder that he'd been sliding down for most of his career.

"Mark, they want you to report immediately. All of us here wish you the best of luck. Now, go home, get packed and get the hell out of here. You've got a ballgame to play in eight hours. Before you go, I've got one piece of advice for you."

"What's that Mr. Cook?"

"When you get down there, you look at some tape. Look at lots of tape of when you're on, hitting the shit out of the ball. But spend even more time looking at tape of when you miss. You have to fix that hole in your swing. The pitchers you'll be facing in the higher leagues will exploit that. They'll make adjustments and they'll find that hole every time."

"I will sir, I will. Thank you, Mr. Cook, thank you very much."

"Good luck, Mark."

They shook hands and Mark made an immediate about face and ran to his truck thinking how great this was, going to Delmarva to play for the Shore Birds, and only twenty-eight miles from Ocean City.

As he climbed into his truck, he only had three thoughts; maybe everything he'd done was finally starting to pay off, he had to keep doing whatever he had to do, at all costs, to move up, and he had to call Jules to invite her to come down to Ocean City and spend some time with him.

Chapter 16

Standing at the wooden rail and looking out at the waves hitting the jetty was mesmerizing. Add in the smells of the salt water and fish, combined with the sweet aroma of caramel popcorn, boardwalk fries and vinegar, Mark was in Heaven. As he stood there at the Ocean City inlet, he started reflecting on how his fortunes had turned around in the nine short days since the Albert accident.

Here I am, standing on the boardwalk waiting for a girl who two weeks ago I never would have given a second thought unless I was back home and horny. Now I'm standing here as nervous as a kid waiting for the first day of school. All I think about when I'm not playing ball is Jules.

Mark kept telling himself that he should be thinking about his swing. He should be studying film. He should only be focusing on baseball, but whenever he tried, his mind would wonder back to Jules. He was starting to think he was losing his mind.

"Mark, Mark is that you?"

He turned around to see Jules. Julie looked so beautiful. She was wearing a white summer dress with spaghetti straps and had on a bonnet, the kind you see the ladies wear at the Kentucky derby or the Preakness.

Around her waist, she had on a thick leather belt pulled tight to show off her figure. She also had on a pair of lite tan sandals with three-inch solid cork heels.

"Damn, you look stunning," Mark said as they approached each other.

"You look pretty spiffy yourself. The beach seems to agree with you."

As Mark put his arms around her and drew her tightly up against himself, the feel of her body and the smell of her hair were very arousing. This girl had put something on him that Ajax couldn't wipe off, and he liked it!

"Where did you park?

"Right over there. I got lucky. I guess everybody likes to get as close to the beach as possible. I got a spot between Boog's Barbecue and the lifeguard building."

"Well, you want anything to eat sweetheart?"

"No, it's too late for breakfast and way too early for lunch," she said as they started heading for her car.

As she got out her keys and started to unlock the door, Mark grabbed her outstretched arm and wheeled her toward him. Then he moved forward and wedged her body between himself and the car door. Mark pressed his weight against her as he put his arms around her thin, firm waist.

He started kissing her passionately. As their tongues entangled he held her tightly, feeling her heart beat against his chest.

After a long and passionate embrace, Jules said, "Wow, big boy, what was that about?"

"I don't know, I guess I'm just really glad to see you. I've missed you and thought about you so much."

"Well, it's about time. Don't you just love when a plan comes together, even if the plan has taken me six years to finally hear you say something like that?"

"Well, Jules, you know what they say. Good things are always worth waiting for.

She just shook her head and proceeded to get in the car. As they left the inlet parking lot and made the right onto Baltimore Street, Jules said she wanted to go to the hotel room and freshen up from the long five-hour drive. Mark said that was fine as he looked out the passenger window at the amusement rides at Trimpers.

"My room is at the Clarion hotel on hundred and first. A couple of the guys on the team also have rooms there. They gave us some great weekly rates because we're on the pet floors. They one of the few places here that allows pets. So we put up with a few barks for a great place to stay. Besides, you only live once so you might as well try to live it in style. Jules, I should be at the ballpark in Salisbury no later than 3 o'clock. Our game starts at 7:05. What the guys usually do is get up early and hang out at the beach until noon. Then we take a power nap, get up and grab a bite to eat and leave for the ball yard at 2:30. The only drawback is that the skipper forbids us to swim before games. He's afraid it will wear us out. It still leaves us plenty of time to do whatever else we want."

"Mark, there's something that's been bothering me. Do you know Buck?"

"The dude that works at the body shop?"

"Yeah, that's him," she paused.

"What about him, Jules?"

"Well, he seems to have some sort of hard on for you. He comes over to the restaurant all the time and asks me about you. He asks if I'm seeing you, wants to know if I have been in touch with you. He bugs me nonstop about you. He's been doing it since way before you came back this last time."

"So, what?"

"It just creeps me out. He's really weird. He used to ask me out all the time, even as far back as high school. I always shot him down because I had a thing for you."

"Had?"

"Well, have. He just scares me Mark."

"Don't worry about that overweight, out of shape, country bumpkin. He's harmless. Besides, he has no idea what I'm capable of doing. If you want, when I get back home I'll have a long talk with him."

After finding a parking place in the hotel lot, they entered the lobby, got on the elevator and headed to the sixth floor. Mark opened the door to the room and followed Jules in. He couldn't help but notice her silhouette as the sun shone through the sliding glass doors leading to the balcony.

God, she has a banging body, he thought as she reached the large dresser and looked at herself in the mirror. Mark dropped her bags and walked behind her as she untied the silk ribbon that held up her hair. She gently shook her head and her long, beautiful, blond hair fell to her shoulders.

Mark reached for her hair with his left hand and gently brushed it off her right shoulder, all the while lowering his mouth to just below her right earlobe. He began to gently kiss and lick her neck while his left hand reached around her waist to pull her closer to him. Jules arched her back and pressed her firm rear into his groin as she released a small moan. He took both of his hands and reached around the front of her to caress her ample breasts. She started to grind her ass harder into his groin. Mark slowly turned her toward him and ever so gently started to lower the spaghetti straps of her dress to her shoulders. As he did, Jules gently pushed them back until they fell onto the bed.

They fell to the bed in a passionate embrace, and Julie paused long enough to ask about his roommate. Mark assured her he wouldn't be around the whole weekend, having paid him off earlier in the morning. They continued to kiss and caress each other and explore each other's bodies in ways he'd never known or experienced before.

As he was drifting off to sleep, Mark knew that he would never see or think of Jules the same way again. He knew their relationship was evolving, moving into unchartered waters.

Chapter 17

Back at the office in the state building, Guinea and I were no further along in the Brannon investigation then we were nine days ago. We had gotten the ballistics back from the C.S.I. guys, plus we got the make and size of the tire from the print, but not much else.

As we entered the conference room, complete with our own version of the round table, I surveyed the people assembled in the room. I was glad to see that Smitty had made it back from vacation. To his left was Attorney General Dewayne Wilson. To my surprise, Lieutenant Governor Robert Brandt was also in attendance, "Mike I'd like to introduce you to Lieutenant Governor Robert Brandt", Dewayne said then continued, "Robert this is Detective Mike Carrier and his partner Roger Ginavan, he's already met everyone else here Mike." After exchanging pleasantries, I continued to look around the table; they were followed by Detective Molly Swift from our office and Detective Freddie Hunt, who I had asked to join us. I was glad to see him in here, too.

As Guinea and I took our seats. I addressed the assembled team.

"I want to thank you all for coming in today. Lieutenant Governor, I'm surprised your here, but you certainly welcome."

The Lieutenant Governor stood up and said, "I hope I'm not intruding, but I want to make sure I'm kept abreast of what's going on in this murder investigation. As I am sure your all well aware, this investigation and its outcome are very important to a lot of people in this building, including the Governor. Not to mention the people of this state. I can't stress how important it is to find the person responsible for carrying out this hideous crime."

Spoken like a true politician I thought as he sat back down. What he meant to say was, *you guys need to find this killer to save our asses before the election.* Like most politicians, they think of their careers before they think of the people they're supposed to be representing.

Like a good soldier, I kept my thoughts to myself and proceeded on with the meeting. "Gentlemen I'm going to defer to Molly to bring us up to speed on where we are at this point. Molly."

Molly took the floor. She was the glue that held all the parts together in our office. She collected the data that we gathered, sorting the bullshit from facts, checking and rechecking leads, and organizing it all. Needless to say, we'd be lost without her.

"Well, gentleman, we really don't have much. C.S.I. came back with the ballistics, and, as Freddie had suspected, the weapon of choice was a Cheytac M-200. There two versions of that model: the civilian, and the military, with minor differences in both weapons. Last year the manufacturer sold over six million worldwide. Per Freddie's request, I collected the data to see how many were sold in the tri-state area. There were over fourteen thousand sold legally."

She paused, and then looked around the table before continuing.

"The tire print they found is a size thirty-eight Mickey Thompson made by Goodyear. On average, one in every eighty-three trucks in the tri-state area has some type of similar tire. We are in the process of cross-referencing the data to see if we can narrow it down to who owns both. But in all honesty, it will take a while. We also have a time of death. The coroner figures the victim died at 8:45, right around dusk. Nightfall that evening was at 8:53. She paused again, then, shaking her head slowly she said, "A lousy eight minutes and the kid may still be alive."

"Do you have anything else Molly?"

"No, that's about it Mike."

"Well, Molly, you've done your usual outstanding job." I looked across the table at Fred and asked, "Do you have anything to add?"

"I've got a bunch of people claiming to have seen a truck on the shoulder of I-70 the evening of the murder. Almost all of them are conflicted on the make and model.

Of course, no one got a tag number. But they all said it was black with big tires. More than half of them said it was a truck, while others thought it was an SUV."

"How in the hell can a guy pull over on a major highway going into a major city without people seeing him, or at least, get a halfway decent description of his fucking truck?" Dewayne blurted out.

"Hey, pal, how much attention do you pay to someone pulled over on the side of a highway unless it has a skirt on?" Guinea asked, somewhat agitated.

I continued, "Fred, I want you and any men your department can spare to go back to Brannon's town house and go door-to-door again. Have them ask about anything unusual that anyone may have seen in the days or weeks leading up to the murder. Ask if they saw any vehicles in the area that they normally don't see. We need something to work with. Somebody at that complex had to see something. Hopefully, your guys can canvas the area again and find us something.

"Michael, we need time. Do what you do with the press and keep them at bay. Tell them we are looking for any information on a black truck that was on the shoulder at the times Molly gave us. Maybe more people will come forward with some info. We need all the help we can get."

Chapter 18

... *Recon*

This weekend had been much more than I ever expected. I knew my feelings for Julie ran very deep, but now things were much clearer. I also had a better understanding of Julie's feelings as well. I had always known there were others vying for her attention so I decided to do what had to be done.

I was now much more focused on the task at hand. I entered the lobby of the Clarion Hotel thinking, *in order to get all I want out of life I have to succeed, if not only for myself, but now also for the love of my life, Julie.*

I'll have a whole day to do recon. If there was one thing I know, it was that ballplayers are creatures of habit. They'll get into a routine and do the same thing for years or until they go into a slump, only then will they change their routine. Ballplayers are very superstitious. Their motto is, "If it ain't broke, don't fix it."

I surveyed the lobby. There were between ten to twenty people milling around. Past the lobby desk, which featured paintings done by Randy Newman, was a great painting of Cal Ripken throwing out a base runner. Across from the lobby, a little to the left, was a wide staircase. Across from that were two elevators.

I overheard a couple talking about getting a drink and a bite to eat at Lenny's Bar and Grill, so I decided to follow them. They ascended the staircase that only went up one floor. Once they got to the top, they made a right, passing a snack shop and jewelry store. They kept going until they made another right that led to the pool.

Right before I entered the double doors out to the pool, I looked to my left and saw the entrance to Breakers Pub. I glanced inside as I passed and saw that there were only two people in there, and neither was the one I was looking for. I continued through the doors and looked to my left, seeing a poolside bar. Beyond that, again to the left, was a set of doors that led to a large deck which, in turn, led to the beach.

As I passed the bar, I couldn't help but noticed a drop-dead gorgeous girl with long red hair who was working behind it. The bar was packed, no doubt because of the well-built red head, but I still did not see my target. I continued walking, and as I hit the outside deck, I went to the railing to look down at the beach.

Directly below me and to the left was Lenny's Bar. It was packed, but from my vantage point, I could see everyone. Mostly what I saw were bikini-clad women. I figured I can spot my prey from the poolside bar where I knew he would pass on the way back to his hotel room.

I found a seat at the bar. Here I had a great vantage point of the bottom of the steps leading up from the beach. It was perfect. I looked away from the steps into the greenest eyes I had ever seen.

"Hi, my name is Kelly. I'll be your server today. Would you like to see a menu?"

"No thanks, green eyes. What do you have on draft?"

"We have Icehouse, Amstel Light, Bud, and Bud Light."

"I'll have a Bud, please."

"Twelve or twenty-two ounces, sir?"

Looking at my watch, I saw it was only 11 o'clock. "Make it twenty-two, green eyes."

As Kelly grabbed a frosty stein from the cooler, I couldn't help but admire the view. At about 5'8", she had legs that went on forever and the bright orange bikini barely held in her ample breasts, while a light tan wrap complemented her shapely waist. On a scale of one to ten, she was a solid nine. But by no means was she in Julie's class.

Julie was a natural beauty, while this girl Kelly obviously had to work at it. She could become a distraction while I was here, and I had to focus on the task at hand.

Around 1 pm, I saw my mark starting up the steps, accompanied by a female companion. I hurriedly put a twenty and a five on the bar and told green eyes I'd see her later and headed toward the lobby. I milled around for a few seconds until I saw my target going toward the elevators.

I followed right behind the couple. As the elevator doors opened, an older couple got out. The target and his companion entered the elevator, followed by a mother and her little boy. The little boy nudged forward and pressed the number seven. Timmy, the intended mark, asked the little boy to press five. The young child looked at me and asked if I was going to get off at five also. Just then I caught a break when I saw the key card in Timmy's hand it read 509 so I wouldn't have to follow him immediately. I told the little boy to press thirteen, please.

Timmy and his companion got off when they reached the fifth floor. As the door closed, the little boy started to give his mom the itinerary he wanted her to follow. I could hear him continue as the doors closed behind them as they got off on their floor. I continued to the thirteenth floor and then took the ride back down to the lobby.

I picked up a local paper and milled around the lobby for a few minutes until I saw what I needed to see. There, just as I had suspected, was Timmy's companion getting off the elevator. I checked my watch. It was 1:20. I smiled and muttered, '*creature of habit.*'

Chapter 19

I drove around for a while before heading back to the Clarion at 10:30 am. I still had some things to go over in my head, so I decided to take a walk on the beach to sort some things out.

As I got out of my truck, I put my black bag behind the seat and covered it up so that a passerby wouldn't notice it. Then I locked the door and headed toward the beach.

At 10:40 am, the sights and sounds, as well as the smells, were alive and well. The seagulls were chasing the large sand sweepers looking for morsels and tidbits of food. The chair and umbrella rental businesses were up and running, doing a brisk business. The smells of the morning sea breeze swept through the air.

I took a seat close to the sand dunes and went over the details of my plans, which were quite simple in design but could be dangerous, with the chance of being caught or identified. My identity, to a large degree, was protected in the other murders. This time it would be different. This time it would be up close and personal, and it would be messy.

I didn't want to get into a pattern. I also knew that the police would start to connect the dots after this murder.

They would know it was all connected. It was only a matter of time before they would figure it out.

Now the game had changed and I was more committed than ever to achieving my dreams at all costs. Nobody and nothing would get in my way. Now it wasn't only for myself, it was for Julie, too.

It was now 11:30 am and time to get moving. As I walked to the truck to get my black bag, my stomach was in knots. All that I had been taught by maw-maw and pa-paw about up close kills would be applied today.

As I was going through the lobby, I glanced at the clock behind the front desk. It read 11:50 am.. I also noticed I blended in well, wearing khakis with a light brown embroidered Ocean City wind breaker. I decided to go to the bar and saw that Kelly was working again. She had on a purple bikini with a black wrap and she looked fantastic.

"Hey, you made it back. Do you want a bud draft?" she asked.

"Yeah, if you don't mind," and with that, I took a seat on a bar stool feeling cool and confident.

We made small talk and I was surprised to learned she was a Raven's cheerleader in the off-season, which I had thought was cool. The conversation also served my purpose well. I was blending in. Talking to Kelly also prevented me from over-analyzing the task. Before I knew it, it was 12:30 pm., and time to put the plan in motion.

After paying Kelly, I headed for the front desk. I knew the next sixty seconds would either make or break my plan. During their conversations yesterday, Kelly had told me that between 11 am and 3 pm, the hotel's front desk was usually slammed with people checking in and out. The overflow would fill up the hotel's bars while people waited for their rooms to be ready.

"Good afternoon, and welcome to the Clarion. My name is April. How may I help you today?"

"My name is Tim Fallon and I'm in room 509. I think I left my key card in my room. Could I possibly get another one please?"

"It would be no problem at all, Mr. Fallon. I'll get you a new card right away. Will there be anything else?"

"No, that will be all, thank you."

"Just give me a minute. As you can see, we're very busy." Shortly she returned with the key card.

"Thank you very much. I really appreciate it," I said.

Well, that couldn't have gone any better, I thought as I picked up my black bag that I had retrieved from my truck and headed toward the elevator. Once there, I checked the time. It was now 12:42 pm - three minutes ahead of his schedule. The door opened.

Four people emerged from the elevator. It was a typical vacationing family, ma, pa and the kids. I entered the elevator along with two giggling teenage girls. One of the girls asked me what floor I wanted and I told them "Six please". As the door closed, she pressed six, then nine, and the elevator started up. As the doors opened onto the sixth floor, I checked my watch and saw that it was 12:45 pm. I stepped through the opening and headed for the stairway. I went down the stairway to the fifth floor.

I slowly cracked the door open and saw no one in the corridor. I walked down the hallway until I reached 509. I then looked left and then right and still saw no one. I quietly slid the key card into the door. The little green light blinked. Quickly putting on my gloves, I opened the door. As I entered, I mentally thanked April for her great customer service.

The blinds to the balcony were open. As I set the bag on the bed, I checked my watch; it read 12:52. I unzipped my bag and pulled out my R.T.A.K survival knife that maw-maw and pa-paw had bought for me so many years ago, I left the bag unzipped and threw it under the bed, crawling under the bed beside it, thinking the whole time, *I hope this ballplayer keeps acting like a creature of habit.* After a few minutes, the door opened and I heard Tim and his lady friend talking as they came in, getting louder as they came toward the bed. I saw their feet right in front of me. Tim was wearing brown sandals and his lady friend was wearing orange ones.

They both sat on the bed having idle conversation about where they would have dinner after tonight's game, the upcoming road trip that lay ahead, and finally what time he was going to pick her up after her shift ended at Phillip's Crab House. Then they both stood and kissed good night, having no idea it would be their last.

As Tim's lady friend started for the door, Tim followed behind her. I was having a hard time controlling my breathing as I could see their feet as they paused while Tim opened the door. Again, they hugged each other. I almost felt bad for what I was about to do, but I knew what I wanted and I had to get rid of Tim to get it.

After their embrace, she left and Tim came back into the room. He sat on the bed and got undressed, grabbing a pair of multi colored boxers from the bureau as he headed for the bathroom.

I waited and heard the bathroom door close, followed by the sound of the shower being turned on. I compulsively looked at my watch. It now read 1:17 pm. I gave it another minute before I got in position for the kill. As I got out from beneath the bed, I grabbed my black bag and knife and sat them on the bed. I took a deep breath and looked around. I grabbed the knife and removed it from its sheath. I was breathing heavily. I had killed wounded animals by slicing their throats, but this was very different. I was going into foreign territory.

With my knife in hand, I closed the blinds and walked up the brightly painted hallway. Facing the front door, to my immediate right was a door-less closet across from the bathroom door. I locked the security bar latch and went to the wall that separated the bathroom and bedroom and waited.

While waiting, I thought, *"Remember, it's just like in the woods. You've done this countless times; grab the head, pull to the right, rip across the vein with the left. Just like ma-maw showed you. The vein explodes the blood into his throat and lungs so he won't even be able to wail in pain. Boy, the K.G.B. taught them both well, but I'm sure they never thought in their wildest dreams I'd be practicing what they preached."*

Finally, the shower went off and I felt the hairs on my neck stand straight up. It was like being sexually aroused. I muttered to myself, *"Be efficient, be very efficient"*. As I peeked in the mirror across from me, I saw the doorknob turning. Tim was coming out the door, towel-drying his hair as if he didn't have a care in the world. Making an immediate right, suddenly he was directly in front of me.

I stepped out and slid my right arm above Tim's right shoulder, wrapping my forearm tight to his chin. I reached my hand up the left side of his face, palming his forehead and grabbing the crown of his head tightly. Then, all in the same motion, I pulled his head violently to the right while pulling the blade of the knife with my left hand across Tim's bulging and pulsing vein.

Tim never knew what hit him; he was bleeding out before his eyes ever had a chance to roll. His eyes had a look of shock in them; blood was coming out of his mouth. With every gasp he took, blood flowed out of his vein. I held him as he died, and then gently laid him down on the already blood soaked carpet and whispered, "I'm sorry I had no choice."

Immediately, I started to change. I took off the windbreaker and removed my sandals and pants, putting them all in the bag. I took my knife and wiped it off on Tim's shirt. The dead, cold eyes of Tim were staring up at me. As I did this, his body was still convulsing. I started to put the knife back into its sheath but thought better of it. D.N.A. can be a bitch so I just put it in the bag to deal with it later.

I looked in the mirror to see if any blood had soaked through onto the clothes I had been wearing underneath. Satisfied that they were clean, I made sure everything was in the bag as I put on my tennis shoes and a ball cap. Heading toward the door, I turned around to make sure nothing had been forgotten. I unlocked the security latch, turned the knob, and opened the door. As I entered the hallway I looked both ways and then closed the door, taking off my gloves and also putting them in the bag.

Going down the hallway toward the steps, I went back up to the sixth floor and pressed the elevator's button. The door opened and no one was on it. As I entered through the door, I put my sunglasses on and pressed 'T' for the terrace floor. Once I arrived on the terrace, I went to the stairs and walked down the one remaining flight to the lobby and out the front door.

Chapter 20

We were having yet another meeting in the office working on the murders of the ball players. Dewayne had stopped by to check on our progress. As it always seemed to happen, he was called away by his ringing cell phone. As Guinea and I were going over the information on the case one more time, Dewayne was just getting off his cell phone. His face told the story.

"Guys, we've got another one. A player for the Delmarva Shorebirds was found in his hotel room in Ocean City by his girlfriend less than an hour ago, dead of an apparent homicide. It looks like the cause of death was a slit throat."

"Did they get identification on the victim?", Guinea asked.

"Yeah, his name was Tim Fallon. And get this, he played first base, same as Brannon."

"Didn't I read somewhere that the kid who was killed in the hit and run in Aberdeen a few weeks ago, was also a first baseman?", I asked

Molly answered immediately, "Yes, he was Mike."

"Well that can't just be a coincidence. Guinea, I need you to go to Aberdeen a.s.a.p. Get the real story about what happened up there. Three first baseman dead in a two-week span. I'd bet my yearly salary it's more than just a hit and run. I'm going to go to O.C. to lead that investigation, and then up to Salisbury to get a feel for what the players and management are thinking and saying. Dewayne, I'm going to have to take Smitty with me. I need a seasoned pro to help interview witnesses and take the heat of dealing with the press off of me. Can you handle the press up here?"

"Not a problem, Mike." Dewayne responded

"Good. Gentleman, as always, we will continue to run everything through Molly to process and coordinate. Does anybody have any questions?"

The Lieutenant Governor spoke up, "It looks like we might have a serial killer on our hands."

As we all started to get up from our seats I stated the obvious.

"Look, this is all going to go south pretty quickly once the press gets wind of it, so let's get some answers, and get them soon.

I knew the press was going to be all over this like bees to honey. That was the main reason I asked Smitty to come with me. If I went to Ocean City by myself, I wouldn't get much accomplished. Now I'd have a buffer between me and the press corps, which I was sure was going to quadruple in size knowing the story would now draw national attention.

After our initial meeting, I asked Molly to call the Clarion to see if they had a single and a double available, and if they didn't, to find us something close.

Unfortunately for the hotel, but fortunately for us, when the story broke about the murder later that day, they had many last-minute cancellations. We were able to get two adjoining rooms on the floor just above where the murder took place. Molly also told me that the media outlets were booking almost everything available in the Clarion and any surrounding hotels and condominiums. *Thank God Smitty is coming,* I thought after hearing that from Molly.

I talked to Smitty that evening and told him about the media and what to expect. I also reiterated that we would have a lot of interviews to conduct and thought it best to split up and do as many as possible, at least for the first round. Later we would double-team the interviews that panned out. I also informed him that I was bringing my boys to spend my down time with them.

Knowing that this case was going to become all too time consuming, I had to find some way to spend more time with the boys. The fact that it was in Ocean City would make it like a little vacation for them. While I was working, the boys would have the surf and sun to keep them occupied. They could also tag along with me when I went to Purdue Stadium to do the player interviews. They'd be able to watch the team work out, perhaps catch a game, and maybe even learn something.

When I got home in Edgewater, I heard the boys yelling and laughing in the backyard. I was none too thrilled to see what I saw and what they were up to. Josh was throwing deep passes to Shane, who was running flat out toward the end of the yard leaping over our 6x8 retaining wall and taking an 8ft drop into the South River. Not too smart I thought, but boys will be boys.

Shane emerged holding the football high and laughing so loud it was almost unbearable. Out of the corner of my eye, I saw our neighbor Juanita, just shaking her head. It made me feel somewhat relieved to know an adult had been in shouting distance in case something had gone awry.

"Hey," I hollered.

As Shane turned, he rifled a bullet right at me, shouting, "Catch dad."

The pass caught me by surprise and hit me square in the chest, right on the numbers.

"What's up dad, why are you home so early?" Josh asked.

"You guys up for a road trip?"

"Where to?" asked Josh

"O.C."

"are you kidding? For how long?", Josh responded.

"For a couple of days. I have some work down there."

"We heard it all over Sport Center," Shane said.

"Sports Center, really?", I asked.

Shane and Josh nodded their heads up and down.

"Guys, I want you to get enough clothes for three or four days. Make sure you bring a windbreaker, dress cloths for dinner, two bathing suits, toothbrushes …"

"We got it, dad. We've been on a trip before," Josh deadpanned.

While the boys got their stuff together, I went on-line to the Shorebirds website. I saw they had games tonight and tomorrow night before leaving on a nine-day road trip.

We got into Salisbury later that day at about 3:30 pm. As we pulled into the stadium parking lot, the boys were amazed at how different a minor league park looked. It was so much smaller than Camden Yards. Once the game started, I knew they'd love the intimacy and closeness of it all. As we walked up to the gate the boys had their gloves in their hands. I was expecting to see some sort of attendant or security, but there was none to be found, so we walked right through the gates.

As the boys got inside, they saw just how small and how close you were to the field and action. I guess it held five thousand, tops. At the time, there were about fifty people scattered throughout the stands. I told the boys we had to find someone in charge. Josh wondered aloud if any of the people there were scouts.

Then Shane said, "Dad, is it okay if I go to the left field area and try to catch some home-run balls?"

I knew Josh wanted to do the same thing. I said, "Make sure your cell phone is on", knowing I'd be able to find them easily in the small crowd.

As the boys headed off to the left field corner, I saw who I thought might be the equipment manager. I went up and introduced myself, credentials in hand.

"Hi, I'm Mike Carrier with the D.F.V.C. Division of the Maryland State police. I'm here to investigate the murder of Timothy Fallon. Could you please point me in the direction of the person in charge?"

"Timmy was a good kid. He had a bright future- maybe not in baseball as a player, but a good kid none-the-less."

"You knew him?" I asked.

"Yeah. I'm Denny Klein. I'm the guy you're looking for, General Manager, promoter, equipment man. You name it, I do it, or have done it, one time or another. In the minor leagues, you have to wear many hats."

"It must keep you pretty busy," I said.

"Yes, it does. So, how can I help you?"

"Well, first I'd like to speak to all of your players, coaches, anybody who had any contact whatsoever with Timmy. I'll need complete access to everything Timmy and your players have access to.

"Detective, whatever you want or need, you'll have the entire shorebird organization's cooperation. In fact, we received a fax after the Bobby Brannon shooting telling us to fully cooperate with any and all investigations."

"Well, I'm glad to hear that. And please, call me Mike."

What I didn't tell him was that Dewayne himself was having a meeting today with the owner of the Orioles and other big wigs within the organization.

Continuing, I said, "I brought my two boys with me. They're big ball fans. I hope you don't mind"

"No, not at all. Hell, I may even put them to work. Have they ever been in a club house?"

"No, they haven't, but I think they 'd find it interesting."

For the next two hours, I interviewed the players and coaches. It wasn't at all as I thought it would be. They all competed for playing time and promotions, but they all pulled for one another. Everyone wanted everyone else to succeed. I found no animosity from any of the players or coaches. I went in thinking it would be a cut-throat atmosphere, but to my pleasant surprise, it was far from that. I had one more interview to do, a kid named Mark Newman. One of the coaches said he was in the club house studying film.

He's a big boy, I thought as I approached the shirtless young man wearing only shorts, socks and stirrups covered slightly with shower shoes. He was sitting on a wooden bench that ran the length of the room, parallel to a bank of lockers. Even sitting down, it was obvious that he was taller than average. He was watching two monitors that he had setting on a chair being used as a make-shift table.

"Excuse me. I'm detective Mike Carrier. Can I have a minute of your time?" I said as he started to stand up and greet me. I got a better appreciation of just how big he really was.

"No problem, detective. I'm Mark Newman. What can I do for you?"

"As I'm sure you know, I'm investigating the murder of Timothy Fallon. Did you know him?"

"No, not really detective. I just arrived in the middle of the week, and of course I met him, but I really didn't get a chance to get to know him. He was one of the guys who showed me around the hotel when I got here. A bunch of the guys stay there. The hotel gives us a really sweet deal."

"So, you did talk to him? Did he mention any problems or voice any concerns?" As I asked the question, I noticed a little nervousness as he reached into a black Nike bag to retrieve a sports drink.

"No, like I said, he just helped me get into a routine. Everybody helps everyone else around here. I'll do it for the next guy that comes through the door. I wish I could be of more help, detective, but I can't," he said as he took a drink of his Gatorade.

"You say you just got here, where from?"

"I was playing for the Iron Birds in Aberdeen."

"Really?" I said with obvious surprise in my voice. "Did you know an Albert, ah, Albert…."

Mark was quick to respond, "Griffith, Albert Griffith. Yeah, I knew him. We were pretty tight."

Just then, two very excited young men came bouncing through the clubhouse doors.

"Dad, this is so friggin' cool," Josh said.

Then Shane asked, "Dad what are you doing?"

"Shane, I'm busy right now interviewing this young man."

"What are you watching?" Shane asked Mark.

"Shane, he's busy," I started to say, but Mark interrupted me.

"It's okay, detective." Mark stood up and extended his hand to Shane. "I'm Mark, Mark Newman. First baseman of the Delmarva Shorebirds. And you are?"

"Shane Carrier, and this is my big brother Josh." he extended his hand toward Mark. I was proud of the maturity the boys showed. For a brief second, my mind flashed back to their mother referring to them as 'her men' as Mark shook their hands.

"Shane, I'm studying some old film and looking at some new film to see if I can spot any differences or tendencies in my swing," Mark responded.

Josh spoke up and said, "Yeah, I do that. I'll stay up at night and study Albert Pujol's swing. I figure I might as well try to learn from the best."

Mark continued, "Well, the film on the right is when I was smoking the ball and the film on the left is when I was not. Unfortunately, it seems that's been happening more often than not in the last couple years.

"Do you mind if we watch?" Josh asked.

"No, go ahead. I should start getting ready for the game. Besides, I could use all the help I can get. Detective, you were asking me about Albert?"

"Please, call me Mike."

"Detective, I was raised to show respect to authority."

"That's okay. So, you say you knew Albert also?"

"Yeah, we hung out. Albert and I shared our roles at first base and as D.H. We got along great. We would go over scouting reports together. It's a shame what happened to him. Have they found the S.O.B. who hit him?"

"No, not yet. In fact, my partner is in Aberdeen right now collecting information for our investigation."

"Do you think they're related?"

"I sure do. I think Bobby Brannon's murder is, too. Did you know him?"

"No, I never met or played with him."

"Mark, you know they all played first base."

"Yeah, I know. I wouldn't be here if Albert was still alive. I took his spot," he said as he put his uniform pants on.

"We found it," the boys screamed at the same time.

"Found what," I said, somewhat annoyed.

"The hole in his swing, dad," Shane said with a look that said I should know what he was talking about.

"We know what's causing it," Josh answered excitedly

"What? Show me," Mark said.

"Okay, look at the film on the right. Look at your hands, how you're gripping the bat. You're holding it so tight, like you're trying to squeeze it into saw dust. Anything inside and tight, you're too tense to get the bat barrel through the zone and it causes your elbow to drop. And if you do make contact, you'll probably hurt yourself."

"I've strained so many tendons I've lost count," Mark said.

111

"I believe it," Josh said, then continued, "dad always taught us to play the piano."

Shane then added, "Now look at this screen. As dad would say, your hands are loose, you're moving your fingers, just like Josh said. You're playing the piano. Now watch. In comes a high and tight fastball. You get the bat barrel through the zone and bam, three run homer, picture perfect."

"I can't believe this. I've had hitting coaches, managers, all types of people analyze my swing and now two kids figure it out. This is unreal. I was starting to think it was all in my head. I don't know how to thank you."

"Don't thank us, thank our dad. He taught us. Like I tell all my friends, my dad could teach a blind man to hit three hundred," Josh said.

Marked looked at me and I was grinning ear to ear, obviously pleased with what my boys had found and proud as hell of the compliment that Josh had given me.

"You guys are going to stay for the game, aren't you?" Mark asked.

"Of course," Shane replied. "We have to see how good you are, One thing is for sure, you are big enough to hit 'em out."

We all laughed at Shane's remark.

"Mark, one more question?" I asked.

"What's that?"

"What do you drive?"

"A Chevy Tahoe."

"What color?"

"Black. Why do you ask?"

"Just doing my job," I replied. "Have a good game."

Mark had a game for the ages, going four for four with two doubles and two home runs, with six runs batted in. The boys were very excited for him. There was no doubt that the two autographed bats Mark had the whole team sign to give them had a lot to do with that.

As we left I purposely walked through the players parking lot looking for a black Tahoe. When I found it my heart went to the pit of my stomach. In front of us was a 4x4 black Tahoe with 38-inch tires, all chromed out with Virginia tags that read 'BSE B Ply.' My sons' new hero was now my prime suspect.

Chapter 21

Guinea arrived in Aberdeen to find out what he could about the Albert Griffith hit-and-run. He started where the accident took place. The apartment complex was small, maybe sixty units in all. It was located on a small dogwood and oak lined road that dead-ended into wooded area about an eighth of a mile away. To his left was only one intersection between the woods and the complex.

Guinea had the local police department's report in his hand and he knew that the vehicle had come from the direction of the woods. *Man, that's an awful short distance to get up to speed to kill someone and not be intentional,* he thought.

He decided to do some door knocking, He could confirm what the local P.D. had in their report: a black truck was seen numerous times in the area and it had big tires. Unfortunately, no one had seen the tag number or the driver.

Next, Guinea went to the County Coroner's office. There he found out that Griffith had been hit at such a high rate of speed, the impact snapped his spine. The coroner said that when Griffith's body recoiled from the hit it was so violent that it snapped his sixth vertebra in the opposite direction. He estimated that the speed of impact had to be between 53 to 60 miles per hour. In Guinea's mind, that rate of speed and that short distance confirmed that this was no accident.

Guinea also learned that there was some rubber dust embedded in the body and that this was not uncommon on trucks with balloon tires. He was told that there is so much rubber hitting the road that it would wear to dust and form on the wheel wells and rims. Consequently, when you hit a bump in the road, or, in this case, a body, the dust would jar loose from the rims. The dust proved to be from a size thirty-eight Mickey Thompson. Per the lab report from the C.S.I crew, it also matched what the Frederick crime scene guys had gotten from the print off I-70. However, much to Guinea's chagrin, there was no way of telling if it was the same tire. He called Frederick and chastised the crime scene guys for not getting dust on a tire print in the gravel.

When Guinea called me with an overview of his report, all I could think was, '*Really, what did you expect... miracles?*'

About the only thing that didn't add up to Guinea was why the local P.D were calling this an accident. It sure had the look and feel of being deliberate. So much for common sense in police work. Next it was off to Cal Ripken Sr. Stadium to interview the players and coaches. As Guinea entered the stadium, he couldn't help but notice how big league the facilities were for a minor league stadium. It was all smaller in scale, but even the souvenir shop immediately to his left was big league. Guinea thought, '*I've got to bring the boys and Mike up here to check this out.*'

He couldn't help himself. He had to go into the souvenir shop and look around. Guinea stumbled on some old, broken game bats. He had to have them, even though they cost twenty-five dollars apiece. Then he came upon a set of nine dollar coasters with the Iron Bird logo that he thought just looked cool and two pennants for five dollars each. He justified the purchases with the idea of giving the pennants and bats to the boys. Truth be told, he just likes sports junk as much as the next guy but would never admit it.

Guinea had a plan; as he interviewed each player or coach, he'd get them to sign both bats and if any of them ever made it to the majors the price of the bats could double. And if one made it to the hall of fame it would be worth a fortune.

As Guinea finished his last interview with the Iron Birds General Manager Dennis Cook, he thought that whoever committed these murders was not one of the players or coaches he had just interviewed. The vibe he got was that of a love fest within the team. It made him somewhat nauseous

"Dennis, I've got one more question?"

"What's that, Detective Ginavan?"

"Has anyone been released or promoted in the weeks leading up to, or since the accident took place?" Guinea didn't want to use the word murder.

"No, wait a minute, just one. Mark Newman - it was a lateral move."

"And when was that?"

"Right after the accident the Orioles, and I suppose the Ripken family, canceled the weekend series out of respect for the Griffith family and the players. When they returned, we shipped Mark out to the Delmarva Shore Birds. In fact, it was Albert that was ticketed to go, but with his death they still needed someone so we sent our other first baseman, Mark."

"Do you happen to know what Mark drives?" Guinea asked.

"Hell, everybody knows what he drives. You couldn't miss it - a big black Chevy Tahoe."

"Is that so? Well, thank you. I'm sure you've been told this a million times, but tell the Ripkens they really did an outstanding job here. This place is amazing," Guinea said.

"I most certainly will. They love to hear positive feedback." Dennis replied

Chapter 22

As we crossed the Rt. 50 Bridge heading into Ocean City I decided to call Smitty to let him know we had arrived. I was glad I'd brought the boys. As we entered the city and saw the White Marlin sign welcoming us, the expressions on their faces as they watched the hundreds of people walking here and there was priceless.

Making the left turn I remembered how, as a kid, I used to love to read and look at the hundreds of neon signs advertising the various hotels, motels, eateries and shops on what I called the strip. Some of the names and the buildings may have changed, but it was still the same. The smell of the salt water, the families, some of which had large stuffed animals or shopping bags filled with trinkets milling about and, of course, the girls wearing bikini tops or other revealing attire being followed by hopeful boys.

In the distance, I saw the Quality Inn sign. Back in the day it had been called the Palms Hotel, but as much as things changed they still stayed the same. The Quality Inn still advertised the all-you-can-eat smörgåsbord as the Palms Hotel once had decades ago.

We finally came to the end of Baltimore street where the Yankee Clipper once stood and now was replaced in name by the Ocean Voyager. We turned right onto Coastal Highway and made our way out to, what my mom use to call, 'the golden mile' - a stretch of high rise condos that started on 94th street and ended at the Carousel on 118th. As a toddler, I remember my parents driving, what seemed like forever, to go have dinner there. At the time, it was the only building past 27th street. It was then called Bobby Bakers Carousel; a hotel and restaurant in the middle of nowhere, surrounded by sand and surf and nothing else.

Upon arriving in front of the hotel, we couldn't help but notice all the television vans and satellite dishes reaching toward the sky. It looked like I had been proven right when I told Smitty that this case would start to receive national attention. It had, and they were all here from CNN to ESPN, plus the big three, NBC, CBS, and ABC. The over flow parking lot across Coastal Highway was packed with media trucks and vans.

After getting our key card from the front desk, we went up to our room. The boys immediately changed into their bathing suits while I called Smitty and arranged to meet him at the pool side bar. Once at the pool, the boys didn't hesitate to jump in just as I spotted Smitty sitting at the bar.

"What's going on Smitty?"

"You see it Mike, the circus is in town. I already gave them the usual bull shit speech of when we know, you'll know."

"So, what else do you have Smitty?" As I asked, a beautiful red head in a bright orange bikini with a white wrap approached us from behind the bar.

Smitty said, "Mike, meet Kelly."

"Hi Kelly, do you have bud on tap?" I said while staring at her green eyes.

"We sure do. you a detective also?"

Smitty spoke up. "Let me formally introduce you. This is Detective Mike Carrier."

"Nice to meet you," I responded.

"Is Michael the only name mothers giving their children in Annapolis?" she said with a laugh.

"I don't know. I was raised in Hereford, and then as a teenager I worked in Baltimore." As I spoke I wondered why in the hell I was giving this woman my life history, and continued, "We call Michael 'Smitty' to avoid confusion when we're together.

"I know the Hereford area. It's right up interstate 83 going toward PA. I have family that lives in Parkton," Kelly said.

"Mike, Kelly was on duty the day the kid Timmy bought the farm," Smitty said.

"Really," I said just as Shane came up dripping wet.

"Dad, can you get me and Josh a soda please?"

"And who's this handsome young man," Kelly asked.

"This is my youngest son, Shane. The one on the diving board over there is my oldest boy, Josh," I said while pointing in his direction. "Shane, this is Kelly, and you remember Smitty, don't you?"

"Sure do, dad."

"Handsome, what kind of soda would you and your brother like?" Kelly asked.

"Do you have a Dr. Pepper?" A blushing, red faced Shane asked.

After the boys got their sodas, Smitty explained to me what, or more like it, what we don't have.

"Mike, we've got a lot of conflicting reports. We've got a half dozen who say they saw a guy in shorts, tee-shirt, and an Oriole hat carrying a black bag right around the time of the murder."

"What kind of black bag?"

"Just a black athletic bag. Why, Mike?"

"I'll explain later, go on with what you were saying." As he answered, I could tell he was being cautious to make sure that no one like the press was eavesdropping on our conversation.

"Then we've got about two dozen people, including miss sexy there," with a nod at Kelly, "who saw a guy hanging around the bar and hotel for two days who apparently wasn't even a guest here. But his description doesn't even come close to the guy in the Oriole's hat.

"So, we've got two people of interest we need to find and talk to"?

"It looks like the murder weapon this time was a knife," Smitty said while holding up his glass to get Kelly's attention. "Mike, this has the feel of some type of military operation. There's just too much misdirection, you know what I mean?"

"Smitty, this whole thing stinks of misdirection from the start. First the hit-and-run, then the sniper, and now a knifing?"

"So, the hit-and-run ties in Mike?"

"My gut tells me so. Guinea phoned in and things don't add up in Aberdeen. It's too conflicting," I said as Kelly approached.

"Would my Michael men like two more beers?"

"Please, and could you also get the boy's two orders of calamari, if you don't mind?"

"Will that be all?"

"Yes, unless you want something Smitty?"

Smitty shook his head, no, as he took a drink of his beer.

"That will be all, then. They ate before we got in town. I just want them to get something before they go to bed."

I looked at my watch it was already 11:30 pm. "Man, time flies when you're having fun. The boys will sure sleep good tonight. Before I forget, Smitty, was there anything missing from Timmy's room?"

"No, there wasn't Mike."

"Didn't think there would be, but had to get the robbery thing out of the equation. What's the deal with the physical appearance?

"The guy in the shorts most people had at 6ft 180 to 190 lb., the dude in the khakis they got at 6'2 185 to 210."

"That's not much of a difference, if you ask me. It could be the same guy, Smitty."

"Yeah, I thought the same thing, but you got timing issues. One guy can't be in two places at the same time and wearing different cloths."

As Kelly returned with our two beers I asked her, "Kelly, the guy who was hanging out down here, if you had to describe him in two words, what would they be?"

"Country and smart, and polite."

"That was three, but it was very helpful," I said with a grin.

"Yeah, I know. Your calamari will be out in a minute, and as for being helpful, I'm sure I'll see your appreciation in my tip," she said with a returned grin.

As I called for the boys to eat, I thought about what Smitty had said regarding misdirection. Then I thought about my boys' new hero and what Kelly had said; country, smart and polite. But his height bothered me, plus, since he stays here more people should know and recognize him. However, at this point, anything is possible. Misdirection indeed.

"One more thing, Smitty, I need to know if there was any kind of logo on that black bag. And I want pictures distributed of all the ballplayers to all guests who were here at the time of the murder. Plus, I want to see the crime scene first thing tomorrow."

"We can look at it now, Mike."

"No, I'm spent. We'll do it tomorrow."

Chapter 23

In the morning, we awoke to a picture-perfect day, morning temperature already in the low eighties with a nice seven to ten miles per hour ocean breeze. While the boys were getting up and showering in preparation for their day, I stood on the small balcony sneaking my morning cigarette while drinking my usual coffee with two sugars and too much cream.

Below me on the beach, things were starting to stir. People were walking their dogs, while others were collecting shells that had washed up on shore the night before. The raft and umbrella vendors were readying their wares, while the sea gulls combed the beach and sang their morning songs.

As I took a sip of my coffee, I exhaled a cloud of blue smoke from one of my two daily cigarettes. I grabbed the phone and called Smitty.

"Hey, would you like to join the boys and me for breakfast at the Bay Side Skillet on 79th Street? The breakfasts so big that we'll only have to order two. Shannon and I use to go there before the boys were born."

"Yeah, I've been there Mike and the food is excellent. "

On the way, back from a very filling and satisfying breakfast, Smitty and I started game planning for the day ahead of us.

"Mike, did you get a chance to see the Baltimore Sun this morning?"

"No, not yet."

"Well, you may want to. They are already reporting that the hit-and-run was now a murder and that they're all connected. Seems somebody from the Iron Birds leaked that Guinea was up there snooping around. And the paper feels we are withholding information."

"I don't give a rat's ass what they think."

"Dad, watch your blood pressure," Josh said.

I had forgotten for a minute that the boys were in the truck.

"Sorry guys," I said while looking in the rear view mirror.

"Look, schedule a press conference for 4 pm. and we will give them everything we've got, which right now is squat."

As soon as we got back, I gave the boys twenty bucks to get some lunch and told them to call me at 4:30. Later, we'd meet, shower, and shave and go to the all- you-can-eat smörgåsbord on the boardwalk and then go have some fun.

The boys headed to the beach and Smitty and I headed to the room where the murder took place. The hotel was clamoring to clean the room so they'd be able to use it. I purposely decided to look at it on my schedule and not be dictated to by anyone. It just rubbed me the wrong way, money before a murder, so I made them wait. Besides, I had already told Smitty I called our cleaner and knew he would be here soon. I looked at my watch. It was 8:15 am and I knew it wouldn't take long to give it the once over, but I instructed Smitty to release the room at 2 pm.

"Smitty, I know I told you to distribute pictures of all the Shore Birds to the guests that were here. After giving it some thought, I want to have pictures of every minor leaguer in the Oriole's organization passed out, as well as, those recently released if possible. I know it's a hassle, but it must be done. And if any of them match our two guys, I want to know about it yesterday! And if Kelly doesn't recognize any of the players, I want a sketch artist here to give us a face and then have someone, better yet two people, who saw the guy in shorts give their descriptions to the sketch artist.

Walking into the hotel I told Smitty that I called Molly and arranged for us to have a conference call with her, Guinea, Freddie and Dewayne at 1 pm. and that the hotel had set it up in one of their conference rooms on the second floor. Once we were inside the lobby, I looked to my right, and sitting in the lounge was my old friend, the cleaner; the one and only Robert Romberger. When he saw me, he stood with a wide smile and outstretched hand.

"How you doing, old man," I said extending my own hand and giving him a hearty handshake. "Bob, have you met Smitty?"

"I believe so, a couple years ago, at the Glen Burnie barracks."

"Yeah, we did. I did a year's tour there right around the time of 9/11," Smitty said.

Bob was the absolute best forensic expert in the state. That's why his closest colleagues called him 'the cleaner'. In fact, the Feds had been trying to lure him away for years. Luckily for us, he hated how the Feds operated. I tried to get him on board when we first formed the unit but budget constraints wouldn't permit it. However, I continued to hold out hope. *Maybe it will come to fruition this year; his help on this case can only help swing the pendulum in our favor if he is in some way able to help us solve this case,* I thought to myself.

He hadn't changed a bit since the last time I saw him - 5'10", about 160 to 170 pounds, gray and balding with a close-cropped graying beard. He looked like he should be teaching at a university somewhere.

"So, what takes me out of my cozy confines of Glen Burnie to come to O.C., Mike?"

"Bob, I really need you to find me something, anything, that gives me a starting point to finding this asshole. The local C.S.I. guys came up empty. They couldn't find anything."

"Nothing against the locals down here, but murder cases aren't really their forte, Bob," Smitty said.

"Well, I'll give it the once over to see what we've got. What else you guys need?"

"Could you also go up to the County Coroner's office in Berlin and let me know what you think? Somebody had to miss something."

"Mike, I passed Berlin on the way in, didn't I?"

"Yeah, Bob, Berlin is six to ten miles out on route 50 on the left."

"All right. Let me get my stuff out of the van and then you can show me the room."

Bob turned to exit from the lobby, pulling out a pack of Marlboro Reds. As he did I saw our golden boy, Mark Newman, coming out of the elevator. The boys had been right. I was more than just a little bit perturbed, and who better to take it out on than the guy benefiting the most from the murders.

"Hey Mark, you got a minute?"

"Yeah, detective. How are the boys? I owe them a lot. I've been lights out since they spotted my flaw."

Great, he has to bring up my kids while I'm trying to put him away for life. If that's not misdirection then I don't know what is, I thought.

"Let me get right to the point. You were at Aberdeen when the Griffith kid was killed. You own a big black truck that has Mickey Thompson tires."

"So?"

"Let me finish. Griffith was run over by a black truck with the same type of tires. Then you get here and low and behold the Orioles lose another first base prospect. You see, the problem is my kids and I love the Orioles and all our good first base prospects are being murdered. And it just so happens that you keep moving up the ladder without doing shit on the field. It seems to me like you could be killing all of our prospects for your own gain."

"you're out of your fucking mind"? Mark blurted out.

"Watch your language, kid," Smitty said.

"I never killed anyone in my life," Mark said in a frantic voice.

131

"Calm down, big boy. I got nothing yet. I will, though. It's only a matter of time, and I'm a fast worker. So, my advice to you is to play each game as if it were your last big boy." I retorted in a matter of fact manner

"I'm telling you, detective, I never killed anybody. I liked Albert. You never played professional sports. We all pull for each other. Nobody wants to see the other guy fail."

"Kid, I know this: if you don't make it in baseball, you got a real shot as an actor."

"I swear on everything I love that I never hurt anybody."

"Sure kid, sure," I said as I turned away. Then I saw the cleaner enter the hotel lobby with all his equipment. As I walked toward Bob, I knew I had left a long-lasting impression on a very stunned prospect. Then I turned toward him to deliver the coup de grau,

"Oh, and Mark, I'll will get you for the Bobby Brannon murder, too."

Chapter 24

"Honey, have you seen the Northern Virginia Daily?"

"No, I haven't, but I did read the Washington Post."

"I'm afraid our baby maybe in trouble."

No sooner had she stopped speaking than the phone rang. On the phone was their grandson, Mark Newman.

"Hi sweetheart, how's my boy doing?" Victoria asked. A pause and then, "Yes, your grandfather and I have seen it."

The conversation continued that way for more than half an hour before she finally said, "Sweetheart, I'll only ask you this once, and your grandfather and I will continue to love you, support you and help you in any way you wish. We will move on regardless of your answer. Sweetheart, did you kill those boys? It's okay, your grandfather and I will protect you. You know our past and what we did in the old country."

"Well, what did our grandson have to say, Victoria?" Vladimir asked.

"Does it really matter? He's our daughter's son, and we will protect him however we have to, regardless, Val."

Victoria and Vladimir Glasgow were originally from Stalingrad, Russia. At the early ages of seven and nine, respectively, they were unexpectedly thrust into World War II. They were recruited by the Red Army to do recognizance, and later trained to become expert snipers and assassins during the defense of Stalingrad.

For the duration of the war, they had seventy-three and sixty-one confirmed kills between them. Both had been awarded the cross of Stalin during the defense of Stalingrad, one of the highest honors given in the Russian Army. Also, they were the youngest to have that honor bestowed on them. It was during this period that they met and worked together, and later started a torrid love affair filled with passion, romance, and adventure that culminated in their marriage in 1947.

After the war, they were both recruited by the K.G.B., first being assigned to West Berlin and then later to England where their work as political diplomats was their cover. In the summer of 1959, they were assigned to the Russian embassy in Washington, D.C., during the height of the cold war. During that fourteen year span they became very well versed in the art of espionage and political assassination, mixed in with a little bit of cold blooded murder, all in the name of the state.

With the election of John F. Kennedy, the political landscape was changing and Moscow was determined to flex its muscle every chance it got. That, coupled with the birth of their daughter, Janie, in January of '61, made the Glasgow's feel that the Mother Land was heading in the wrong direction, especially for a family in their line of work. So, on the 22nd of February of that same year they defected.

Vladimir and Victoria were not alone. From 1960 to 1963, there were forty-seven defections from communist bloc countries for a variety of reasons; from political asylum and persecution, to leaving for financial gain. But for the Glasgow's it was simply they wanted a better and safer life in these troubling times for their baby girl. So, on that February day they started their journey toward becoming American citizens.

As with other political defectors, they had a three to six-month dance with various state departments, with the warning that they could be called back in at any time. But for now, they were free to assume a life in America.

Vladimir and Victoria, while disposing of a foreign operative many years ago, found an area with which they just fell in love with. The area reminded them of some of the villages in mother Russia. It was up Route 66 in the Shenandoah Valley, a place called Front Royal, Virginia. Far enough away, but still close to Washington D.C., the center of the world, as Vladimir liked to say.

They found the perfect place to settle down and build their dream home just a couple miles out of town. Once settled, Vladimir took a job as a game warden at the George Washington National Forest, while his wife, Victoria, took a part time job at Warren County High School.

There they lived and raised their daughter and enjoyed what many thought was a simple American life. For the most part it was, except for the occasional request from a certain U.S agency that always had a need for their special skill set. Their daughter Janie had a wonderful but uneventful childhood. She would eventually graduate from the same high school where her mother was now working full-time.

In 1983, Janie graduated from the University of Maryland and immediately found a job working for, S.T.G., a defense contractor based out of Sterling, Virginia. Then, two years later, while working in the Pentagon, she met a charming young Lieutenant Commander in the U.S. Navy named Jack Newman. Soon after, they began to date. On March 17, 1987, they were married. One year to the day, their son Mark Val Newman, was born on St Patrick's Day.

While driving home On September 10, 2011, Janie received a called from work. She was told to report to the Pentagon at 8 am. the following morning to go over some military procurement with weapons development officers in the Army. Janie was ecstatic. It was a good opportunity for her company and she knew she would be able to have breakfast, perhaps even lunch, with her husband. They both felt that their careers had kept them apart far too much. As fate would have it, they drove to the Pentagon together enjoying the rare opportunity to spend some time together during the work week. They even met that morning for breakfast after their early morning meetings. It would turn out to be their last breakfast together. At 9:37 am on the 11th of September, they along with 184 others, were killed by five terrorists who hijacked American Airlines flight 77. Of those killed, 125 were in the building and the remaining victims were the 59 passengers on the plane.

Mark was just thirteen at the time. He learned about it just like everyone else on that fateful day. He heard about it on the news while sitting in a science class. Mark immediately jumped up out of his seat and ran to his grandmother's foreign history class. His life was forever changed in a matter of minutes.

For the next five years, his grandparents would raise him. In that short period, they often reminded him that the world was at times a cruel and unforgiving place. They made sure he kept up his grades and graduated at the top of his class and were always at all his sporting events supporting him.

More than anything else, they taught and told him everything they had learned throughout the war and then later in the K.G.B, a subject they had never breached with their daughter. What he learned was take advantage of every opportunity. He learned it was survival of the fittest, and he carried that mentality with him in everything he did, including sports.

Now both in their mid-seventies, Victoria and Val were in better shape than most people twenty years their junior. They still both ran two and a half miles every other day. Both were still avid hunters and expert shooters. Both still were involved occasionally in espionage and had numerous underworld contacts all over the world. They both knew they would call on all their past training and resources, if necessary, to help their grandson in his time of need. They were responsible for all this attention on their grandson in the first place. They were going to make sure he succeeded.

Chapter 25

As the elevator door closed behind the three of us, Smitty asked me who the kid was.

"Guys, with what little we've got to go on, that young man is our prime suspect. We can place him in Aberdeen and here at the time of both murders. In addition, his truck matches the description of the truck seen on the side of I-70 in Frederick and in the neighborhood of the hit-and-run in Aberdeen. So, I just figured I'd shake his tree and see if anything would fall out."

"Well, did anything fall out?" Bob asked.

"No, not really. He swore up and down that he never killed anybody, but then again I've never had anybody say, 'Yeah, I'm guilty,' right out of the gate either."

"Mike, I don't know if I would have put my cards on the table so soon. You just made him aware we suspect him, and now he'll be on the defensive," Smitty said.

"I concur, that wasn't such a bright idea, Mike. If he is guilty, you just gave him a head up," Bob replied.

In hindsight, maybe I did overreact, so I said to both of them, "We'll just follow the evidence and see where it takes us. He did sound sincere, though, I'll give him that."

As the elevator doors opened before us on the fifth floor, we entered the corridor and headed down the hall. Bob nonchalantly said, "if I was facing capital murder charges, you bet your ass I'd sound sincere."

When we got to the room where the murder took place, Smitty spoke up. "Fellas, if you look two doors down at the exit sign, that's the stairs. If I'd just taken someone out, and I watch any crime shows on T.V, I'd know that the police will be able to determine the time of death. Why in the hell would I take the elevator and risk being seen when all I had to do was go up or down a couple flights to prevent being identified on the hotel security video?"

"Smitty, it all goes back to misdirection. Remember what we talked about at the bar?"

"That's what I mean, Mike. It's playing out like this is a professional hit and we're purposefully being led, we're being sucked in," Smitty concluded as he opened the door to room 509.

As we entered, I noticed a door-less closet to my left across from what was the bathroom door. A few steps further was the spot where the victim was found. There were still chalk lines on the carpet at the edge of the hallway entering the sleeping area. In the center of the room to my right was a queen-sized bed and to the right of that was a reading chair. A lamp hanging above it, and two nightstands flanked the bed. There was a cheap oil painting of the surf pounding the shore on the wall.

Bob laid his bag on the balcony to take out the tools of his trade as I started applying mine. I asked Smitty to sit down at the writing desk and take some notes as we began to piece this puzzle together.

"Smitty, we know the killer came in first. He got the key card from the desk clerk between 12:30 to 12:35 pm. The girlfriend said they got to the room around 1 pm."

"He may have waited in the stairwell," Smitty said.

"Nah, He had to make sure the girl had left. It's possible, but I'm not buying into that. He needed to make sure she was gone. I think he was already in here. But check with the front desk. Maybe they have monitors on those cards or something."

"But how did he know the girl was going to leave in the first place?" Smitty asked.

"You know the answer as well as I do. He did his homework, and I bet the cocky son of a bitch did it the day before. Kelly said he was at the bar at lunchtime, remember? I'm thinking he saw them go up and followed them. I'd bet a year's salary on that. Smitty, I know ballplayers are creatures of habit. If it works, they keep on doing it. They're famous for sticking to a routine."

"Okay, Mike, but if you're right, then that kid that you just brow busted is innocent," Smitty countered.

"No, not necessarily. He has the most to gain, and he could have had an accomplice. That would explain the two different descriptions."

"Mike, so do about two dozen other players in the organization."

"Point taken," I replied. Just then Bob interrupted.

"Hey, I think I may have something."

"What you got?" Smitty asked.

"What I've got are some C.S.I. guys who, like you, assumed he waited in the stairwell and weren't very thorough," he said as he looked at Smitty. "I found some hairs that are human on the underside of the box spring, right here at the edge of the bed. Plus, the carpet is somewhat matted. Something heavy was underneath here. I'll bet you guys a dinner our boy hit his head either getting in or out from underneath the bed. And Mike, I think you're right. It only makes sense that he would wait in here to assure that there were no surprises, and the only place to hide would be right here," he said, pointing under the bed. "I'm going to keep checking the room, but I don't need you guys here. In fact, you are kind of distracting me and are both in my way. In addition, if there is a next time, and I hope there isn't, don't move the body or touch a thing, and seal it all off till I get there. Trying to process a crime scene that has already been done is like trying to eat an already chewed piece of meat."

"Bob, I'll try. I'll put the word out to all the departments who are in the locations where the O's have minor league teams, not to disturb or process the crime scene till you arrive. I can't promise anything, though. Besides, if I knew where he was going to strike next I'd stop him before it got to that point."

Chapter 26

The hotel was gracious enough to set up and let us use one of their conference rooms on the second floor for our conference call. Again, the room was bright, with a green and yellow color scheme and a splash of turquoise mixed in. It was excessively big for what we needed, but I appreciated it, nonetheless. At 1 pm, the connection was made as Smitty dialed in. On the other end were Guinea, Molly, Freddie and Dewayne. After greetings were made, we dove right in.

"All right guys, if we can get started: at 4 pm today we have scheduled a news conference here at the hotel. Smitty will be giving them everything that we deem appropriate and informative. There is so much press here that you can't sit down for a meal without fear of being overheard by someone sitting at the table beside you. To that end, we had no choice but to schedule a press conference a.s.a.p. Holly, if you don't mind, I'd like you to make up a generic copy of anything that Dewayne feels we can give the press from the information we gather from this meeting. you on board with this Dewayne?"

"Of course, Mike, whatever you need. If I could make one suggestion to Smitty, I would have a prepared statement with all information in it. Keep the questions to a minimum, and when asked, revert to the statement. Just repeat the information you already gave them and keep your answers short, Smitty. I can't stress this enough."

"Rhetoric. Sounds like a true politician," Guinea said with a laugh that was shared with all on the call, including Dewayne.

Then Dewayne continued, "We'll have the same information up here in case the press tries to double play us."

"Mike, I felt that your first concern would be getting the press off your back and out of the way, so I've already begun to put some tidbits together. I figured that you and Dewayne would want to feed the wolves," Molly said.

"Fantastic. I'm glad to see we're all on the same page. With that being said, Dewayne, what is the status on ownership and the front office of the O's and their affiliates?"

"The owner and the entire organization is in crisis mode. Both the owner and the General Manager have pledged their total support and access from ownership to the bat-boy in the lowest league in the system. We have free rein to do whatever we feel is necessary to catch this killer or killers. I've also asked them to beef up security at all levels in the organization, which they gladly agreed to do. The General Manager, as of 6 pm today, will be implementing a buddy system throughout the minor-league level, where all ballplayers will be paired with other players between 9 am and 11 pm. That's the best they can do, due to contractual obligations. It will be in effect until further notice."

"That's not good," I heard Guinea say, and I had to agree.

"No, I don't like that at all either. I don't think the killer cares how many he takes out to reach his objective, and if it is a ballplayer, it wouldn't impede him one bit. He'd just wait until lights out. Dewayne, call the G.M. and tell him not to do that and explain why, okay? Does everyone agree?" I asked. "Also, Dewayne, I want a background check on every first baseman in the system; pictures, hometown, hobbies, etc. Get them to Molly, she'll know what to do with them from there."

"Mike, that's going to be a problem. When I talked to the G.M., he told me that they often transfer third basemen, corner outfielders, and even catchers to first base. It's a numbers thing. You can hide a poor fielding player at first base if he has a good bat," Dewayne replied.

"So, we need to do a background check on everyone in the system," Guinea said, obviously frustrated.

"If it's alright with Mike, I'll come up in the morning and help work on it with you, Molly," Smitty said.

146

"And I can help, too. My Division Commander has transferred me here until we wrap this case up," Freddie responded.

"Great," I heard Holly say.

Dewayne jokingly asked, "what does your Commander drink, Freddie?"

"Scotch, good Scotch."

"Great, I'll send him a bottle of Glen Fiddich with a thank you card."

"Freddie, did you have any luck?"

"No, not much Mike. My guys went out and beat the bushes and we got the black truck seen in the area numerous times, but no one got a tag number. My gut tells me this isn't the killer's first rodeo. Everything seems so thought out, too clean."

"Yeah, Mike, I'm getting that vibe too. With all the info I've been collecting from you guys, this dude is what my mom would call a slick Willie," Molly said.

"What about you, Guinea?"

"Mike, like I told you earlier, that was definitely no accident. The driver had less than an eighth of a mile to get up to speed on a small, and I mean small, street. Hit him so hard it severed his spine. From what the coroner told me, it's no question it was a murder. There's absolutely no doubt about it. Additionally, the coroner found some rubber dust on the body from the same make of tires, those Mickey Thompsons.

"Is that it, Guinea?"

"Mike, this kid was really well liked. Everybody loved him. It seems he didn't have an enemy in the world. Maybe it's someone that has a score to settle with the Orioles."

"Mike, do you have a kid down their named Mark Newman?"

I looked at Smitty and said, "Sure do, why?"

"The Iron Birds General Manager, Dennis Cook, said he got what he called a lateral move to Delmarva."

"Yeah, I got the pleasure. In fact, I told him he was my number one suspect. It seems he not only was there at the time of the murder, but also has a black pickup truck with Mickey Thompson tires. Not to mention, he plays first base, plus the fact that he hasn't moved up in two years either because of slump or injuries. Fact of the matter is, I told him he was running out of time to make it to the show. I tried to put the fear of God in him, but to his credit, he stuck to his guns. He kept denying his involvement in any murders."

"Brother, I don't think that was such a good idea," Guinea said.

"Yeah, you're not the only one who has said that." Again, I looked at Smitty.

"I've got a question. What's the show?" Holly asked.

Freddie replied, "the major leagues."

"Mike, how're the boys doing?" Guinea asked.

"Good, why do you ask?" I said somewhat puzzled

"I got them two autographed bats with all the players on the team to sign. The damn bats cost me a small fortune though, and they were broken."

"Well, you're not going to like what I'm about to tell you. "I said

"What's that?" Guinea asked.

"It seems our number one suspect is the boys' new hero. The boys found a flaw in Mark's swing and, in turn, Mark gave them each a bat autographed by the entire Shorebird team."

"That bastard," Guinea yelled as everyone on the conference call broke into laughter.

While still laughing, I continued, "We need give the press as much as possible, except for Mark Newman being a suspect and the dust from the tires. Make sure we mention that the Orioles are giving us their full cooperation. I'll see you all tomorrow night or early Thursday morning."

Chapter 27

Victoria and Val left an hour after receiving the call from their grandson Mark. They had made good time on the way to Ocean City. There was almost no traffic from Manassas to 495, which was odd, plus they caught a break when they got to the Woodrow Wilson Bridge. There was just a little bit of traffic leaving Virginia as they entered Maryland off the bridge. From there it was clear sailing to route 50 east. After they crossed the Bay Bridge, they stopped at Kent Narrows to get a bite to eat. As they did, Val recalled the first job they did when they got to the states; taking out a C.I.A. operative and disposing of him in beautiful St. Michaels, Maryland.

Victoria smiled sheepishly and said, "My love, you were so full of piss and vinegar back then. There was nothing that you couldn't, or wouldn't do. I remember how handsome and strong you were. I've been a very fortunate woman to spend my life with you. It has been so adventurous and exciting, and of course, wonderful."

"Honey, you're saying I'm not strong and handsome anymore?" They both laughed as they took a bite of their crab cakes on crackers with just a touch of mustard on them.

As they continued down route 50 towards Ocean City, the talk turned to their grandson. Upon entering

Salisbury, Victoria asked, "Shall we stop and watch Mark's game, my love?"

"I don't think so, honey. I think we'd both serve his interest better if he doesn't know we're around just yet. I think we need to study what has been going on and find out exactly where the police are in their investigation. Learn about them personally. Discover their weaknesses, find out what they've been doing and what our grandson has been doing. We will learn about our adversaries as we once did, then proceed and act."

"Of course, you are right my love. This is so exciting," Victoria said as she slid to her left and put her hand on her husband's knee.

He turned and looked in her eyes and said, "Yes, it is honey. It reminds me of our world a long time ago."

As they entered Ocean City, it was now 4:15 pm. They had made excellent time, just five and a half hours from Front Royal. They decided to stay at the Clarion. On their way, they had made the reservation. As it turned out, it was just one floor above their grandson's room. Victoria and Val decided that if they ran into Mark they would just say they were concerned and came down to support him. But the truth was, they had come down to protect, and perhaps even save him. They had much work to do.

"My love, I think we should visit with Mark's chief adversary. From what I've read in the Post, the lead investigator is a man named Mike Carrier. What do you say we try to get to know our new friend?"

"I couldn't agree more. I'll go to the front desk and get us registered and ask the desk clerk what room our new friend is in, and we will take it from there."

By this time, they had made it to the Clarion, and the first thing they noticed was all the network news vans.

Val commented, "In all my years in this country, I have never understood the fascination Americans have with murders."

"I don't know, my love, but again, I have never understood your fascination with sports either."

After finding a parking place they grabbed all their luggage, including two bags that resembled old makeup cases from the sixties. But it may have been what was left in their car that was of far greater importance - two large military style duffel bags.

As Val went to register, Victoria found a bellhop cart and put their luggage on it. She methodically looked around the lobby, and, in her mind, took mini snap shots of the surroundings and even the people and staff that was there. As Val returned, he acted every bit his age, walking like he was a beat and broken down man. Victoria thought he looked pathetic and would be sure to tell him later. She would not be playing that charade. She was proud of the way she looked, and worked hard to stay in shape. She would not degrade herself for this or any mission.

When Val returned with the key card, he took the last bag from his wife and put it on the cart. As he started pulling it to the elevator, he said to his wife in a puzzled voice, "Our friend is staying in room 710 and Mark is in 603. Our friend brought his two boys with him."

"Well, why should this surprise you, my love? He is just like you - he likes to mix a little bit of pleasure with his business. Besides, it should be easier to spot him with the boys. Also, I downloaded a picture of him before we left home that I got from the Washington Post. I think we should start buying the Baltimore and local papers to perhaps get more information. It could be useful," Victoria said.

The elevator doors opened on the penthouse floor. Victoria smiled at her husband in loving appreciation as he said, "Only the best for you, my dear."

Inside their suite, Victoria could see that her husband, as he always did, surrounded his wife in luxury. The suite was huge. As they entered, they both saw the ocean through the large living room. The room sported two sofas with a large coffee table between them, and a large plasma TV. To their right was a large bedroom, complete with a hot tub and Jacuzzi, and of course, a king size bed. To their left was an office equipped with computer terminals, fax machine, and a copier.

Victoria went straight to the balcony to admire the view. Val put the luggage on the bed, mumbling what every man around the globe has thought at one time or another, *why must she bring all these clothes?* Then he came upon the two large cosmetic cases. Opening them, he removed the trays. Underneath them were all kinds of electrical devices. Some looked like old relics, but they would serve his purpose well. After putting all of his and her cloths neatly on the bed and hooking up the computer in the office, he went to the balcony to join his lovely wife.

Victoria was standing tippy-toed at the railing looking down at the never ending beach and sea. There was a late afternoon haze above the Atlantic that was only interrupted by the occasional seagull or prop plane with a large advertising banner. Val quietly walked up behind his wife and wrapped his arms around her waist. She smiled as his breath brushed her face.

"The view is breath taking, Val."

"Not as breath taking as you, my dear. And I can see that you plan to be breath taking the whole time we're here."

"Val, my love, a woman has to be prepared for any social situation and weather condition," she said as she turned and kiss him on the cheek. "Why don't you see if they have good vodka in that mini bar while I put away our clothes, which you so graciously laid on the bed. Then we shall go and see if we can find our friend."

Chapter 28

As I entered the hotel room and looked down the hallway, I saw the boys on the balcony looking out on the beach. As I slowly crept up behind them, I noticed how nice they both looked. Josh and Shane both had on cargo shorts with button down shirts. Shane's was a light brown while Josh opted for a light green. Both shirts were, of course, left un-tucked. They were both wearing solid white Nike's, paired with white ankle socks.

Crossing onto the balcony I hollered, "Hey!" They both must have jumped a foot. *Score a rare one for dad*, I thought.

"Well, boys, I finally got you."

"Every dog gets a bone occasionally," Josh said.

"You both look good. Give me fifteen minutes to clean up and we'll get out of here."

"Dad, is your friend Smitty coming with us?" Shane asked.

"No, I thought it'd be just us fellas tonight." With that I smiled and turned to go get ready. The boys returned their attention back to the beach.

As we waited in line at the Paul Revere restaurant located on the boardwalk below the hotel, we took in the sights and sounds of this resort city. Ocean City had grown rapidly. As a small child, I could remember Ocean City ending at the boardwalk where the Dunes and Diplomat Hotel were located. It had continued to grow, and by the mid-seventies, there were so many condominiums that they glutted the market and started auctioning and foreclosing on them. All the wetlands that use to be natural barriers to storms and hurricanes were now covered in asphalt and buildings.

Finally, we entered the restaurant. The place was packed. After we were shown to our table, we immediately got in the huge buffet line. Of course, the boys and I went right for the seafood. They had steamed, fried, and raw clams and oysters, steamed crabs, and soft crabs, and of course, Maryland's world famous crab cakes. Then there was the other food – spareribs, corn on the cob and enough Eastern Shore fried chicken, courtesy of the Purdue family I bet, plus loads of other stuff.

We ate and ate and then ate a little more. We were having a blast, laughing and talking, just the three of us. I treasured these moments and I vowed to myself to find more time to spend with them. I knew, as they got older, the window for these opportunities would dwindle. Leaving the restaurant fully stuffed, the boys wanted to walk down the boardwalk toward the inlet. We stopped at one of the many t-shirt shops that advertise three tees for

$10.99. We each got one. I thought it was the second-best deal of the day.

As we were heading toward the inlet, we enjoyed looking at all the people, another great activity down here. The boys kept staring at all the 'young honeys', as they would call them, and I looked at the ones who were more age appropriate. There were so many people of all ages, shapes, and sizes. *The more things change, the more they stay the same*, I thought. Little kids were pulling on their parents, older folks were sitting on the benches watching the people, the rent-a-cops were patrolling the boardwalk trying to make their presence felt.

As we got to the inlet, we entered the carnival-like atmosphere. We were at the beginning of the fishing pier when the boys saw the Star Shoot game. They both wanted to shoot the BB machine guns and I was up for it, too. When I paid the attendant for our games, I noticed an elderly couple getting ready to shoot. The couple saw the boys and decided to watch them first.

The boys fired away, trying their best to shoot out the small red star. Josh did the best of the two, shooting out almost the entire star. Shane got ¾ of his out. Now it was up to me to show them how it was done.

"Let's see how the big, bad cop does," Shane said sarcastically, trying to egg me on. I took aim and depressed the trigger to fire, shooting small bursts. I felt confident I could knock it completely out. I was sadly mistaken. I got it all, except one small corner in the lower left of the five-pointed star.

The boys sighed. We turned to leave, then the elderly lady said, in what I thought was a slight Eastern European accent, "Wait a minute boys. Why don't you watch us? If we win, we won't be able to carry those big stuffed animals, and you can have them."

The boys looked at each other, shrugged their shoulders, and then turned to me and rolled their eyes as if to say, *"Sure lady,"* but we were polite and stayed to watch.

The older gentleman went first. He also took short bursts drawing a circle around the star. Then he started at the top and shot a straight-line right down the middle. Next, he went from left to right of the target. It looked like a cut pie. He proceeded to shoot the pieces out, getting them all, except one that was hanging on by a thread. When he fired again he was out of BBs.

The boys and I just looked at each other in amazement as the elderly gentleman said something to the woman in a foreign language. She nodded and raised the machine gun to her shoulder. Then she did the exact same thing her husband had done. She took short bursts, being very methodical and deliberate. She, too, had shot it all out except for a sliver that was still hanging. She then depressed the trigger, and amazingly, she still had rounds left. She knocked it out with a couple rounds to spare.

The boys jumped up and down. They were amazed, and I was stunned as well. As the boys offered their congratulations, the woman asked them what stuffed animal they would like to have. I told her she didn't have to do that and she replied, "If it wasn't for the boys and you shooting first, my husband and I would have never figured out the pull."

"What do you mean?" I asked.

"After you and your boys shot, we noticed that the weapon pulled a little to the left. After my husband fired, he determined it shot left and down. From there, it was like ... how you say ... taking candy from a baby."

"Where did you learn to shoot like that?" Shane asked.

"Many, many years ago, in Russia," the elderly man said.

"We were about the same ages as you two boys ," the woman said looking at them both, while her husband instructed the still stunned game attendant to give the boys the 4 ft. Raven bird with the famous 52 jersey on it.

"So, have you both been here in the states long?" I asked, as we all started walking toward the rides at Trimpers together.

"Oh, yes, we have been in America since the early sixties. We're both retired now. We came here to Ocean City to visit our grandson," the gentleman said.

As the boys got in line to get some tickets to the Zipper, one of my favorite rides as a child, the lady continued, "We just got here and decided to take advantage of the senior discount at the Paul Revere Restaurant before we make our way to our hotel. Plus, we have to wait for our grandson to get off work, so we decided to take a walk."

"Where are, you staying?" I asked.

"At the Clarion," the woman replied.

"Really, so are we. In fact, we ate at the same restaurant. Small world isn't it".

"You have no idea," the gentleman said aloud.

"What are your names," I asked.

"This is my wife Victoria, and I am Vladimir Glasgow, but my friends call me Val. You may call me Val."

As he said that, I thought, *well, yeah okay,* somewhat puzzled as he asked our names.

"I'm Mike Carrier and these are my boys, Josh and Shane," pointing to each of them as I adjusted the big Raven bird that I now was stuck holding. "Again, I want to thank the both of you for this Raven bird. You really didn't have to."

"Oh, it was really our pleasure. The love and the smile of a child is priceless. As parents and as grandparents, we have found that you are willing to do anything for your young," Victoria said.

"I couldn't agree more," was my reply.

Chapter 29

The boys and I awoke late in the morning and got showered and dressed. I had decided that we would spend at least half a day here before heading back home. I knew everyone else would be back at the office pouring over all the information that they had collected on the players. I'd be more in the way than helpful. At least that's what Smitty said when I spoke to him before he left earlier in the morning.

As the boys and I were walking down the corridor heading to the elevators, I couldn't shake the thought that this guy is going out of his way to be seen hanging out at the bar and getting on the elevator with a boat-load of people. *What was this guy up to?,* I wondered as our elevator door opened.

The sketches drawn of the two suspects were similar, but they didn't look much like Mark. There was a slight resemblance, but not much, plus the height and weight varied a lot on the suspects. I wasn't convinced it was just one person involved, but what would be the motive if it were more than one?

As I was checking out at the front desk, I noticed Kelly coming in through the lobby doors. As the hotel manager handed back the department's Visa card, I thanked him for comping Smitty's room and asked the boys to take our bags to the truck. Then I thought of something.

"Hey guys after you put the bags in the truck, see if you can find that black truck we saw at the ballpark. If it's not in the parking lot, check the side streets. If it not there, check the parking lot across the street, but be careful crossing. If you find it, call me. If not, meet me back at our truck. And boys, don't lock my keys in the truck, please."

"Dad it's been three years already since we did that - you need to let it go," Shane said.

While the boys headed out the lobby doors, I made my way to the poolside bar. Kelly was in the process of getting the bar open for the day's business.

"Hey Michael, have you finally worked up the nerve to ask me out?" she said as she cut lemons and limes.

"Kelly, you know I'm too old for you. You'd wind up breaking my heart."

"Michael, when I met you, you came off as a much more confident man than that. I'm truly disappointed."

"Kelly, when I was sixteen I started tending bar at my parents' place. I learned to be a marriage counselor, shrink and a financial advisor, but, most of all, I learned how to read people doing that job. It really helped me to become a good cop. I need to know - what was your read on this guy, besides being smart and country?"

"Michael, when I said country I didn't mean 'hillbilly' or 'redneck.' His slang, his mannerisms, being very polite and proper, he seemed well organized and meticulous. He was constantly straightening his coaster, repositioning the ashtray everything had to be in a certain place. Even his clothes were well thought out. You could tell everything had a purpose."

"Is that it, Kelly?"

"No, but I doubt if this will help you any."

"What is it, you never know."

"He has a hard time with the ladies."

"What do you mean?"

"He has no self-confidence with the girls. Most guys like that have problems talking to women because they must think on the fly, they can't prepare. Then you take a girl like me, we can help a guy feel comfortable. Every time I talked to him he kept looking around, never looking me in the eyes. And when he did engage in a conversation, he became nervous and fidgety, peeling the coaster and putting it in a neat little pile. At first a girl may think that's kind of cute, but after a while that becomes pretty pathetic."

"Damn, I just learned something. You just threw his manhood right under the bus, and now I know what women think and want. I should just retire right now and call it a day. After all these years, I've finally been told how to figure you ladies out!!!"

"Michael, we've been telling men since the beginning of time. It's just that this time, it went in one ear and not out the other."

"Yeah, well maybe next time I'm down here we can talk about all of man's other great blunders over dinner."

"See, there is hope for mankind after all," Kelly said while she jotted down her phone number.

As she was handing it to me my cell phone rang. I told her goodbye as I turned and headed for the lobby. I answered the phone. It was the boys, and I told them I'd be there in a minute.

My boys met me at the front door. Shane said they found the truck in the parking lot across Ocean Highway.

After getting a couple of evidence bags out of our truck, I followed the boys across the street to the black Tahoe. Once there, I asked them to watch and wait and to let me know if someone was coming. I climbed under the truck and tried to scrape some of the rubber dust from the inside wheel well, but there was none to be found. The whole underbelly of the truck was spotless. It was cleaner

than a kitchen counter top that had just been bleached. I
was amazed. *Who the hell cleans the bottom of their truck?*
I thought as I climbed out from under it, disgusted and
puzzled.

Chapter 30

The time spent in Ocean city had been somewhat productive to the case, but very productive to my family. The boys had a blast, and the time I got to spend with them was priceless. I was glad I had taken advantage of the situation. Being a realist, I knew that the opportunities were going to become fewer and farther between as both the boys got older.

I felt good that we got to spend some quality time together. Even the drive home was nice, as we talked about the upcoming school year, sports, and just life is general. We stopped in Kent Island before we got to the Bay Bridge to have dinner at Skipper's Pier. As we were crossing the Bay Bridge after dinner, I saw the beach at Sandy Point State Park. I was brought back to the realization of the task at hand. Tomorrow we'd all be rolling up our sleeves and continuing the hunt for the murderer or murderers.

Once I got back to the office the next morning, everything returned to normal. I went over everyone's reports on the case and then the weekly expense reports. The only thing that was out of the ordinary was when Guinea came into the office with the two baseball bats, along with the peanuts, and laid them across my desk, saying, "I guess I'm second fiddle to a potential killer." It was all I could do not to break out laughing.

Later in the afternoon, I asked everyone to meet so we could get an action plan together. Taken our seats, I asked Molly how all the background checks were going.

"We've gotten all the Aberdeen Iron Birds done, and half the Delmarva Shore Birds. Freddie's gotten almost all of the Frederick Keys completed, but we haven't even started with the Bowie Bay Sox or the Norfolk Tide yet.

"Of all the ones, you've completed, does anyone stand out?"

"Well, we've got an interesting cast of characters. The backgrounds that we got back on almost all our Latin players are pretty vague. When I asked the organization about it, they were quick to point out that they're not even sure the birth certificates are correct. When I asked them to explain, they said that if a player is good enough to sign, age is a big factor; the younger the better. Years later after the player has already made it to the major leagues, some organizations have learned that a player's real age is older. And the Cuban players - you can forget that. Most of them don't even have attainable records. Mike, the minor and major league system have people from all walks of life, ethnic backgrounds, and cultures. It's a small melting pot of what makes up America. It's really fascinating, but in answer to your question, nobody really profiles as a cold-blooded killer, at least not yet."

"What about Mark Newman?" I asked.

"Yeah, Molly, tell him about our boy," Guinea responded.

"He doesn't profile to be a killer. He's had some tragedy in his life, but he's otherwise stable. He had excellent grades and made a 3.8 G.P.A. in high school, plus he has a girlfriend. He seems to be a well-rounded young man, who you and Guinea seem to think is a serial killer. He doesn't fit the stereotype or profile. Then again, my field is collecting data and analyzing it. You guys are the murder experts."

"Point taken, Molly, you give us everything you have and rest assured, the people in this room will figure it out. We have what I feel is the crème de la crème of law enforcement in this room, and that includes you. It is my hope that in the not so distant future, when Dewayne gets the state bureaucrats to give us a bigger budget, we will be able to have Freddie and Bob on our team full time, too."

"You think I'd leave my gravy job for this outfit?", Freddie said sarcastically.

Bob chimed in, "and if you think I'd leave Glen Burnie for this picturesque two-bit town you're out of your mind."

"Yeah, I do, because you both love me," I said, and then continued to ask Molly, "what else do you have on our so-called golden boy?"

"He was born Mark Jackie Newman, March 17, 1988, to a Lieutenant Commander named Jack Newman and his wife, Janie. It also should be noted that the Commander played baseball right down the street at the Naval Academy. Janie was formerly known as Janie Glasgow, but I'll get back to that in a few minutes, because that in itself may open up another can of worms. They all resided in Front Royal, Virginia. Both of Mark's parents commuted daily to Sterling, Virginia, where his mother worked for S.T.G., a defense contractor. His father would catch the metro at Sudley Station into the Pentagon."

"Molly, let me interrupt for one minute, if you don't mind."

"Sure, Mike."

"Freddie, I noticed your facial expression when she mentioned Front Royal."

"Yeah, Mike. Remember what I told you and Guinea in Frederick, that hunting was like a religion there and all points west? Well, Front Royal is like an hour southwest of there. Our boy Mark had the weekend pass from Aberdeen after the Griffith hit-and-run, or should I now say murder, so we can possible put him there."

172

"Imagine that. Okay, continue, Molly.".

"They lived in a subdivision called Hensalstone. Mark went to A.S. Rhodes Elementary, then later the family moved to 564 River Drive in town. Later he went to Warren County Middle school. From the age of six to thirteen he played in the Front Royal little league where he was coached by his father from tee ball to the senior league." Molly paused as she took a drink of her diet coke and then continued.

"Then, on September 11, 2001, his life would change forever." Molly looked up at me and again paused for a moment. I could feel my stomach starting to churn and form knots. I knew what was coming, when she said, "From what I can gather his parents were together eating a late breakfast in the cafeteria when the plane hit." Molly looked right at me and said, "Mike, I'm trying to confirm this, but it looks like she was there to attend the same meeting as your wife. There is a strong possibility that Mark's mother knew Shannon. Mike, I'm sorry to bring all this up, but it gives us a good picture of his upbringing and mental makeup."

"It's alright, Molly. A lot of people lost loved ones that day. I'm certainly not alone."

"Janie's parents were left as guardians of Mark. His paternal grandfather lives in Fairfax, Virginia and his wife died in August of 1999. Mark's parents were both only children. Mark then moved in with his grandparents, Victoria and Vladimir Glasgow."

When Molly said that I abruptly jumped up out of my chair and said, "What did you say?"

"Victoria and Vladimir Glasgow, Vladimir's friends call him Val."

"I know what they call him, Molly," I said in an agitated tone.

"Do you know these people?" Guinea asked.

"Do I know them? I met them in Ocean City when the boys and I were playing an arcade game, you know, the machine gun BB game. They both gave us a clinic in shooting."

"What do you mean?" Bob asked.

"I mean both showed us what we did wrong after they took out their targets!!!"

"Both of them took the targets out?" Bob repeated.

"She took it completely out - he left a piece hanging by a thread. He said something to her in Russian and then she took it out in short order, with shots to spare. Then they both explained to the three of us how they saw our guns pulling to the left. If you had heard them explaining it, you'd have thought they were friggin' science teachers

174

explaining the shot. On top of that, we hung out with them for the rest of the evening. She just talked about being a parent and grandparent and I remember her specifically saying that a parent would do anything to protect their young."

"Mike, are you sure were talking about the same people? Those two are in their seventies," Freddie asked.

"They're the same people, trust me, and they're in outstanding shape. They look like they are both in their fifties. In fact, I remember her telling me they ran two miles a day. Molly, what else do we know about them?"

"Not much, Mike. I traced them back to 1961, and then they fall completely off the grid. It's a big red flag, but I have a theory and I have a friend checking it out."

"Well, you've got our attention, Molly," Guinea said.

"Yeah, we're all ears," Bob said.

"They showed up in '61 and deposited over 1.75 million in U.S. savings bonds and other treasury bonds, plus 1.25 million in cash. I don't need to tell you that was a boatload of money back then."

"It still is, from where I'm sitting," Freddie said as we all shook our heads in agreement.

Molly continued, "After they had their home built, Vladimir landed a job as a game warden with the United States Forestry Service. His wife went to work as a substitute teacher - not exactly lucrative jobs, but we all know how tough it is to get a job with the government. You must know somebody, plus a game warden has more power than us. Hell, they don't even need a warrant to knock down a door."

"Girl, how do you find out this stuff? You amaze me," I said, and then asked, "so what is your theory?"

"I think they defected."

"They what?"

"They defected. Back in the day, the government was giving bonds away to defectors, like it was candy. Read your history, Bay of Pigs, Cuban Missile Crisis, the cold war gentleman. It is widely thought that hundreds of Russians defected during this time."

"Who's your friend?" Guinea wanted to know.

"Sherry Kraiss - she works for N.C.I.S and is an expert in political science, computer science, and is one of the best data analysts in the world."

"The Navy can afford her?" I asked.

"Hell, no. She graduated number one in her class at M.I.T., and she made her millions writing various books in her fields. She just works there to stay in the loop," Molly informed the group.

"She must be a typical nerd," Guinea said.

"I resent that, Roger."

Guinea had upset her and I knew the slam dunk was imminent.

"There's not a man or woman in this building that can hold a candle to her. In fact, she was even asked to pose for Penthouse back in college - beauty AND brains, asshole!!!"

"Geez, Molly, it slipped out. I was just thinking it, I didn't mean for it to come out. I'm sorry, Molly," Guinea said in full retreat.

"Can we get back to it guys, before Guinea digs himself in deeper?, I said then continued, "Molly, when do think your friend will have anything for us?"

"Sorry about the outburst. It's just a touchy subject. Women should be able to be smart without having to apologize for it. Anyway, not long. Like I said, she's that good. She can find a needle in a haystack. I'd bet she'll have something for us by day's end."

"Alright, then give us the rest of what you've got on Mark Newman."

177

"After the death of his parents, Mark moved in with his grandparents. They live right outside of Front Royal on route 522, on Thunderbird Road. It's close to a small town called Bentonville. They have 27 acres, and there's one way in and one way out. They have only two neighbors within a half mile of their property, per the county records. As I said earlier, he was enrolled in Warren County High School, where he lettered in football, basketball, and baseball while earning a 3.8 G.P.A. He was offered over thirty-eight scholarships from various colleges, but from what I was told, he took some bad advice from his high school manager. He advised him to turn pro in the hope of furthering his own career, while his grandparents tried to persuade Mark to further his education. It's important to understand, guys, that I obtained all this information from public records and a couple college coaches. I haven't called any of his schools or known acquaintances. I wasn't sure how you would want to proceed with this   I thought it would be wise not to contact anyone that might alert him or his grandparents. I know how small towns operate - if one person knows it, they all know it."

"Does he follow any set social patterns? Is there a girlfriend in the picture?"

"Guinea, from what I've been able to obtain from looking through his yearbooks and hundreds of press clippings, it's safe to say he was a ladies' man. He played the field, and played it well, and he had a lot of friends in school. Typical jock. Everybody loved him. In fact, the whole town thought he'd turn pro and put Front Royal on the map."

"That's a lot of responsibility and pressure to put on a young man. That alone could make anyone unstable. That could be our motive. The fear of failure and rejection is a powerful motive," Guinea said.

"Just one more thing of importance and one observation," Molly said.

"Go ahead, Molly, the floor's still yours."

"He has been an avid hunter since he was eight, checking in his legal limit of animals during every hunting season since then. He also has a handgun permit for three guns, a 9 mm, a 38, and a 44 magnum, plus various hunting rifles, including a Cheytac M 200."

As Molly said that, the rest of us just nodded at each other.

"I'm sorry, guys, but even with all of this I still don't think he fits the profile. If he failed at baseball, with his smarts, demeanor, and determination, I think he'd land on his feet. Not to mention the millions that his grandparents have and will eventually be leaving him – he would be set financially. Plus, he isn't a social misfit. He has lots of friends, and judging by all the pictures of him with girls in his yearbook and his press clippings, that department wasn't a problem."

179

"But, Molly, the thought of fame and making your own fortune, along with your face being plastered on every TV in America and half way around the world, can be very enticing. The dream of fame and fortune has gotten a lot of people killed," Guinea said.

"I understand, Guinea. The world is your oyster type deal," Molly sighed.

"Do you have anything else, Molly?" I asked.

"I've got two more players that may be a possibility. One has serious social issues and the other seems to be a little unstable mentally."

"Okay, let's get some fresh coffee and go to the head and we'll come back and finish this up."

"Hey, Mike, how close did you come to hitting out all of the targets that grandma and grandpa knocked out? Did you embarrass yourself and the boys?" Guinea asked as we were getting up from the table.

"Go to hell, pal," was my reply, as everyone in the room got a laugh at my expense.

Chapter 31

About an hour later, we finished the beginning of a profile of a first baseman named Zach Ryan, we were just about to conclude with a third baseman named Alex Santo when the phone rang. Molly answered it after only two rings.

"Hey, Sherry. Yeah, we're all still here. Do you mind if I put you on speaker phone?" There was a slight pause as Molly switched it on. "Sherry, can you hear us?" Molly asked.

"Just fine," the voice said from the other end.

"Sherry, you're here with detective Mike Carrier, Roger Ginavan, Steve Smith, Freddie Hunt, and from our C.S.I. division, Bob Romberger."

"Hi everyone. If you don't mind, I'd like to get right to it. I've got a lot of work to do. Molly, your instincts were right. Victoria and Vladimir did, indeed, defect. What you didn't know is that Victoria and Vladimir were K.G.B. agents, two of the finest they ever had - first rate in intelligence gathering, special ops, and assassination. They were very well versed in their trade, and I assume you only need their background prior to 1961? "

"Yeah, Sherry, I think we're up to speed from '61 until now, but I want it all. We need to know exactly what we are dealing with," I said.

"Well, these two led a very adventurous and colorful life. They both were forced into World War II at the ages of seven and nine, respectively. They both became snipers almost immediately, accumulating one hundred and thirty-four confirmed kills between them. Both are also highly decorated, receiving the cross of Stalin, their version of our Congressional Medal of Honor."

We all looked at each other, and I could tell by the expressions on their faces, everyone was as impressed and bewildered as was I. Sherry continued to brief us on their backgrounds.

"They met on the battlefield in Stalingrad and it eventually led to a torrid love affair that culminated in their marriage in 1947. After the war, they were both immediately recruited by the K.G.B., serving in many different locations throughout the world, until being transferred to the United States at the height of the cold war in 1959. It is worth noting that in their dossier it was believed by the Russian party that the Glasgow's themselves did not believe in the socialist party doctrine, but were loyal to mother Russia and her people. They both often missed socialist party meetings and were under close watch by the political party liaisons. In short, they were loyal to Russia but thought of as dissidents. On February

22, 1961, they, along with their one-month-old daughter, defected. It is my belief that the reason for the defection had something to do with their baby girl being born. Maybe it was because of all the uncertainty of the times. But, after six months of intelligence debriefings by all our government agencies, they were given a king's ransom in bonds, a kiss on their cheeks, and sent on their merry way."

"Awful generous of the C.I.A.," Guinea said aloud.

"I agree," Sherry responded, then added, "Back then it was all the game to get agents to flip. In the late seventies and early eighties, Mother Russia started turning Americans, so it really came back and bit us in the ass."

"One more thing of interest, and I believe of extreme importance, when they defected I'm sure they were offered new identities. But I'm guessing they refused them, which is rare. It's like they were daring the K.G.B. to come after them. So, I investigated a little further on a hunch and, not to my surprise, I found that since the fall of '63 until the summer of '78 there have been fifteen Russian operatives found in various national parks in the area, including seven in George Washington National Park, where Vladimir works. Now stay with me boys and think outside the box. "From September of '63 until July of 2003, there have been twenty-seven deposits of one hundred twenty- five thousand dollars each, deposited in an off-shore account in their name. These are from a dummy corporation. I found out it is a front for our friends at

Langley. Gentleman, what I am about to tell you could get me fired, not that I really care, but you need to know what you're dealing with. The C.I.A. is not allowed to do business inside our borders as you know, and its common knowledge that they believe that a dead foreign operative is just as good as a flipped one. It is my belief that the Glasgows are working our side of the fence. That would explain the large cash deposit when they first arrived, a down payment of sorts. Again, this is just my professional opinion, but I've been doing this a long time and all my expertise tells me these grandparents are doing some of this country's dirty work. Please, I ask that what you just learned does not leave the room. It could have a catastrophic effect on a lot of people, including myself."

"Sherry, this is Detective Mike Carrier. I want to thank you for your time involved in this research and for giving us this information. This brief has given us valuable insight into what we may be dealing with. Rest assured that this room is like Vegas - what goes on in here stays here. Again, thank you, and I think I speak for everyone in this room when I say, we look forward to meeting you."

"Thank you, Mike. "Until next time. Molly, I'll call you later."

"Okay, Sherry, bye-bye," and with that the line went dead.

We all looked at each other, knowing that Sherry may have just opened a whole new can of worms. I could not help but to think, *what have we gotten ourselves into?*

Chapter 32

"Molly, I want to thank you for bringing Sherry into the loop. What she gave us could prove very beneficial to this case."

"Mike, remember when we were in Fredrick and you or Guinea said it looked like a professional hit? At the time, I had my doubts, but I'm not so sure now. I may have to re-examine my thought process." Freddie said.

Guinea spoke up, saying, "Well, I've got a completely different take on this. I still like the kid for it. I'm sure grandma and grandpa took the boy out on their estate and taught him how to shoot and cut jugulars to put animals out of their misery, and everybody learns how to drive. Plus, he's got motive."

Smitty said, "I'm liking the grandparents. For one, we showed Mark's picture around in O.C and we didn't get a hit from any of the witnesses. Two, I like them in the Aberdeen hit-and-run, and the Frederick murder is close to their home. Remember our discussion on misdirection. I'm sure they're good at coercing people to doing things for them. That would explain the two different men the witnesses saw. And the hit and run is a no-brainer for a pro, and they are snipers. We all know that was one hell of a shot."

"Well, we can't jump to any conclusions. The fact of the matter is, we are no farther along with this case than when we started. Truth be told, we probably just widened the gap," I remarked to the group.

"So where do you want to start Mike?" Smitty asked.

"First, let's get twenty-four-hour surveillance on both Zach Ryan and Alex Santo. See if we can get some local uniforms to do it in street clothes to save us some money in the budget."

"Freddie, I'd like you and Smitty to watch the grandparents they look awful good to me. They have the expertise and I could see them wanting to help their golden boy succeed by taking out the competition. But then again, they are smart enough to know we'd be looking at their grandson, so why would they put him in the position to possibly take the fall? These people haven't lived this long in their business by being careless and stupid, this whole case has been about misdirection. It could be part of their master plan."

"Guinea, you and I are going to force the issue. I'm going to speak with Dewayne and see if we can get a search warrant for Mark's hotel room and truck, plus his residence in Front Royal. If he's involved, we may find something or at least ratchet up the pressure to force him or even his grandparents into a mistake.

"Molly, in your report did you mention if he lived by himself or with his grandparents?"

"I'm sorry Mike, I thought I covered that. He lives alone at 118 Kerfoot in Front Royal. His grandparents rent it to him."

"Guys, I want to thank you all for getting this information together today. Molly, please send Sherry a thank you note. Make it personal - no e-mails - do it the old-fashioned way, through the post office. She was a big help."

"Guinea, we'll go to Ocean City first thing tomorrow morning. You might want to pack an overnight bag just in case. I'll call you later. We'll probably meet at my house, but I'll confirm. "Molly, can you handle the reservations for us?"

"Everybody, as usual, we'll run everything through Molly. Let's finish up early today. Tomorrow starts the long hours associated with the legwork. I don't know where to tell you guys to begin in finding the Glasgows. You may want to call the Clarion in O.C., or better yet, see if you can find out where they last used a credit card. Molly will help you with that. When you do find them, be extremely careful. They'll spot a tail, and as seasoned pros my guess is they won't think twice about killing you. Freddie and Smitty, make sure you get the best team you can find as your relief. I don't want anybody getting killed, we clear"?

"Crystal clear. I know just the two," was Freddie's reply.

"Good, then go ahead and get out of here. You've got the longest drive home. Go spend some time with the Mrs. This could turn out to be a long stakeout."

As everyone filed out of the conference room, I called Dewayne. "Hey pal, this is Mike, you busy? Good, I'll be down in a minute. I've got some stuff to go over with you."

After taking the steps down the two flights of stairs to Dewayne's office, I saw the door was open. I walked right in, by-passing the reception area, and saw Dewayne on the phone waving me in from his office door.

Dewayne's office is big with lots of space. He has a large oak desk with a half-inch piece of protective glass covering it. There is also a very nice matching high back swivel chair behind it. As with most lawyer's offices, there were all the diplomas and law degrees adorning the wall behind his desk. Surrounding the room were various plants and ferns, and on the wall to the left was a fifty-gallon fish tank.

As Dewayne hung up the phone he must have read the expression on my face. "Man, I know what you're thinking, but this wasn't my idea. My wife decorated the office. She says I'm always too stressed out. She thought a relaxing work place would change that, but personally, if I jump out this window you'll know the real reason why."

"Who am I to argue?" I replied.

"Well, what can I do you out of Mike?"

"Dewayne, I need a search warrant for Mark Newman's hotel room in O.C., as well as his truck and his residence in Virginia."

"Do you have enough to arrest him?"

"No, that's why I need the search warrants. We can prove that he has means and motive."

"Have you thought this out Mike?"

"What do you mean, Dewayne"?

"On what little we have, If I can get a judge in Maryland and in Virginia to do this and you serve him a warrant, the media will be all over him and your team, not to mention my department. It could cause a hornet's nest of problems, especially if we're wrong. May I make a suggestion?"

"Go ahead," I said, somewhat annoyed.

190

"Just ask him if you can look around. He hasn't left O.C. since the murder of Tim Fallon, so if he's got something it may still be there. Besides, asking a judge in his home town for a search warrant on what little we've got, hell, I'd have a better chance of my wife redecorating this room. Go to him, tell him if he doesn't he must have something to hide. You know the drill. Threaten him. Say that you'll tell the Oriole brass and the press that you think he did it. Tell him he'll get released by the Orioles. Use your imagination. A warrant is the last thing we want to do, trust me. You're a great cop. You do the cop work and let me get the conviction."

"All this political B.S.. Now I know why you make the big bucks, Dewayne."

"Sometimes you've got to walk softly and carry a big stick, but stay focused on the end goal. And that's to get these whackos off the streets, however, you've got to do it within the parameters of the law."

"Yeah, it's the last part I sometimes have a problem with."

"Yeah, you and your team, Mike."

Chapter 33

In the morning, I awoke, showered, shaved, got my coffee, cigarette, and morning paper and headed to the back deck to wait for Guinea. After talking to Dewayne yesterday, it was clear I had no choice but to do it his way. But I really wanted those warrants as intimidation. He finally said that if push came to shove, he'd get them for us and fax them down to the State Police barracks in Berlin.

I could hear the boys coming down the steps. I had planned for Juanita to check in on them from time-to-time. If I had to spend, the night they could sleep over at her house. After getting their Fruit Loops, they joined me outside to have their breakfast and both reached for my sports section that was laying on the table. About a minute later, I looked over their shoulder and saw their Uncle Guinea in the kitchen helping himself to a cup of coffee and a bowl of cereal.

As he came out the sliding glass door, the sports section became a thing of the past. I often felt that the boys thought of Guinea as nothing more than a big kid in a man's body. Whenever he's around, their faces always light up. Leaving the boys behind is always tough and it's not made any easier when Guinea is around, but we finally got on the road after a couple promises were made. Guinea had already spoken to Freddie and Smitty. They had already left and were about forty-five minutes ahead of us, having just crossed the Kent Narrows Bridge.

After a long ride with only one stop for a bathroom break in Cambridge, we finally arrived in Ocean City. Things had worked out well for us. It happened to be an off day for the Shorebirds. We would be able to search Newman's hotel room and truck without raising a lot of eyebrows. I liked him for the murders, but I also thought his grandparents could have done it or helped him do it. However, Dewayne was right, I had to think of the consequences if I brought him in and charged him. Just bringing him in for questioning could raise suspicion and could cause him to get released and lose his job, and even his baseball career.

Dewayne had made me start thinking about all the cases I'd been involved in over the years. I never gave much thought to the people that we had suspected and brought in for questioning, only later to be found innocent. How had that affected their lives? What about their careers and family? It had to have a negative impact on their lives, I thought, and moving forward my team and I would have to be more considerate of that fact.

Pulling up to the hotel, I knew this was going to be different. I expressed my concerns to Guinea. He is, and most likely will always be, an 'in your face' cop. It worked well for him. It was his style, but today he would have to tone it down a notch and keep it in check until we were at least behind closed doors.

As we approached the front desk, I happened to notice Kelly walking down the hallway toward the pool. She was in front of us and didn't see me. I couldn't help but wonder if it was possible for a man my age to have a relationship with someone sixteen years younger. After finding out that Mark Newman was still believed to be in his room, we started walking toward the elevator. We were just about to enter when I turned and said, "To hell with it."

"What?" Guinea said.

"Wait right here. I'll be back in a minute."

As I was walking through the double doors that lead to the pool, Kelly looked up and noticed me walking toward her. She looked stunning in a bright orange bikini top with a white wrap around her waist.

"Michael, I'm glad to see my charm and sex appeal is so irresistible that you just couldn't stay away."

"Am I that easy to read? I asked. 'Just how many bikinis do you have?"

"If I told you that I would have to kill you. Would you like something to eat or drink?"

"No, actually I'm working, but I was wondering...." she cut me off.

"I get off at eight o'clock. I'll meet you here, and please don't be late because this lady won't wait!"

"I wouldn't think of it." I responded

Boy, she made that easy, I thought as I turned to walk away, and ran into a wide-eyed Guinea.

"Whoa, dude, who is that?"

"I thought I told you to wait, and that, my friend, is my dinner date."

"With any luck, she'll also be your dessert," Guinea smirked as he pulled the door open for us. I didn't dignify his comment with a response as we walked toward the elevator.

We reached the sixth floor without saying a word. As the door opened, my instincts and muscle memory took over. Without a thought, I unzipped my jacket and unbuttoned my holster on the way to Mark's room. I glanced over my shoulder and was glad to see that the corridor was empty, and I was hoping like hell it would remain that way, avoiding a public display.

Reaching room 613, I knocked as Guinea pulled his 9 mm and had it in what I call the prayer position. Mark answered the door wearing plaid short pants with black Nike shower shoes and nothing else. I could tell he was more than a little surprised to see Guinea and I.

"Detective, what are you doing here?"

"Mark, this is my partner, Roger Ginavan. May we come in?"

"Sure, what can I do for you?"

"Let's step inside, shall we?" Looking at Guinea, I could tell he was shocked to see how really big Mark was. You couldn't help but think he'd be quite a load if this would happen to go south.

Standing between the bed and the writing desk, I again introduced Guinea. Mark, out of good upbringing or reflexes, brought up his hand toward Guinea, who ignored him. Instead, he reached into his inside pocket and pulled out a pair of latex gloves.

"If you don't mind, we'd like to look around," Guinea said.

"Don't you need a search warrant or something like that?" Mark asked.

"If I have to, Mark, I can have one here in a half hour. But by then, the two news trucks that are still outside, not to mention the Orioles front office, will know all about it. Roger and I figured you would want it this way, but ..." then I flipped open my cell phone.

"Yeah, yeah, you're right. I have nothing to hide. Help yourselves. I'll wait outside on the balcony 'til you're done."

As Mark started walking toward the balcony, I followed him. Standing outside, both of us leaning on the rail and looking out on the semi-crowded beach with the waves pounding the surf, I asked him in a very friendly tone, "Mark, you got anything you want to tell me?"

"No." His reply was fast and very curt.

I continued, "You also know we're going to have to search your truck. Is that cool?"

Just then, Guinea said, "It better be cool, because we got your ass, you son of a bitch, we got you dead to rights!!!" Guinea was holding a Cheytac M200. He continued, "It was in a big green duffel bag under his bed, plus I also found clothes matching both descriptions of the man or men seen in the lobby the day of the murder here. All we're missing is the Orioles hat and the knife."

So much for restraint. Guinea just couldn't help himself, he had to get right in his face.

I asked, "Mark, you sure you don't have anything to say?"

"I haven't killed anybody. I swear, I've never killed anybody in my life. I use that rifle to blow off steam and to relax. I'm an avid hunter."

"What are you hunting down here in the middle of the summer, you over-sized prick?" Guinea asked, turning up the heat.

"I go target hunting and skeet shooting. That's not breaking the law, and it sure as hell is not killing anybody." was all Mark could say.

"Mark, you do know that we have ways of testing that rifle to tell if it was used in the Bobby Brannon murder?" I said in a very even and non-dramatic tone.

"Detective, you can test it all you want. It wasn't used to kill anybody. In fact, I just got finished cleaning it when you knocked. I had just come back from the shooting range. I had been there since 8 o'clock this morning."

"You arrogant bastard. You think that just because you cleaned your friggin' rifle it will hide the fact that you killed Bobby Brannon? If you do, you're sadly mistaken, asshole."

In the same even tone, with no sound of panic in his voice he had maintained throughout, Mark said, "No, but it should make the ballistic test easier. Being a detective, I'm sure you know that, asshole."

"You friggin' jerk, who are you to mock me? I'll.... "

I stepped in between them and said, "Mark, get your shirt on. We're going to get in your truck and take a little ride."

Before we left the room, I stepped out on the balcony and called Dewayne. He answered on the third ring. "Hey, it's me. Listen, we found a Cheytac M200, like the one used in the Bobby Brannon murder, plus some questionable clothing. We're getting ready to take Mark Newman and his truck to Berlin to search it and question him. Thing is, he's cooperating fully and he's maintaining his innocence. I know we have enough to arrest him, but I'd like your input. I don't want to book the wrong guy after our discussion yesterday. The media would have a field day if we were wrong. I don't want to ruin this kids career or yours, not to mention mine. So, my question to you is, how good is your rapport with the Orioles General Manager?"

"Why, what are you thinking Mike?" By this time, both Guinea and Mark had come out on the balcony and were listening.

Guinea was already putting Mark in cuffs as I continued my discussion with Dewayne. "I'm thinking we be honest with the G.M. We tell him we have Mark in custody for the possible murder of Bobby Brannon and

199

suspect him in the other two, but until ballistics come back on the weapon we found, we don't want to charge him. We feel he might even be getting set up and because of that, we'd like to keep this on the down low between the G.M. and us. We also feel it's in the best interest of the club and our department, also Mark's career, that we not rush to judgment. When we take him out of here, we are bound to be seen by reporters, so we are not going to cuff him as he has agreed to cooperate fully. We'll follow him to Berlin so we don't raise reporters' suspicions.

Dewayne said, "It sounds like you've given this a lot of thought. I'm sure I can get the G.M. to play ball, but I'm concerned the local press down there, and then the rest of the media, will wonder why Mark isn't playing. Then they'll put two and two together."

"Have the General Manager put Mark on the disabled list."

"For what?" Dewayne asked

Looking at Mark still in cuffs, I said, "A wrist injury."

Chapter 34

I asked Guinea to take the cuffs off Mark. He thought I was crazy. I said to him, "You heard the conversation. If we blow this and we happen to be wrong, we'll all have egg on our faces and our asses will be on the line. you willing to risk that? With a high-profile case like this is, moving forward we would have no creditability, every move that we made would be second guessed. That is, if we still had our jobs."

"What makes you think I'm going to play along?" Mark asked

"If you don't, Mark, your career is already over," was my reply.

While we waited for the elevator, I had second thoughts on what I had said to Dewayne. I didn't want Mark to play rabbit on us, so I told Guinea to drive Mark's truck. Mark would ride with me.

We caught a break as we made our way through the lobby, and then to our vehicles. What little bit of press was still there didn't pay us any attention.

After the twelve-mile ride to Berlin, we arrived at the State Police barracks and pulled around back, just in case there were any media-types lurking about. Seeing that there were none to be found, I escorted Mark into the barracks, cuff-less of course, just in case any press was inside.

Meanwhile, Guinea had pulled the truck inside the garage and started looking through the Tahoe. I immediately came to join him and crawled under the Tahoe to look for some rubber dust from the tires, which I was sure to find from the trip up here. When I found it, I grabbed an evidence jar from the workstation and scraped some into it with my pocketknife.

With that complete, I went to help Guinea, who had already found two M200 clips in the console. As I was looking through the driver-side door, I looked up on the visor and saw a picture of a gorgeous young woman in her early twenties. She had wavy, long blond hair and big blue eyes - a real looker. *Our boy sure has good taste in women,* I thought as I laid the picture down and continued my search.

I stepped out of the truck and kneeled down to look under the front seat. When I did, I saw a long knife in a black leather sheath. I thought this and the rifle could turn out to be the murder weapons. Add the rubber dust from the tires, we could tie him into all three murders if we were lucky. But something didn't feel right. It was all too easy, but as in any case, you go where the evidence takes you. With what we might have, it just could be the final nail in Mark Newman's coffin.

As soon as we got back inside, I called Bob Romberger and told him we needed him down here A.S.A.P. to process two possible murder weapons. I wanted the best on the job, so I wanted him to do it personally. When I asked him how long it'd take to get down here, he said he'd be here in two and a half hours.

Looking at my watch, I saw that it would put Bobby here around 4:30 pm. I called Dewayne again and told him what else we had found. Also that Bobby was coming down to do ballistics on the rifle and check out the knife. He in turn told me that he'd spoken with the Orioles General Manager and he was completely on board. The G.M. was going to notify the Shorebirds brass and tell them to place Mark on the fifteen-day disabled list, retroactive to today.

Things were coming together fast so I decided to call Josh and tell him I wouldn't be coming home tonight. His phone rang five times before he picked it up.

"Hey pal, what took you so long to answer the phone?"

"Dad, we're playing Halo and I just can't get up in the middle of the game. Besides, I saw it was you and I knew you would call back."

"Look, pal, I'm going to have to stay down here tonight. I want you to fix you and your brother that

203

Stouffer's frozen lasagna for dinner, and then later, I want you both to go over to Juanita's. She'll be expecting you."

"No problem dad, anything else?"

"No. Does your brother want to talk to me?"

"Shane, do you want to talk to dad?"

"Nah, just tell him I love him." Shane replied.

"Dad, did you hear that?" Josh asked.

"Yeah, I did, and I love and miss both of you. I'll call Juanita's later tonight to see how your day went. Be good, okay?"

"We will." Josh said

After hanging up, I called Juanita to let her know what was going on. She assured me that she would check in on them during the day until they came over for the night. With that taken care of, it was time to turn my attention back to our golden boy.

I went to find the Watch Commander to ask him if there was a private room where we could talk to our boy. After pointing me in the right direction, I found Guinea and asked a uniformed officer to bring Mark into the room. The room was small, maybe ten by eleven. It had an old, gray metal desk and a matching chair with worn, green upholstery on the arms and seat. There was another chair in similar condition in the corner of the room.

When Mark arrived, I asked him to take a seat. Guinea had gone to find another chair. I purposely waited for him to return before I spoke. I thought a couple more minutes of silence with me sitting across from him, would make Mark a little more uncomfortable. When Guinea returned, I began.

"Young man, you've got some serious problems. If there's anything you need to tell us, now is the time. If you don't talk to us right here and right now, we won't be able help you in any way. And trust me, you'll be putting yourself in a no-win-situation, do you understand?"

"Do I need a lawyer, detective?" Mark asked

"If you want one, you have that right, and I can't stop you from exercising that right. But you haven't been charged with anything yet, and we have gone to great lengths to protect you and your career."

"Who do you think you're kidding? You're protecting your ass, as well as the Orioles. I overheard your conversation. You couldn't give a rat's ass about me."

"You ungrateful bastard. We've got enough on you already to put you away for the rest of your life, even if you happen to be innocent, you asshole!" Guinea shouted.

"It's a shame you feel that way. I was just told that the Orioles' front office had put you on the fifteen-day disabled list to protect your roster spot while you're cooperating with us. But if you want to get your attorney involved, all bets are off. Trust me, we will charge you with all three murders, and make them stick. Even if we don't, when I notify the Orioles that you refused to cooperate with us, you can kiss your career goodbye." As I was telling him his options, I did so in a very non-chalant tone, trying to suggest with my voice that I didn't care what he decided to do.

"Detective, I swear I didn't do anything wrong." Mark had lost his smugness and his composure as he pleaded with me to believe him. From our previous conversation, and up to this point, he had done a good job of keeping his composure. I attributed it to the fact that he was used to being in pressure situations. I found myself briefly feeling a little sorry for him, but he may have been responsible for the deaths of three young men. Just how much compassion could I have?

Then Guinea spoke up in a harsh tone, "Kid, you don't get it. If you don't talk to us right now, when this is all over they're going to put you away in some harsh prison where you must fight for your life day in and day out, just for the chance to slowly rot away. You will never see the light of day again. Think about that, kid. It doesn't get any clearer than that, pal. Now, we're going to ask you one more time, you going to help us help you, or what?"

"Detectives, I don't know what you want me to say. I swear to God, on my parents' graves, that I never killed anybody, I swear!!!"

With that, Guinea stood up and slammed his chair against the desk and said, "You stupid son of a bitch. Your parents can't help you now. The only place you're going is straight to hell." With that said, Guinea headed toward the door and walked out, slamming it behind him.

"Alright Mark, this is what I know, and this is how it's going to play out. We've got your rifle which probably killed Bobby Brannon. I also found the knife that killed Timmy Fallon in your truck under the driver's side seat."

Mark stood up and shouted, "I use that knife for lots of things!"

"Sit the fuck down!" I said, finally raising my voice. Guinea walked back in as I continued, "I've scraped some rubber dust off your truck tires that I'm certain will match some of the dust that was found on Albert Griffith's body. I've got dozens of reports of a truck matching yours being seen in both Aberdeen and the Frederick area."

"You're guilty, and we've got you. You're in the big league now, kid. Some District Attorney isn't going to prosecute you. No, the State's Attorney is on this like stink on shit. You're going down, and down hard!" Guinea shouted.

That did it, he broke the kid. Mark was crying now. The game was over. All that was left were the reports from Bobby.

"Here what's going to happen next, Mark. We are going to hold you until my C.S.I. officer arrives. He is the best in the state. He'll match the rifle to Bobby's murder and the knife to Timmy's and the dust from your tires to Albert's death. Once that is confirmed you will be charged with three counts of first degree murder. Then, you'll be tried, convicted, and sentenced to a couple life terms. You will die in jail, Mark. You made these choices and we can't help you now. Only God can."

"Detective, I was framed." Was all that Mark could say

Chapter 35

On the way, back to Ocean City, neither Guinea nor I felt good about what had just transpired. Ninety-nine percent of the time we feel a great sense of accomplishment for putting a murderer behind bars, but other times we feel that there are no real winners. This was one of those times.

"Guinea, sometimes it seems like such a waste. Here's this kid, twenty-two years old. That's only seven years older than Josh, and his life, for all intents and purposes, is over."

"Mike, he knew exactly what he was doing. We don't make the rules, we can only enforce them. Besides, don't lose sight of the fact that three other twenty somethings were killed by this guy. Who knows how many others have now been saved."

"And that makes it right, Roger?" I asked He knew I was serious when I called him by his birth name.

"No, of course not, but what else can we really do. It's the system. The whole world revolves around the almighty dollar. Some people put that above all else. This kid did and now he's going to pay for it. You know what they say, what goes around comes around. It's a shame some people have to be that shallow."

"Yeah, that's what's bothering me. From the report about his upbringing, he seems better than that. Besides, I'm sure Mark knew he was in store for a big payday when his grandparents died. So, are we to assume he murdered these kids for a chance at fame? The odds of him making it to the majors aren't great and he knows that. They all do." I said

"I agree with you, Mike, but some people think with their wallets, others think with their balls, but so few think with their hearts. You're going to have that. Maybe the chance of fame was too overwhelming for him." Guinea countered.

"Or he could be telling the truth, Guinea."

We rode the next couple of minutes in silence, no doubt pondering my last statement when Guinea finally asked, "What time is it?"

"4 pm., straight up. Bobby should be getting to the barracks soon, so we should be getting some answers later tonight or early tomorrow."

"Mike, I don't give a damn about Bobby. I'm in Ocean City and I'm ready for a cold beer. How 'bout we go to the poolside bar back at the hotel and pound a few back?"

"Let's not. I know another place. You know I have a dinner date with Kelly. I don't want to push it and look desperate."

"Mike, it's me. I know you're desperate."

After I found a place to park, we walked up to the boardwalk and entered the Purple Moose Saloon, finding two stools at the bar. We were soon approached by the bartender. I was beginning to think there wasn't a bad looking girl tending bar in all of Ocean City. April was a brown-eyed brunette with short hair. She was a real knock out in a pink bikini top and white shorts.

"What's the deal with the girl at the poolside bar?" Guinea asked.

"Not much, really. We met last week when Smitty and I were doing interviews. It seemed to me that she was flirting and she kind of dared me to ask her out. I wasn't going to, but I thought, what the hell."

"How old is she, Mike?"

"Twenty-eight, and yes, I know there is a fifteen-year age difference between us," I said after taking a big gulp of beer.

"Well, it's good to see you are finally getting off the sidelines."

"Guinea, you act as if I never go out."

"You don't, it's been six months since your last relationship."

"Guinea, you know I was undercover, and she was aware that I was going undercover and would be gone for two months. She knew what I do for a living and sometime there's some risk involved. After all the time we had been together, she up and decides she can't handle it. That's bullshit! Then, when the assignment is over I try to contact her and patch things up and she blows me off - not once, not twice, but a dozen or more times. Screw that."

"Man, calm down. I must have hit a nerve. I can tell you're still hurting after six months. You still love her, don't you?"

"What do you think?"

"Well, pal, all I can tell you is to either keep trying if you feel she's worth it, or move on. It's that simple. In the meantime, go out tonight and have a good time with the red-headed bombshell. I hear she's a cheerleader for the Ravens."

"How the hell did you find that out?" I asked as Guinea ordered two more Bud drafts.

"I'm a detective, too, remember? Mike I really hope you get laid tonight. If anybody deserves or needs it, it's you."

212

"I don't know if I should thank you or tell you to go to hell."

We both laughed, and then my cell phone rang; it was Bobby. He was in Berlin, and he said we needed to talk.

Chapter 36

My cell phone kept ringing off the hook. As I picked it up, I saw it was already 8:32 am, and Bobby was on the other end.

"Hey Bobby, what's up? All right, I will. I'll be there in an hour," I said, while still trying to get my bearings and not recognizing a thing. I reconsidered and said, "Bobby, we better make that two hours," and hung up.

As I hung up the phone, I looked at Kelly approaching, wearing my shirt and looking very beautiful in it. She was carrying two cups of steaming hot coffee that looked equally appealing.

"Good morning, Michael, did you sleep well?"

"It's funny you ask. I haven't slept like that in months, and I haven't seen anything quite as stunning as you this early in the morning for a while either. You sure make my shirt look good."

"Yeah, it's something I just picked up." We both grinned.

"Kelly, I 've got to ask you, do you always look good?"

"Yeah, I do." We both laughed. She had a great sense of humor and made me feel at ease in what could have been an awkward situation.

"So, what's your plan, Michael?" Kelly asked as she sat down beside me on the bed and wrapped the blanket around both of us.

"I have to run out to Berlin and see what's up. Then I'll shoot back up to Annapolis I guess"

"I was afraid you'd say that. When will you be coming back down?"

"This is going to sound terrible, but I really don't know. The up-side is, I'm only two and a half hours away."

"Well, let me ask you this; do you want to see me again?"

"Of course, I do."

"After last night, so do I, Michael. Your performance gave me another reason to not date younger men," she said with a sly grin.

"Kelly, that was just my warm up act," I said as I took her coffee and sat it on the end table. I gave her a passionate kiss as we fell back on the bed.

Forty-five minutes later, I left Kelly's condo in English Towers which was right beside the Clarion. I had to hustle back to the hotel and get cleaned up and check out. During that time, I could not help but to reflect on my date and agonize over the twenty questions that Guinea was sure to ask me. I couldn't help but feel guilty though. Guinea was right. I was still in love, and it wasn't with Kelly.

After getting cleaned up, I called Guinea and arranged for him to meet me in the lobby. When I got there, he was grinning ear to ear, looking like a neon sign. I was hoping he got lucky and spent the night with a beautiful woman, too, but it was highly unlikely. As we both checked out, Kelly came walking through the lobby. She walked straight to me instead of going toward the bar. When she reached me, she cupped my face in the palms of her hands and gave me a long, passionate kiss. I instinctively put my arms around her, but she pulled away after whispering in my ear, "That should stop him from asking any questions now." Then she walked away, looking over her shoulder and telling me to call her.

As I turned toward the front desk I couldn't help but notice Guinea's jaw had dropped halfway toward the floor. I think it's the only time in my life that I've ever seen him totally speechless. That surprised me, but I loved it. As we turned and headed for the front doors, I saw the Glasgow's walking in. As they passed, they nodded and said, "Detective".

I said to Guinea, "Did you see that older couple?"

"Yeah, why?"

"That's the Glasgow's."

"You're shitting me."

"No, I'm not. I told you they don't look seventy. Did you hear what they said?"

"No, I didn't," Guinea replied.

"When they passed, us they said, "Detective.""

"So?"

"Guinea, I never told them I was a detective. I knew they were playing me. The whole thing on the boardwalk was a set-up. They knew who I was and that I was investigating their grandson. Well, I got a surprise for them," I said, as I saw Bobby walking through the door.

Chapter 37

"Sweetheart, I believe our detective friend has put a tail on us." Val said as he adjusted his rear view mirror.

"Really, Vladimir? How thoughtful of him. Perhaps we should play a little game of cat and mouse."

"What do you have in mind, sweetheart?"

"Well, after we pick up our package at the call center, we'll head back toward the hotel. We should be able to get at least a three-block lead on them, without letting them lose sight of us until we get to the hotel. Then, make the turn into the parking lot, losing them long enough for me to deliver the package. After you find a parking space, meet me in front of the lobby as if you dropped me off. They'll look and feel like fools," Victoria said.

"For such a beautiful woman, sometimes you can be mean-spirited."

"It's just my little way of saying; yes, we may be older, but we are also wiser. And we're the professionals that they can only one day hope to be."

"Speaking of being wiser, have you been monitoring the bug I put in our detective friend's truck?" Val asked

"Yes, I have, and, as you said, it has proven to be very useful, Val."

Pulling into the call center and parking the car, Vladimir was very careful not to get out of sight of his newfound friends, thinking all the while that these two gentlemen were not good at playing this type of game.

"My love, do you have any cash on you? I don't think it would be wise for us to pay for the package with a credit card."

"How much do you need, sweetheart?"

"I think six hundred should do. The last one was four hundred."

With that, Vladimir pulled out his wallet and gave his wife four hundred dollar bills and four fifties.

"Are you sure that will be enough?"

"Yes, my love. You are such a kind and generous man." She gave him a soft kiss, the same way she had always done for the last sixty years whenever she left his side.

As she got out of the car, she didn't even bother to glance at the two detectives watching her. She was an expert at this game. It reminded her of her days working for mother Russia, leading the lambs to slaughter. After getting their package, she couldn't help but think how dashing Vladimir looked in their new B.M.W. IL 740. As she approached, Vladimir, always the gentleman, got out of the car to open her door, giving the detectives a glance as he did so.

"Well, sweetheart, are you going to tell me what our little bug has been saying?" Vladimir asked as he checked the rear-view mirror to make sure their new friends were still behind them.

"They believe they have our grandson, hook, line, and sinker."

"What else is new?"

"It also seems our single father of two has some love issues with an unnamed woman, and dulls the pain by sleeping with another."

"And to whom did he tell this?"

"His brother in-law. That seems very troubling indeed. After this is all over, you may need to sit down and have a little talk with that young man. He has children to raise."

"Sweetheart, we must first make sure that we will be able to keep he and his friends alive. Blood is thicker than water. Our first responsibility is to our grandson. Whatever transpires will be predicated on him."

"I agree, my love. This whole affair has gotten so out of control for Mark. We must do whatever is necessary," Victoria responded. "They have no clue to the lengths we have already gone to protect our grandson. Soon they will suspect something is up I am sure, but it was just a precaution, anyway."

"But a good one, Victoria. It is of the utmost importance that we keep them guessing until we can figure this whole thing out for ourselves," Vladimir said as he made the first of what would be three straight lefts. After he made the second one, he told his wife that he would catch up to her in a couple of minutes.

She smiled and leaned in, giving him that familiar kiss, and said, "I will be with you shortly."

Chapter 38

Heading into the parking lot, we ran into Freddie and Smitty, and by the expression on their faces they weren't too happy.

"What's up, guys?" I asked, standing on the sidewalk as they approached."

"That old lady just played us. I friggin' can't believe it," Smitty said in obvious disgust.

"What do you mean, she played you?" I asked.

"I mean she played us like two fools. We followed them to the call center, the old lady goes inside and comes out carrying a long box, maybe four or five-foot-long and a foot wide. We got pictures of it. Anyway, we followed them back here. The old man circles the lot a couple of times looking for a parking space. He finally finds one and gets out, walks to the entrance without his wife, and waits. Next thing we know, she comes walking up from the opposite direction and walks right by us and has the nerve to say, "Good morning, detectives," Smitty said.

"You sure she made you? you sure she just wasn't being polite?" Guinea asked.

"I'm sure," I replied. "I told you how they played me on the boardwalk, and you just saw how they put it in my face. They just did the same thing to them. Those two couldn't care less about us and our presence. We don't faze them and their agenda even in the slightest. This is child's play to them, and frankly, that scares the hell out of me. We need to find out what was in that package, and to whom she dropped it off. Break off the tail, go back to the call center, and try to find out what was in the package and who sent it. We're heading to Berlin to meet with Bobby. Call me when you have something."

"No problem, Mike, we'll be in touch with you the minute we get some information," Freddie assured me.

The drive out to Berlin had been somewhat quiet, as Guinea and I were lost in our own thoughts about what had just transpired. As we pulled into the barracks parking lot, I finally broke the silence with an off-the-wall question.

"Guinea, when I met you in the lobby, I expected a bombardment of questions. Instead, I got nothing. What gives?"

Staring straight ahead, Guinea dead panned, "Mike, I'm a detective. I can pretty much figure out what went on." He paused for a second. slowly turned his head and stared straight at me, and suddenly burst into laughter. Little did I know, it would be the last laugh of the day.

Entering the barracks, both of us were still grinning and talking about what could possibly be up Mark's grandparents' sleeves. As we approached the Watch

Commander's desk, I asked where we could find Mark, and asked him where Bobby was. He pointed down the hall and told us to make two lefts and it will be the first door on the right. He'd have Mark in an Interview room when we needed him. I thanked him as we headed down the hallway to meet up with Bobby.

Entering the room, we found Bobby staring at the computer screen. He never even looked up, he just motioned us over and said, "we've got some problems."

"What do you mean, we got some problems?" I asked.

"Like I said, we've got some problems, Mike. This is not coming together like I expected."

"Like what?" Guinea asked, his voice showing obvious agitation.

"Let's start at the beginning, shall we? I ran the rubber dust that you collected through all the tests, and it came back as the same that was found on Albert Griffith."

"Great," I said.

"You would think. It seems rubber is made in large batches. It's sold to the various rubber vendors and logged in. Then a company like Mickey Thompson buys the batches, has them shipped to their manufacturing plants and made into tires. After that, the tires go to the various

224

distributors. Here-in lies the problem. That one batch of rubber, after being processed, is shipped to fifteen or more different distributors. I think we all assumed that one batch would be shipped to one distributor, and once we found the distributor we could look at their sales records and find our suspects name on a bill of sale. However, we can't pin the sale on our suspect, or any of his family or known associates. In short, all we have is circumstantial evidence. And, gentleman, I'm afraid that was our best shot. It only goes downhill fast after that."

"What do you mean?" I started to say when my phone rang. It was Freddie on the other end, so I immediately answered it. "What do you have, Freddie? You're kidding me, are you sure? Anything else? All right man, get back on the tail and I'll talk to you later."

"What did he say?" Guinea asked.

"The package that the Glasgow picked up came from Langley, Virginia. The contents were unknown, but there was a lot of insurance on it, close to six hundred dollars. Freddie said he pressed the clerk and learned that usually an item with that much insurance was something hi-tech. Also, cash-only-receipt usually means it was either a down payment or final payment, agreed upon by the sender to cover the insurance. The clerk said they also picked up a similar package two days ago."

225

"Two things are for sure. One is they must still have friends in the C.I.A. and two, they're either involved in all of this or are getting involved now."

"So, Bobby, what other good news do you have for us?" Guinea asked.

"The rifle is virtually spotless and the barrel is practically brand new."

"What do you mean brand new," I asked.

"This sniper Rifle is designed to have interchangeable parts. That's what makes them so appealing to the military and gun enthusiasts. I put this rifle through our ballistic tests and it came out clean. It's definitely not a match."

"What about the firing pin?" Guinea asked.

"Good thought, Guinea, but without the casing we don't have anything to match up."

"Did we get anything on the knife?"

"Sure did, Mike, we found some blood on the handle where it meets the blade. Unfortunately, it was from a snake, a Copperhead to be specific."

"So, we don't have friggin' shit?" Guinea said. We were all pretty frustrated.

Then Bobby responded in a somber tone, "All we've got is circumstantial evidence, and I don't think Dewayne will run with that."

We had nothing on Mark, so we had no choice but to let him go. What made matters worse was he had been put on the disabled list and wouldn't be able to play for the next thirteen days.

Before we let him go, I still had a few more questions I wanted to ask him. In the meantime, I asked Guinea to call Dewayne and tell him what had happened. This was one of the times when I could really use a cigarette.

I was in the same office we used when we first brought Mark in for questioning. As he came in, I took off his bracelets and leg shackles and asked him to sit down.

"Let me ask you a question, when did you buy the new barrel for your gun, before or after you killed Bobby Brannon?"

"I don't know what the hell you are talking about. I never bought a new barrel." Mark shouted

"Really, how long have you had the rifle?"

"I don't know, maybe three, close to four years. Why?"

227

"Mark, I'm asking the questions here. So, you have no idea how the barrel got on the gun. So, tell me this, is their anybody who would want to see you spend the rest of your life in jail?"

"Hell, no."

"Alright, does anybody have access to your truck or your hotel room?"

"No, nobody has access to my truck, and only people who work in the hotel go in my room."

"What about a spare key?"

"Detective, nobody has a spare key. Well, nobody except my grandparents."

As Mark was answering the question, Guinea entered the room. Without a word, he just nodded his head as if to say, *it's been taken care of,* so I continued to question Mark.

"Your grandparents have a set of your keys. Do they know what kind of rifle you have?"

"Of course, they do. They bought it for me. What are you getting at, detective?"

"I'm thinking that they are either involved or trying to protect you."

"My grandparents are both very smart and worldly, and they both know how the world works. But I don't need their help because I did nothing wrong. Besides, they're some three hundred miles away."

"Are you telling me you didn't know they're in Ocean City?" I countered

"They're what?" Mark replied astonished.

"They have both been here for a while, Mark. You should give them a call. Better yet, you are free to go. If I were you, I'd take them out to dinner and catch up on what's been going on. Sounds to me like you haven't been kept in the loop, son."

As Mark stood up, I continued, "Give them a message for me. Tell them that we'll be in touch with them real soon and that I look forward to picking up our conversation on raising and protecting children. Heck, I may even come out to Front Royal and explore the park. I hear there's a lot of interesting things to see. Mark, just one more thing and then you'll be able to get your belongings and leave."

"What's that?"

"Do you know what they did for a living before they came to America?"

"Sure, they worked at the Russian Embassy. They were both Diplomats."

"Mark, you may want to ask them if that's all they did. I'm here to tell you, all these murders were either committed by you or center around you. My training tells me that, and my gut tells me that, so you think about it, you think real hard about it!"

Chapter 39

Mark made his way down the concrete steps, holding onto the metal rail as his eyes tried to adjust to the bright sunlight. Spending twenty-four hours in lock up tends to do that to a person. Finding out that his grandparents were in town and had not come to see him, adding to the fact that they may somehow be involved, would make anyone's head spin.

As soon as he got back to his room, he was going to call his grandparents and find out what the hell they were doing. Then he was going to come up with an action plan for the next thirteen unwanted days off. It was imperative that he take advantage of these next two weeks off, he thought as he climbed into his truck.

About an hour later, there was a knock on Mark's door. Answering it, he was greeted with two big smiles and then even two bigger hugs, first from his maw-maw then his pa-paw. After their tearful greetings, he ushered them through the door. As he closed it behind them, he noticed two liters of Stolichnaya in his grandfather's hand and he knew they'd come prepared to talk.

Mark got three plastic cups and a bucket of ice and made his way to the balcony. After exchanging more hugs, his grandfather took the cups from his grandson and filled them with half ice and half vodka.

"How long have the both of you been in Ocean City?" Mark asked.

His maw-maw reached across the white resin table and touched his forearm and said, "Long enough my child, long enough."

"But why, why would you come down here?"

After taking a long drink, his pa-paw answered, "to protect and support you, my son."

"Protect me; how in the hell can you protect me? I've got two cops breathing down my neck, a million things going through my mind, and a lot of tough decisions to make, so how can you help?"

As Mark downed his vodka, his pa-paw said in a stern voice, "Boy, there's much you do not know about your grandmother and I. But, believe me when I tell you, we are the only ones who have the means and the expertise to get you out of this mess. From this moment on, you will do exactly what we say, when we say to do it. Do you understand, my son?"

"Yes, sir, but ..."

He was abruptly cut off, "There are no buts, my love. Your grandfather did not have to be so dramatic to make his point, but you will listen to us if you want to survive this whole ordeal, do you understand." She squeezed his arm to bring the point home, while also flashing a stern look in her husband's direction. "What did the detectives ask you at the police station?"

"They're convinced that I killed those three ballplayers'. They searched my room, my truck ..."

His pa-paw again interrupted him. "My son, we know all of that and have taken measures to safeguard you, just answer your grandmother's question. What did they say to you in the police station?"

"Measures to safeguard me? What ....?"

Again, he was cut off, this time by his grandmother. "We will explain it all to you later. Just answer the question, my dear." Her tone of voice rising.

"He said at the beginning that he could tie me to the murder in Aberdeen with rubber shavings found on my truck. The knife they found in my truck was the same kind of knife that was used in the murder here, and my gun was used in the murder in Frederick. But this morning he backed off a little. First, he asked when I had gotten the gun and when I bought the new barrel. I told him I never bought a new barrel, so then he asked if I knew anyone who would want to see me in jail. I told him no. Then he wanted to know if you two were aware of the rifle and if I knew you were both in town. Finally, he suggested that you two may be trying to protect me or are somehow involved. He also said that I should ask you about what you did before and after you worked at the embassy. And he mentioned a conversation with you about raising and protecting children that he looked forward to continuing."

His grandfather couldn't contain himself any longer. With a burst of laughter, he stood up and grabbed he and his wife's plastic cups and filled them with more vodka, and ice cubes.

"You have to love America. In mother Russia, with what they found in your room and truck, or if they even suspected you did the things you are now being accused of, you would have already been put in front of a firing squad and killed." he said as he walked around the white raisin table filling his grandson's glass with more of the Russian vodka. Continuing he said, "Here, circumstantial evidence does not get you killed or even convicted. They have to have proof, my son. They backed off because they have none, and I will tell you why and what we know."

"Your grandmother and I changed out your rifle barrel. We also bugged the detective's truck, and we plan to bug his and his cohorts' offices when we go to visit them. We knew that at some point they would want to talk to us. In fact, we were anticipating that. Am I correct?"

"Yes sir. Mark replied and then said, "Besides the conversation about protecting children, he also mentioned something about coming up to Front Royal and visiting the state park."

His maw-maw interrupted and said, "He is a little smarter than I thought. There is no doubt he knows who we are and who we worked for, and, more importantly, what we did and can do. He must certainly know that he is of no relevance to us."

"Maw-maw, pa-paw what are you talking about?"

"My son, we will sit and order some food, and drink much more vodka. There is a lot you need to know.. Your grandmother and I will tell you everything, including why we did the things we did, and sometimes still do. But you must remember and understand, everything that we did, we did first for your mother, and now for you."

The one thing his grandparents had failed to mention during their little speeches was that they also had his truck and room bugged. They would safeguard against being surprised.

"Vladimir, what about the packages from Langley?" Victoria asked.

"By now they know where the packages came from, but can't possibly know what they contained, and they won't know. They can, and will, suspect the first one being the barrel for the rifle, but will never be able to prove it. And until someone uses the second package, they won't find out what it is or where it was hidden. Trust me, my love. When all is said and done, where it is placed is where it will eventually be needed. Of this I am certain."

235

"Do you think it will be safe there?"

"Again, have faith in me. They will never suspect a thing. Sometimes, the most obvious place is the best place to conceal what you don't want found."

"You always have been so good at this type of deception, my love. Of course, I trust you," Victoria replied.

Chapter 40

On the way, back to Annapolis, Guinea and I
decided we should go to Front Royal and snoop around
while the principals were still in Ocean City. Having
Smitty and Freddie tailing them bought us some time to go
to the Glasgow's place to look around and see what we
could find. Also, since it was the beginning of the
weekend, we thought we could mix a little business with
pleasure and have my boys again tag along.

Guinea had been on his laptop looking up Front
Royal. He saw that they had some neat things to do. There
was going to be a wine and crafts festival this weekend,
with free live music and some discounts at Skyline Caverns
and Skyline Drive. We knew the boys would find this
interesting, so Guinea went ahead and booked us two
rooms at a Holiday Inn just outside of town. It was
overlooking a golf course. We thought we may all get a
chance to play Sunday morning if we were lucky.

But, most importantly, I wanted to check out where
the Glasgow's and Mark called home and what they were
all about. Freddie had told us that in many small towns like
Front Royal, everybody knows each other and everyone
know everybody else's business. A detective's dream, I
thought. I also realized that we would have to keep a low
profile. The Glasgow's and Mark probably have some deep

roots in that small community, so we would have to be careful.

We woke up at 5 am., extremely early for the boys, but we had to get an early start. Their uncle arrived an hour later and proceeded to make a thermos of coffee for us, and packing some V-8 and a couple of sodas for the boys. Meanwhile, the boys and I finished getting ourselves together. After reminding them not to forget their hygiene items and two changes of clothes, we were ready to go.

As we stepped outside, I heard the boys yelling. I turned around after locking the door and was surprised to see Guinea's bright red Jeep 4x4 with those huge chrome rims. Then I noticed the four fishing rods in their holders in front of the grill, complete with hook, line and sinkers.

When Guinea saw, me staring at them he said, "I guess I forgot to mention that Front Royal has these little things called the Shenandoah and North Fork rivers. It is also the canoeing capital of Virginia." I turned around and unlocked the door. Guinea asked, "What are you doing?"

"We forgot something, our bathing suits." I replied.

At 8:45 am, we arrived at the Holiday Inn. The ride up there had been a blast. Guinea had his CD player cranked full blast to Nickel Back the whole way up Route 66, our faces in the wind and all of us singing along. We were out of our rooms by 9:15 and driving through Front Royal ten minutes later. I got the sense that time stood still in this town. They did a good job, I thought, of mixing the old with the new. It was actually somewhat intriguing. As we got closer to the outskirts of town, we began to see signs for Skyline Drive and the caverns.

We headed out Route 340, passing the entrance to Skyline Drive and then the caverns. As we continued, we passed numerous canoe companies along the banks of the river and the base of Skyline Drive on our way to a place called Bentonville. About ten minutes later, we knew we were getting close when we saw a sign that read, 'Andy Guest State Park' up ahead. Per our GPS, it was on the right before the park. Turning right onto Thunderbird Road, we immediately passed three young girls playing. The boys took notice. and the girls in turn, stopped what they were doing to check out the boys. We continued down the road for about ¾ of a mile when we suddenly came to a large metal gate. As Guinea made a three-point turn, I noticed a roof to a large home barely visible further down the lane.

After Guinea completed the turn, we pulled to the side and parked. We could hear nothing but the rushing of water as we got out of the Jeep. I looked in the direction of the noise and could just barely see the bank of the river through the woods. I noticed the river flowed left to right, then made a dog leg around the back of the house. I told the boys to go to the river on our left. It was the closest to the Jeep.

"I'll holler for you when we were ready to go. Don't wander off too far."

In unison, they replied, "Yes, sir."

Guinea and I walked through the woods toward house. We went about five hundred yards when we noticed a camera to our left in a tree about thirty feet high. We went about seventy-five more yards. Guinea spotted another one about the same height, but this time to our right. We knew we were on candid camera. The question was, did they have tape running, or was it a direct feed to a security company? We knew that they'd know we had been here, so it made no sense trying to hide it.

We went about another hundred yards or so when all hell broke loose. Motion-detecting lights were flashing from the trees and the eves of the house. We were two hundred yards away from the front porch of an absolutely stunning ninety-foot, two-story, L-shaped log cabin that followed the dog leg of the river. The porch wrapped around the entire house. As we approached the steps, I thought I'd put on a little show for the cameras. I walked right up the steps until I got to the front door and then knocked for the cameras, and more importantly, the Glasgow's.

They would know that the knock was just for effect and that I was mocking them just as they had mocked me. It was my way of getting just a little bit of payback. After another knock, I peered through the door window and decided to walk around the porch. As I did, I kept stealing glances through the windows to see what I could see. As I rounded the second corner, the river opened in front of me and the porch turned into a large, 14 ft. wide deck that overlooked the Shenandoah River. You could see for what seemed like miles in either direction. Guinea emerged from the other direction and appeared as equally impressed as I was. We were about seventy-five to a hundred feet above the river, and the view was spectacular.

But it wasn't just the view that impressed us. It was the killing field below. In order to get to the house from it, you had to climb an impressive set of steps made of 6 x 6 Landscape timbers and brick pavers. You were a sitting duck either in the water or on the steps. It was all wide open. Then you had woods surrounding the house, no doubt filled with heat sensors, motion detectors, and cameras.

Guinea took one look at it and said, "That, my friend is one hell of a view, but an even better killing field. They have height at every angle except the front."

"A lot of thought went into building this fortress. When the Russians, or whoever sent someone in here to try to take them out, they in turn, killed them. Then they made a deposit for a hundred K. There is no safe way to get in here."

241

We turned around and faced a wall of sliding glass doors, no doubt made of bulletproof glass. Looking through them, we saw a large walk through fireplace made of stone. On the one side of it was a big kitchen with built in ovens and range encased in the same stone. They were accented with some type of brown marble counter tops. On the other side was a huge, sunken living room. What caught our eyes was an eight-foot-wide, light brown metal gun cabinet complete with a tumbler lock. It was the biggest civilian one I had ever seen.

As we walked around the front, Guinea wondered aloud, "How many bodies that the K.G.B. sent do you think are still lying out there, that haven't been found?"

"Just subtract all the deposits from Langley from the bodies that have been found, and whatever you have left, I'll bet, is your answer."

We just looked at each other as we started walking toward the garage. Once there, we peered through the windows. Looking in, we saw a dark blue, almost black, Dodge Ram and an old orange Kubota tractor. To my surprise, there was another large, metal gun cabinet.

"They sure as hell have a large enough collection of guns," I said.

"You think?" said Guinea.

242

As we started walking up the lane, I called for the boys. I noticed in the distance what looked like a bow window of a house some twenty-five hundred yards, off to the right. A little further to the right of that was what appeared to be a lane that I hadn't noticed coming in. Once we were back at Guinea's Jeep, I called for the boys again. As we waited, we heard a vehicle approaching. I glanced up the road and saw nothing, and then turned in the direction of where the boys had entered the woods. I saw them running towards us. I screamed for them at the top of my lungs to stop, but they kept on coming. I screamed again, and the boys stopped suddenly. I noticed out of the corner of my eye that Guinea had pulled out his service revolver.

I directed my attention back to the road, and my fears subsided. Coming towards us was a police cruiser. Guinea immediately holstered his weapon as the cruiser pulled up. By this time, Josh and Shane had made it back to the Jeep.

The officer rolled down his window and said, "Excuse me, may I ask you what y'awl are doing out here?"

I noticed it was a Warren County Police officer. Guinea answered, "We're just looking around."

"This is private property, are you aware of that?"

"No, we weren't, officer," I replied.

"Well, I must ask you to leave immediately, if y'awl don't mind."

"No, not at all officer," I said.

"One more thing. The owner requested that I check your IDs before I let you go."

"They what?" Guinea said.

"Look, mister, either you show me some ID. or I lock you up for trespassing. That was the owner's request, and in all honesty, it seems awful generous of them, if you ask me."

"My dad and uncle both cops," Shane blurted out in our defense, as Josh nudged him to calm down.

"It's alright," I said as I pulled out my shield and presented it to the officer. Following my lead, Guinea produced his.

"Let me ask you a question, officer. How did you know we were out here?"

"The owners, Mr. and Mrs. Glasgow, called us and said someone was on their property."

"You don't say," Josh responded.

Guinea and I looked at him, puzzled.

244

"Well, if you don't mind leaving, I'd appreciate it. The Glasgow's are well respected people in the community and all, so we kind of look out for them."

"Not a problem, we'll be on our way," I said.

With that, the officer started to roll up his window, but stopped and asked, "What were y'awl doing out here, anyway?"

Shane suddenly spoke up and said, "We were looking for a place to fish."

With that being said, the officer rolled up his window and pulled off.

"That was quick thinking, Shane," Guinea said.

"I'm used to dealing with cops. Remember, I live with one."

We all chuckled and then I asked Josh, "What did you mean when you said, 'you don't say' to the officer?"

"Dad the woods are full of cameras and little red and green lights in boxes nailed to trees, even in some of the ground cover."

"Really," I said as I held the door open and motioned the boys into the Jeep all the while looking at Guinea.

Chapter 41

After leaving the Glasgow's residence, the boys decided that they wanted to go to Skyline Caverns. It was already ninety-some degrees outside, plus the humidity about took your breath away, so it sounded like a good idea to their uncle and me too.

As we opened the door to enter a rustic looking cabin, the cowbell above the door announced our arrival. To the right of us, as we entered, was a large souvenir shop. The boys went straight for it. Guinea and I went to our left, where a half-circle counter stood, an attendant behind it with information about the cavern tours. After getting some information and four tickets, we joined the boys, looking at all the different souvenirs and artifacts for a few minutes while waiting for the next tour to start.

When they started the tour, it began with a descent into the cavern. The boys were amazed at how cool the temperature was getting. They were equally amazed at all the different formations and colors of the cool, damp rocks and stalactites. I was glad that I could mix a little business with pleasure. Upon finishing the tour of the caverns, we were hit in the face with the July summer heat. After being in the caverns, it was like walking into a sauna, so we went straight across the parking lot into an air-conditioned mirror maze.

With the maze complete, it was off to Front Royal to have lunch. Hitting the outskirts of town, we came to a red light at the corner of Keiser Road and 340. To our left was a 7-11. The boys clamored for a Slurpee, and Guinea needed some gas, so we stopped.

I was surprised to see that gas was seventeen cents cheaper here than in the metropolitan area. You would have thought it would have been just the opposite, with the longer distance in travel to the major seaports in Baltimore and other coastal cities. Entering the 7-11, I thought that they were giving something away. The place was packed. Everyone was buying sodas and beer, and bags upon bags of ice. Mixed in were chips and other assorted snacks. I was wondering what the heck was going on until I overheard two young ladies talking about rafting and the detective in me figured out the rest.

With Slurpee's and two waters in hand, I asked the young lady behind the counter about the eateries in town, especially where the locals preferred to eat. Before she could answer, three or four people behind us started rattling off the names of various restaurants. First there was the Old Mill restaurant on Main Street, then someone suggested the Royal Oak Tavern, which we passed when we first came into Front Royal. Another said that if we wanted something inexpensive with some local flair, we should try the Knotty Pine.

When I heard inexpensive with some local flair, that sold me. After we paid for our drinks and got a receipt for the gas, we were on our way. As we were driving to the Knotty Pine, I went over in my mind what Freddie had said about small towns, and how everybody wants in or knows everyone else's business. We saw a glimpse of that at the 7-11 when I asked the counter person about restaurants and got multiple responses from other people.

Within a matter of minutes, we were at the Knotty Pine. As Guinea looked for a place to park, I noticed all the motorcycles and trucks that lined the parking lot. The bikes were all Harley's, and all of the trucks were mostly four-wheel drives, and seventy percent of them had those big balloon tires. Of course, there were a few cars sprinkled in, but not many.

Entering the restaurant, we were greeted by a bell above the door and a mixture of different food odors, and the smell of cigarettes that about knocked even me out. I thought this place was a health violation just waiting to happen, but once we got inside you could no longer smell the cigarettes, just the aroma of home cooked food.

I had that same twilight zone feeling I'd had when we first crossed the bridges entering town. As I looked around, it was as if we'd stepped back into the fifties. Judging by the general appearance and decor, it was likely that the restaurant had never been remodeled since it first opening the doors.

248

An older woman, perhaps in her late sixties or early seventies, showed us to an old wooden booth. As we took our seats, I continued to look around at the old pine walls decorated with black and white photos of days gone by. The place reeked of ambiance. From the jukebox selections on the counter and table tops to the old green milkshake and malt machines behind the counter, this place was old time America at its best. We could and would go back to Annapolis and tell everyone about this place, but would anybody believe it?

Even though it was three in the afternoon, we all decided to have an assortment of different breakfasts. We saw that numerous patrons were doing the same, and the bacon smell coming from the kitchen was too good to pass up. Our hostess mentioned that they serve breakfast from opening until close, and that they also have daily specials which were posted on the chalkboards behind the counter. After taking our drink orders and giving us menus, the hostess, who reminded me of the stereotype of any American grandmother, told us our waitress would be with us shortly.

About a minute later, a young and very attractive blond waitress approached us who gave me an immediate sense of déjà vu.

"Hi, my name is Julie and I'll be your server today. you ready to order yet?"

"Yeah, I think we are," I said, still trying to place her. While we were ordering, I kept stealing glances of her, trying to figure out where I had seen her before. Then it dawned on me.

As soon as she completed our order and left the table, I told Guinea that I recognized her from the photo in Newman's truck. I explained to my two would-be-detective sons not to say anything. I repeated myself, as all of us parents do on important issues. I was going to be coy with her and try to feel her out to see what she knew. I didn't need anything coming out of left field from the boys.

As she came by the table, I asked her if I could get some change for the jukebox for the boys. As I handed her a five, I asked her if they were getting bigger crowds for the games since they renovated the stadium that sat two blocks behind the restaurant, and if the valley league had gotten any more popular.

"To some of us, hell yes," she said enthusiastically. "This area will always be football first, but some of our best athletes were baseball players. In fact, we've had a few make it to the majors and we have one in the minors who is bound to become a superstar."

"Yeah, I know of Daryl Whitmore and Dana Allison, and I also know Mark Newman. I even remember a kid named Josh Michael who use to light up the American Legion and the high school ball in this area," I

250

said. I'd done a little homework before I came up here, just in case I needed a ground breaker. As it turned out, I was glad I did, because in an instant it had paid off.

"You know Mark?" Julie asked.

"We work as part-time scouts for the Orioles," I said, motioning to Guinea. I knew that the lie I was telling would be exposed the minute she spoke with Mark and told him about us. I had no choice but to play it for what it was worth and continued, "So how do you know Mark?"

"We've been dating on-and-off for a couple years, but recently it's been heating up. In fact, he called me this morning and told me he was coming home for a couple days because he was put on the disabled list.

"Hey Jules, can we get some more coffee over here?"

"Be right there, Bo. Excuse me while I get them some more coffee and check on y'awls food."

"Go right ahead, don't let us keep you." I said

"Aw, it's alright. I could talk about Mark and baseball all day."

Guinea and I just looked at each other and smiled. When Julie returned with my change for the jukebox, she also volunteered a personal perspective. She told us that since Mark had been in Salisbury, he had been doing great.

251

She also said that she would not have been surprised if, at some point soon, he would have gotten another promotion to either Bowie or Frederick. But this unexpected setback could really impede his progress. After telling us that, Guinea asked the question that we already knew the answer.

"What setback are you talking about?"

"He was just put on the disabled list. He called me this morning and said he and his grandparents were on their way home, but first they had some business that they had to take care of. I wish I had known earlier, because I have to work at my full-time job tomorrow and I just know my boss won't give me off."

"Why can't you explain the circumstances to him?" I asked, trying to sound concerned, before taking a bite of my omelet.

"It won't matter. Tomorrow is the wine festival and I have to work the kiosk. There will be a lot of people here from northern Virginia and the District; the type of people that could make a big difference in the business."

"This place is setting up a kiosk?" Guinea asked.

"No silly, don't you listen? I work for a guy whose company sets up hi-tech security for homes and businesses. We adapt it to your specific wants and needs. He's been trying to expand, hoping to land some government contracts because the private sector has not been working out."

"Still, isn't Mark like a local icon around here?" I asked.

"At first, he was, but a lot of people feel he let them down by not reaching the majors by now. Besides, my boss has always had some animosity toward Mark ever since high school. I think a lot of it has to do with me."

"Come again?" I said.

"I know this is going to sound a bit conceited, but there are a couple guys in town who have always tried to take me out over the years. And my boss, Billy, is one of them. In fact, his brothers Brady and Buck have asked me out numerous times, too. But I have always said no because of Mark, even though I know he has slept with half the girls in my graduating class. I guess it must sound weird, but I knew that one day he would come around. I just know in my heart that he is worth the wait," she said, as she acknowledged another table waiting to place an order.

When the boys finished their strawberry pancakes and blueberry waffles with extra bacon, I asked for the check. I also asked Julie if she had a business card. I was curious about the security company.

After paying for lunch at the front counter, I had the boys leave a generous tip on the table. As we headed out the door, the conversation was on the great food we had just eaten.

Guinea said, "I'll catch up to you guys, just give me a minute, I'll meet you at the jeep." With that, he threw me the keys as he headed across the street toward a body shop. I saw what had caught his eye. In the parking lot across the street sat a black GM.C Yukon Denali with those big tires.

As Guinea walked around the truck, a heavyset young man in his mid-twenties came out of the body shop and approached him. I couldn't help but think that, if I worked across the street from this place, I would be out of shape too.

After a brief conversation with the young man, Guinea returned and said, "You saw the truck, right?"

"Yeah, it fits the description, that's for sure."

"Did you notice the gun in the gun rack? It's the same type of rifle that Mark has, the tires Mickey Thompsons, plus it seems that the kid knows our golden boy. Judging by his tone of voice, I'd say he's not too crazy about him. I'm telling you, Mike, this case is getting more complicated by the minute."

"Did you get his name?"

"Yeah, its Charles White."

We headed down 7th Street towards the stadium, which we later learned was named 'Bing Crosby'. We reached the end of the block when Guinea suddenly slammed on the breaks and put the Jeep in reverse. Reaching the end of the Knotty Pine parking lot, he made a left, and sitting there was a black Chevy Cheyenne that also could have passed for Mark's truck. Guinea asked me to call in the tag number for shit and giggles. I thought he was losing his mind, but at that point we had nothing to lose.

I finally got hold of Molly, but the reception on the cell phone was terrible. "Hey Molly, its Mike. I need you to do me a favor - can you run two plates for me please?"

While we waited for the tag numbers to come back, Molly said she had been trying to get in touch with us all day, but it just kept ringing and ringing and wouldn't go to voice mail on either of our phones. Finally, the tag numbers came back. The first was registered to Charles White, as expected, but the other one caught me off guard. It was registered to a Julie Wines. What she said next really shocked me. The Glasgow's had come by for a visit. I just looked at Guinea and shook my head.

"The plot thickens, pal, the plot has just really thickened."

Chapter 42

The investigation had reached Front Royal. I knew it was only a matter of time. Eventually all roads would lead back home. Soon it would all be over. Perhaps, in time, it will become the most publicized unsolved case of all time.

What started out as a move to better my position had now turned into a national media circus, but with the glaring spotlight comes much more added pressure. The first kill was designed to level the playing field. The second kill was really a matter of convenience, being in the right place at the right time. I'd just stopped in Frederick to get a bite to eat on the way back from Aberdeen and had come upon the local sports paper. When I saw the Keys schedule, with that large cut out of that Bobby fellow, it was a no-brainer, it had to be done.

The Oriole organization would be forced to make some moves, and again it would put me in a better position to achieve my objective. The third killing came out of necessity. The love of my life, Jules, was now center stage. I had to change my thought process. Every move I made from here on out would have to be calculated with Jules foremost in my mind. I had to shift my priorities. There had to be a greater sense of urgency. The blame had to be shifted. They had gotten close, so close in fact, I had to divert their attention with another murder victim. To shift the blame, another innocent life had to be taken. It was time to make another move, but how and when, was the question. What would best serve my needs? I could go to Bowie, or I could stay close to home and go back to Frederick. They wouldn't expect that, even though Bowie would probably be safer. It would keep the police at a further distance.

In the end, the decision came down to giving the police more options, even if those options may involve my own family, by sticking close to home. I had to think of my future and my life with Jules. So, Frederick it was. I at least knew the area. I wondered who was playing first base for the Keys now. I rather felt sorry for the poor soul. He had no idea his life was about to end; his fate having been decided for the promise of another's dream. No one was going to stand in the way of what I wanted and had worked so hard to get.

It was now just a question of how and when. The name of the person didn't really matter. I could kill him in many ways. I am skilled in them all, but I had paid for the shipping and handling of the package. It was delivered on time and at such a high cost, so I might as well use my new toy. It would definitely put a new spin on the game. I was going to change the rules again. This would take everyone by surprise. It would shock the police, the Orioles organization, and perhaps even shock the nation.

As I prepared myself for the task, I had another brilliant idea. I had to act fast though, on the information that Jules had so graciously given me. I realized I had to do it right away. It all made perfect sense. The Keys would be going on a road trip for eight days, so an opportunity like this would only present itself once. I had to make the most of the opportunity that was being presented to me.

The wine festival would also give me the perfect alibi. I could be seen there and then sneak away without even being missed. Everybody in this town knows me. I'll make sure I'm seen by everyone. They won't remember, or won't be sure of the time they saw me. They will be confused. This was perfect. Once again, the perfect crime, performed at the perfect time, by the perfect killer.

Chapter 43

I awoke to a beautiful day, but I was dead tired from all the travel and preparation for today's task. As I sipped my coffee, It was already in the mid-seventies with a slight breeze coming in from the west, per the report I heard from the Warren County cable station.

I arose feeling confident and sure of the plan, even though I had diverted from it last night. I knew it was a smart play in keeping the police off balance. It hadn't gone as I'd expected, but it would still serve my needs well. This whole plan had been hastily put together, but it all made perfect sense. It would assure that they would never suspect me. How could I be in two places at the same time? And all the while, my vehicle was parked in the same spot. After last night, I would be cleared of any suspicion for all of these crimes once the police did their due diligence.

I wanted to get an early start. I knew people from all over the state, plus all the local merchants, would be putting up there stands in preparation for the day's festivity at the wine festival. As my computer came to life, I thought about missing one of the better events Front Royal and Warren County put on, with all the in-state vineyards coming together to show off their wares. Not to mention, all the local businesses trying to get their hands in the cookie jar as well.

As I typed in "The Frederick Keys," it took me straight to their home page. In the top left hand corner, there was a box that listed a series of different options. I clicked on rosters and then scrolled down the page. There were numerous first base/third base combos and right fielder/first base combos, and one catcher/first base combo, just as it had been when I checked out the Bowie roster yesterday. I looked at how many at bats the players had. By doing this, I eliminated the catcher and one right fielder and two third base combos for lack of at bats.

Next, I read the bios of the three remaining players. One of them stood out because of where he was from, the other because of his hitting numbers. He, in my mind, was the better target because his absence would be missed the most by the Orioles. It would mean that they would have to promote somebody. The third, he had just turned eighteen but looked more like he was fourteen, so he would be spared. I kept coming back to where the one fellow was born and raised. I just couldn't make up my mind between those two, so I decided to settle it the old-fashioned way. One of these promising young men would lose his life by a simple flip of the coin. Heads, it's the player with the better numbers; tails, it's the guy who was born and raised in Dundalk, Maryland. *And the winner is ...*, as I flipped it, the coin landed on the vinyl floor - tails.

Tommy Burger was the winner, but would become the loser in the game of life. Tommy, a Maryland native, was twenty-two years old, 6'2" and 210 lbs., a right handed hitting first baseman. Born and raised in Dundalk, Maryland, to Thomas and Tammie Burger, he had attended Dundalk High School, lettering in baseball, football and track. He was a three time all-metro selection in baseball, and once made all state. He was picked in the eighteenth round of the draft by the Detroit Tigers, but was later traded to the Orioles in a 'player to be named later' deal.

So, Tommy was the unlucky soul that, later this afternoon, would be making headlines all up and down the east coast. *Such was his fate,* I thought as I turned off the computer and headed toward the kitchen to rinse out my coffee cup before I headed out the door. After locking the front door and getting in my car, it was time to go into town and make sure that all the vendors and merchants setting up their wares saw me. I would mingle and mill about for a while, and stop by to see Jules. I had to see her anyway to put the plan in motion. She would unknowingly play an intricate part in my plan.

I wanted to make sure my car would be seen all day, and what better place to park it than right in front of the Warren County Sheriff's Department. If I got a ticket, so be it. It would be worth the fine to have such an airtight alibi. Every cop that was on duty that day would surely see my vehicle. As I walked down Main Street, exchanging greeting with friends and acquaintances, it was already alive with a flurry of activity as the various vendors were setting up shop. Vineyards from all over the state, even from Wise and Tazewell counties, were here. Just about every local merchant had some sort of stand or poster up on Main Street, including the Front Royal Chamber of Commerce and the Warren County Sheriff and Front Royal Police Departments.

As I continued my walk, I saw Jules setting up her stand in front of the Schewell's Furniture Store. She noticed me at about the same time.

"Hey you," Jules said. "What are you doing down here so early?"

"I felt like being a nice guy so I thought I'd come down here and give my favorite girl a hand in setting up the stand."

"You mean your only girl, don't you?" she said as she picked up a security system incorporated box and started unpacking it.

"Hey Jules, I noticed you parked your truck at the loading dock entrance at the store. You know you'll get towed there today if you don't move it, don't you?"

"Damn, I forgot all about that. Could you…."

"Give me your keys and I'll move it."

"You sure you don't mind?"

"No, but I got a bunch of errands to run. It may be a while before I can return your keys to you."

"You know, I have to go back to the Knotty Pine for an hour or so to finish my shift, but I'll be back here until at least eight o'clock tonight." With that, she tossed me her keys, and I thought to myself, *step one complete.*

I left and walked toward Jule's truck. As soon as I got inside and got it started, I headed to Ramsey's Hardware Store to get a duplicate key of Jules' truck made. Then I made a beeline back to my house to pick up the package and the gel I had made for the task. After last night's episode, I had to make sure that today's mission was a complete success. Once I had retrieved all the things I needed at the house, I started back into town.

After parking Jules' truck, I walked back toward Main Street. As I made the right on Main Street, I was greeted by people that recognized me, with a nod of the head, or a pleasant smile. The one block walk back to the security stand was proving to be very productive in providing me an alibi. I most likely would not even need it, but I learned a long time ago that it's better to be safe than sorry.

"Here's your keys Jules. I parked your truck on Luray Avenue, but I'll be around all day, so maybe later on I'll stop by and see if I can find you a spot closer."

"I'd really appreciate that, but you don't have to."

"I know I don't have to, but I want to."

"You're so sweet," she said.

We made some small talk as I helped her put up displays, all the while trying to be as visible as possible to others passing by. A little while later, I checked my watch. It was 11:45 am - time to get moving. As I left, I walked all the way down to the Old Mill Restaurant and turned around, then made my way back up. I stopped by the gazebo to talk to some of the members of one of the local bands that were setting up there. I continued to do all I could do to be seen at the festival to cement my alibi. I checked my watch again. Now it was 12:05 pm, and time to leave.

Chapter 44

We all awoke early. As I got ready to jump in the shower and sneak my morning cigarette, I asked Shane to go to his uncle's room to make sure he was awake. By the time I got out of the shower, Guinea was already in the room, sitting on one of the beds and watching an old Road Runner rerun.

"Man, you need to get a new phone. Molly and Dewayne have been blowing my phone up since late last night. There was an apparent attempt made on another player, this time at Bowie."

"Why didn't you wake me?"

"Are you still asleep or what? I said an attempt was made. Why would I wake you for that? Bobby went out there a.s.a.p. and did all the dirty work."

"Well, what happened?"

"It seems our killer is trying to add to his resume. This time it was a car bomb, but according to Bobby, it was done in haste and was very sloppy. It seems it went off sometime in the middle of the eighth inning, and, luckily, no one was injured. The bomb was on some sort of timing device. Bobby is still going through the wreckage to see what he can find. And, in answer to your next question, yes, the car belonged to a first baseman by the name of Howard Small."

Guinea filled me in on the rest of the previous night's happenings. As he did, I couldn't help but think that the Glasgow's and Mark were in the area, having visited my office earlier in the day. Was it a coincidence? We all decided to go back to the Knotty Pine for breakfast. Our tee time wasn't until 10:15 am, and the boys loved the place. Besides, Guinea wanted to try the western omelet and I was up for some more of that delicious fried scrapple to go along with those fried potatoes.

After a very satisfying and filling breakfast, we headed back to the hotel. From there, we walked to the golf course. The last time we played, the boys had beaten us pretty good, and that was about a year ago,. The boys had played a couple times since then, so they fully expected to win again. How bad the boys were going to beat us and the great breakfast dominated the conversation on the walk over to the course. In the back of Guinea's and my mind was the fact that our number one suspect was now back in town with his grandparents. Neither Guinea nor I had ruled them out, and add the fact that they were a half hour from Bowie the previous day, only added fuel to the already burning fire.

As expected, the boys dominated both Guinea and me. The Blue Ridge Shadow course played a lot easier then it looked, but Guinea and I both stunk. Guinea shot a ninety-six and I followed that up with a ninety-nine. Shane shot an eighty-six, and Josh shot a very respectable eighty-one. It would be a while before we lived that down. It was obvious that my baseball swing and approach was not working well on the links, which the boys often reminded me during the match.

As soon as we finished, we headed back into town to the Wine Festival. Guinea and I discussed the possibility of running into our suspects, which I hoping for. I had many questions for the Glasgow's and I wasn't intimidated by their past or impressive contacts at all. In fact, I relished the idea of trying to get inside their heads. I wanted to know why they stopped by my office, where they were at the time of the bombing last night, and what they had up their sleeves.

While Guinea and I were talking, I happened to notice a truck that looked a lot like Julie's sitting at the red light at the exit ramp to Route 66. It was in the far left lane heading out of town towards Winchester. I pointed it out to Guinea and we all took a hard look. Unfortunately, we couldn't make out who was driving. We all thought that she said she would be working at the Wine Festival, but it looked like her truck to all of us. Then Shane spoke up and said, "I bet we see three more just like it before we get into town." We all agreed. He had a point. It seemed to be a very popular model up here.

Crossing the bridges heading into town, you could tell by all the traffic that something was going on. It wasn't D.C or the Baltimore metro area traffic by no means, but it was busy none the less. We finally found a place to park by the post office. We had to walk about five or six blocks before we reached the festival. As soon as we parked and got out of the car, we could hear a band playing and smell the aromas of the different foods. I could tell by the expressions on the boys' faces that they were going to enjoy this.

The foods were vast and diverse, from funnel cakes to spare ribs, crab cakes, which we did not try, to pulled barbecue beef and pork. Plus, all the corn dogs, hot dogs and hamburgers you could possibly eat, not to mention the various cotton candy and ice cream stands.

We had been there roughly two hours among the masses, when Guinea spotted Julie Wines at a security system stand. *I guess it wasn't her truck after all,* I thought to myself.

She saw us coming and said, "You lied to me. You had no reason to do that."

"Would you have been so cordial if I hadn't?" I replied.

"Probably not, but that's no excuse. It's been my experience that once a man lies, you can never trust him again."

"Julie, I think we can agree that can go both ways."

"Well, detective… may I call you detective?"

"Of course, or, better yet, you can call me Mike. And this is my partner Roger, but he would prefer you call him Guinea."

"I think at this point it would be better if I just call you both detectives. I'll also tell both of you that you know Mark did not do those terrible things that you are trying to pin on him."

"Julie, that's what we are here, to try to find out. If he is innocent, we will clear him. If he is guilty, we will bury him. So, if there is anything you know that may help us help him, you need to let either me or my partner know." With that, Guinea and I handed her our cards, knowing that we may well need her down the road.

"Julie, I will tell you this, if Mark did not kill those men, someone is going to great lengths to make it look like he did," Guinea said.

"The killer, or killers, could go after him next. If you know anybody that has an ax to grind with him, you need to let us know."

The look on Julie's face could have sunk the entire seventh fleet. Her expression also proved her love and devotion to Mark.

"Julie, one more thing. Have you seen Mark or his grandparents today?" Guinea asked.

"No, I haven't, but I expect to."

"Well, if you do, give them one of those cards and tell his grandparents we need to speak with them. It would be better for all of us, including their grandson, if they'd contact us before we are forced to find them."

Chapter 45

I managed to get out of Front Royal and onto the ramp of Rt. 66 in fewer than twenty minutes. Traffic was somewhat heavy getting out of town, but I'd expected that due to the festival. Before I left, I checked the trip odometer on Jules' truck. It read seventeen miles, about the same distance between Front Royal and Winchester. I made a mental note to set back the odometer on the way back from Winchester.

On the way to Harry Grove Stadium, I thought over my plan of attack. This time, things would be different. My father use to tell me, never make the same mistake twice. What happened in Bowie would not be repeated in Frederick. This time, everything would be done with precision and timing, with safety devices in place for the unexpected. Last time was sloppy and haphazard. The only sloppiness in this operation will be the aftermath, and even that I considered. I knew it will be messy. The poor kid wouldn't know what hit him, but at least for his sake, he wouldn't feel a thing. It would be over in a millisecond.

As I crossed the bridge going through Harpers Ferry, I noticed the sky was getting increasingly darker. It was beginning to look as if it was going to rain. I had checked the forecast in Front Royal. It said it would be a beautiful day, all day. I realized I had failed to check the forecast in the western Maryland area. *How could I be so stupid?* I thought as I approached the 340 I-70 exchange. It was now raining. This could ruin the whole operation. I was furious with myself for not being more thorough. I have always prided myself on being detail oriented. How could I have possibly overlooked this? Pa-paw always said, "Be prepared for the unexpected." *How in the hell could I be so careless,* I thought?

Getting off at the Harry Grove Stadium exit, I couldn't help but notice all the traffic going down the entrance ramp onto I-70. I looked to my far left and saw the stadium parking lot emptying out. The game must have been called because of rain. I cursed myself for my own stupidity. I had jeopardized the whole operation, not to mention my own safety and freedom. *Careless. Stupid and careless,* I mumbled to myself.

Pulling in to the stadium parking lot was a pain in the ass with so many cars leaving, plus I was being seen by hundreds of people. The operation was starting to border on insanity or suicide. Either one didn't present a favorable outcome.

But I was already here. I could adapt and overcome. I just had to focus on why I had come here. Calming down was the first of my obstacles. I started by controlling my breathing and taking long, deep breaths while I was looking for my target's car in the players' parking lot.

I spotted my target's car, a navy-blue Toyota Celica. I also noticed the last of the fans leaving the parking lot. I had the good fortune of knowing what the make and model was, along with the tag number, courtesy of the Front Royal Police Department. It was nice having close contacts in high places.

Pulling around to the front of the Toyota and checking my mirrors for passersby, I again thought, *this is pure suicide.* I got out of the truck while it was still running. Walking to the passenger door, I quickly opened it, got my black bag out and unzipped it. I took one more quick glance around to see if anybody was close by.

Seeing no one, I took the package out, along with my telescoping connectors and a baseball. Stealing a quick look around again, I got on my hands and knees and crawled quickly under the Toyota. I had the blue prints of the engine and the under carriage of the car memorized, having gotten them off the computer last night. Within minutes, I had the package connected to both a manual and a speed-set explosion, which I had set at seven miles an hour. I wanted to minimize the amount of collateral damage to innocent bystanders, if someone would be so unfortunate as to be close by. That's why I wanted it done here in the players' parking lot, knowing there wouldn't be as many, if any people around. I also considered the type of explosives and the explosion it would cause. The incident in Bowie had been done without much thought, but I'd studied this all night. I'd rigged it to blow straight up, forward toward the firewall, maximizing all the energy to the cockpit of the car, and not out to the sides. This should prevent any metal shrapnel from hitting anybody or anything. The car would, or at least should, blow straight up.

Crawling out from underneath the car, I was suddenly startled by a booming voice.

"Hey, what are you doing?" a voice asked.

As I slowly made my way to my feet, I noticed who it was immediately. It was the 6'2", 235 lb. first baseman for the Frederick Keys, Tommy Burger, looking exactly like the picture from the press guide on the Key's website.

"I was just retrieving this ball I got for my kids that I dropped while unlocking my car. Of course, it would have to roll all the way down here and end up under this car," I said in a voice of annoyance as I extended my hand with the ball in it.

"Well, sir, that happens to be my car that your ball was under," Tommy said in a much more subdued voice.

"Oh, sorry about that," I said. "are you a ballplayer?"

"Yes sir. I'm Tommy Burger, first baseman for the Keys."

"Really? Wow, would you be kind enough to sign this ball? My kids would love it. Something tells me you may become famous someday." The last part wasn't a lie. He was about to get his fifteen minutes of fame, postmortem, he just didn't know it.

"It would be my pleasure," Tommy replied. With that, I handed him the ball and a pen that I had in my shirt pocket, just in case this scenario would arise. I was proud of the attention to detail, that I had every base covered, even a story if I should get caught placing the device.

"Thanks so much, man."

Tommy signed the ball and handed it and the pen back to me. I thanked him once more and made my way back to Jules' truck, waving and nodding my head as I did. I opened the truck's door and climbed in. I started the truck and started to pull away, ever so slowly. Looking in the rear view mirror, I watched as Tommy unlocked his car, opened the door, and climbed inside. I could barely make out Tommy's movements. It looked as if he was starting his car. I could see him adjusting his mirror. He seemed to be admiring his appearance as he took his right hand and waved it through his collar-length blond hair.

Using my cell phone, I quickly hit the seven-digit code to activate the bomb. I now could either hit the send button to detonate the bomb or just wait for him to reach seven miles an hour to activate it, which I preferred. In some odd way, I wanted him to be in control of his own destiny, even though that destiny was preordained by my wants, needs and desires.

Tommy finally pulled out of his spot. It had only been 1 minute, which had seemed like an eternity to me. I hadn't planned on watching his death. I thought I would have been long gone by the time it happened, but fate and the rain had dealt this hand. Pulling out in my direction, he started to increase his speed. As he did, so did I. I did not want to take any chance of becoming collateral damage. I glanced down at the digital speedometer; it read ten miles an hour.

Looking back, I saw a sudden flash of light, then I heard the thunderous explosion. The whole car lifted straight up, a good five to six feet off the ground as it was engulfed in a giant fireball. Debris flew skyward some three hundred plus feet. As it fell back to earth, I noticed that it fell no further than seventy-five to a hundred feet from the flash point in any direction. It was surreal that I would be admiring the precision of my work and not care about the death that it had caused. I felt no remorse or guilt, just the joy of the perfection of it all. The bomb did exactly what it was supposed to do; the device had worked with precision, as the frame and charred body, still in flames, came to rest just feet from the flash point. The Oriole organization now had another first baseman to replace.

I love how a plan comes together, I thought as I exited the parking lot and sped away. What had started out as a simple plan, had now developed into a warlike strategy. As developments changed, so did the tactics that surrounded them.

Now all that was left to do was to get back to Front Royal, reset the odometer at Winchester, buy a couple of bottles of wine, and be seen some more at the festival before going home and watching the day's events on TV.

Chapter 46

The four of us were hanging out at the festival, mixing a lot of pleasure with a little bit of business. Guinea and I had tried several of the local Virginia wines that were available. All of us had tried much of the local fare, which was all very good. While the boys played various games and looked at the local arts and crafts, Guinea and I talked to the local merchants.

As we talked to them, we kept coming away with the impression that most, if not all of them, thought the Glasgow's were the best thing since sliced bread. They also thought Mark was a well-mannered kid. After some prodding, they said that Mark was maybe a little self-centered, and somewhat of a disappointment to most of them. They all hoped he'd become a big star to show the other professional sports scouts, not just baseball, that they could find talent here in the Shenandoah Valley. They had a lot of civic pride, but what stood out to me was the unfairness of putting all those dreams on one young man's shoulders.

Shane was playing in the moonwalk when the call came in. Guinea and Josh were eating spare ribs, courtesy of the Royal Oak Tavern's stand, as I sipped on a glass of White Zinfandel and admiring a blond beauty that looked strikingly like the blond that was driving the beamer in Annapolis.

"Mike, this is Freddie. We've got another one," the voice said at the other end of the phone.

"Another what? Please don't say another murder."

Freddie replied, "Yeah, another murder."

"You've got to be fucking kidding me," I blurted out, gaining the attention of both Guinea and Josh. I tried to regain my composer, then I asked, "Where?"

"Frederick, Maryland, in the player's parking lot at Harry Grove Stadium."

"How?"

"A bomb in his car. I've been told there's not much left," Freddie said.

"Do we know who the victim was?"

"No, not yet, but we're on it."

"Well, we're still in Front Royal. Let me get Guinea and the kids and we'll leave as soon as we get back to the hotel, gather our things, and check out. We should be there in less than two hours. Have Bobby meet us there."

"He's already on his way, and so am I. I was doing some paper work when the call came in. Do you want Smitty to come up too?"

"No. If I'm lead on this, it's time I take some heat for it. But could you have Dewayne issue a press release or make a statement to keep me from having to deal with the press at the scene? At least, I hope it will. You know how much I love the press and the cameras."

"Alright, Mike, I'll get Dewayne to set it up, and I'll be there by the time you arrive. Anything else?"

"Yeah, I need you to have a Virginia State Trooper meet us at the Holiday Inn on 522, it's about eight miles outside of Front Royal, to escort us through Virginia. Then, get us an escort from our friends in West Virginia, and finally, have one of our boys meet us at the Maryland line. We'll be in a hurry."

"What route you taking?"

"81 North."

"Mike, why not come up 522, take 340 through Berryville, Charlestown, and Harpers Ferry to 70?"

"Because I have another stop to make."

"Another stop?"

"Freddie, the boys are with me and I'm not bringing the boys to the crime scene. I think it would be a little too much for them."

"Where you taking them?"

"Hagerstown, my mother live there. I'll be there as soon as I can"

"Not a problem, Mike. Take your time, the dead guy isn't going anywhere."

"I know, Freddie, that's exactly the problem. It seems that the more time we take; the more dead bodies keep turning up. I need to shake things up, and in a hurry."

I got Guinea and we gathered up the boys. I told them what had happened in Frederick, and then we immediately left and headed back to the hotel. We all went up to our rooms and hurriedly got our stuff together. As we did, I called my mother and told her the boys were coming for a visit. Of course, she had plans, but plans that the boys could be involved in and would love. At least that was a bright spot in what was turning out to be a horrible ending to an otherwise good day.

As we were checking out, I noticed out of the corner of my eye the state trooper's cruiser pulling up to the entrance.

"Guys, I've got a little surprise for you."

"What?" the boys asked.

"You are going to visit your grandmother while your uncle and I go to Frederick to check out the crime scene."

"But I want to go with you, dad, to see what it looks like," Josh replied.

"Not this time pal. Besides, your grand-mom is planning to take the both of you to the Hagerstown Suns game. It starts at 7:05. We're going to meet her at the ballpark."

"We'll never make it in time," Guinea replied.

"I planned for that," I said, as I nodded in the direction of the patrol car outside. "See our friend out there? He's going to escort us to the West Virginia line, where we will meet one of their troopers, who will take us through until we cross into Maryland."

"Cool," Shane said, his mouth hanging open in awe.

We left the Holiday Inn and were soon on 66, heading north towards 81, doing a little over 100 mph. At that speed, it wasn't going to take as long as I thought. As soon as we got on 81, the conversation had shifted to the boy's grand-mom.

"So, we're off to see the matriarch of the Carrier family," Guinea said.

"I thought you referred to her as the Queen Bee," I replied.

"No, I refer to my mom as the Queen Bee. Your mom, my friend, is of a higher social status."

"In your mind, Guinea. To us, she's just grand-mom and mom. You really need to just sit down and talk to her one day. She does not sit on as high a horse as you would like to think."

"Hell, Mike, you're her son. When was the last time you sat down with her and had a heart-to-heart?" Guinea asked as we hit the West Virginia border connecting with their trooper.

"Guinea, at this juncture in time, neither you nor I have the time to sit and talk to anyone. It's always go, go, go, next case, next murder. But you're right. I don't make time to talk with her. Where can I find time, you tell me? Hell, I bring the boys on cases just to spend some time with them. There has to be a better way."

"So, how's your mom doing?" Guinea asked.

"She keeps herself busy, too busy I think, for a woman who is eighty-one years old. She seems a little fragile to me, but her mind is still sharp as a tack. She still loves to travel, and is still actively involved in the Elk Lodge in Hagerstown. And she still loves baseball, especially the O's, and sports from any other team from Baltimore.

"Well, are the Hagerstown Suns still a minor-league affiliate?"

"Yeah, they're the class A team of the Washington Nationals. I just hope they play better than the Nationals do, because the Nats really stink," Josh replied before I had a chance to answer Guinea's question.

"Are they as bad as the Orioles?" Shane asked.

"Yeah, bro, they're that bad, just like the O's."

A few minutes later, we picked up the Maryland State Trooper at the West Virginia/Maryland line. Ten minutes later, we were at the ballpark. There, waiting for us at the main entrance to the ballpark, was my mother, in all her glory. She was wearing a nineteen-seventy throwback Oriole's hat, complete with the cartoon faced Oriole bird and a authentic replica Brooks Robinson jersey from the same year. She looked great, but maybe a little out of place since she was attending a Nationals minor league game. But it didn't matter. She gave this family the love of the game. It was in our blood. We all bleed orange and black because of her. Shane spotted his grandmother first and ran full tilt toward her, followed closely by his big brother. I was afraid they were going to knock her down. They reached her and started to hug, and the sight made me feel emotional. Guinea must have sensed it. He put his big paws around my shoulder and said, "Come on, bro, let's take a few minutes and talk to mom."

"Hi, mom," I said, giving her a big hug and kiss. "I appreciate you doing this on such short notice."

"It's never a problem. I love seeing my grandchildren and you. I just wish I could see more of all of you."

"How many times have I asked and pleaded with you to move closer to us, in Annapolis or Edgewater?" I asked.

"And leave all this?" she said, while gesturing with her hands wide, half turning to the old wooden ballpark.

"Mom, I've really got to go. I'm sure you heard what's been going on. I'll let you know what I'm doing later."

"You've finally learned to do that, after all those years of me constantly worrying about where you were and what you were doing when you were a teenager?"

"Well, I guess having the boys has made me a little more responsible."

"And how have you been, Roger?" she asked.

"As well as can be expected, Mrs. C., and yourself?"

"I hate to sound like a broken record, but I'd be a lot better if my boys, including you, would come visit me more often. And please, Roger, call me Charlotte, or mom. You know we have a shared bond," she said, looking down at the boys.

"I do it out of respect, Charlotte."

"That's better, Roger. Now you make sure he doesn't forget to call me," she said as she shot me a glance.

"He won't forget. He always calls the boys to check in."

Not taking her eyes off me, she said, "Well, I guess he is learning. You boys run along and clean up this terrible mess. I hope you can catch this mad man soon, because if he's allowed to continue this reign of terror there won't be a home team to root for. Then I'd have no choice but to become a Nats fan, and, frankly, I'd rather die first."

"Grand-mom!" Josh said.

"I'm only kidding, sweetheart," she said with a wink at Guinea.

"You boys behave and listen to your grandmother," I said.

"They will. They have to be more behaved than you were at their age. Roger, you take care of yourself and take care of my boy."

"I will, Charlotte, I will."

Chapter 47

"My love, I don't want you drinking too much wine. We must keep up appearances."

"I won't, sweetheart," Vladimir replied. "Is Mark supposed to be down here today?"

"He told me last night that he would. He was going to take Julie to Winchester to see Brett Michaels."

"Who's Bret Michaels?" Vladimir asked.

"Some eighties rock star. I had to ask Mark the same thing," and they both shared a laugh.

"Vladimir, my love, I want to keep him on a tight leash while he is home. We can ill afford to have any more accidents while he is here."

"I understand completely. I was just thinking the same thing, Victoria, but he's a grown man. It's easier said than done." He chuckled and said, "It's funny, after all these years together our thoughts and minds think alike, as if we were one."

"Vladimir, it's called true love," Victoria replied.

As they were talking, Brady approached the two of them.

"Hello, Brady. I've been wanting to thank you for being such a dear and riding out to the house to escort those two detectives from our property."

"It was no problem, maw-maw. What did they want, anyway?" Brady asked.

"They seem to think that our Mark is somehow involved in the murders of the baseball players in Maryland."

"Oh, really?" said the Front Royal police officer and neighbor of the Russian couple. He continued as both Victoria and Vladimir took a sip of a Zinfandel from a Rockingham county vineyard. "Do they have anything on him?"

"Of course, not," Vladimir shot back as he wiped his chin with his left hand. "They say they can put him around the scene of a couple of the crimes."

"But, at the time he was playing ball in or close to those same towns," Victoria said, in an effort to defend her grandson.

Just then, Vladimir broke up the conversation and asked, "Sweetheart, what do you think of the wine?"

"I like it, my love. It has a real, nice bouquet."

"Good. Excuse us for just a minute while we inquire about this wine with the vendor." Vladimir gently grab her arm just above the elbow to escort her to the stand. "Sweetheart, you shouldn't give away any information to anyone, especially not to one with the resources and possible motive to frame our boy."

"My love, don't you think for one moment that I don't know what I am doing. I have out-foxed much more professional and dangerous people than him. I was trying to bait him, hoping for a slip of the tongue, and more importantly to read his body language, which told me a lot. Did you notice how he became more erect when I said they could place him at or around the scenes? His confidence showed, like he had gotten away with something."

"Yes, I did notice, my dear, but I didn't like the tactic. We're not even certain that Mark didn't commit these crimes."

"That's enough, Vladimir! He's never lied to us before, and he is certainly not lying to us now." Victoria's usually mellow tone was more forceful and direct as she said, "He's also never killed before, Vladimir. When we first killed, we had to or we would have been killed, either by the Germans or by our own compatriots. I remember that feeling as if it was yesterday. And to this day, that first kill still twists my stomach. And who's to say you aren't behind this. You have the experience and the resources to have it done, and I know how badly you want your grandson to succeed."

"As do you, sweetheart. I'm just saying…," Vladimir stopped, wishing he had not made that last comment after reading her facial expression.

Vladimir quickly turned to the vendor to give him their address to have the two cases of Zinfandel they purchased delivered. And to avoid any further discussion with Victoria. That would surely have come had he not turned away. They returned their attention to Brady, who was now talking to his stepbrother, Buck.

Buck, seemed to be in really good spirits, drinking straight out of a half-filled bottle of cheap Chablis.

"Hey maw-maw, pa-paw," Buck said in a loud and overbearing voice.

"How are you, son," Vladimir said, thinking to himself, *that boy is dumber than a box of rocks.*

"Same old, same old, pa-paw. Brady tells me the Maryland police seem to think Mark is the killer of those ballplayers in Maryland. What Buck didn't tell the Glasgow's was how he hoped the police would lock their grandson's ass up and throw away the key.

"No, no, let's not overreact. They're just doing their job with due diligence," maw-maw said, sensing by Bucks body language and demeanor that nothing would please him more.

"Do they have anything on him?"

"Of course they don't," Vladimir retorted in a tone that would tell anyone with the least amount of sense that the old man's Russian blood was about to boil over.

Just then, the trifecta was about to be complete, as the third brother of the trio, Billy, came strolling up. "Hey, it looks like old home week. The whole crew is here, except Mark."

The Glasgow's were like the trio's surrogate family. Their biological parents had been addicts. Their mother died of heroin addiction when the boys were all in their teens. Soon after, their father left them and moved on. The Glasgow's paid off the boy's house and kept an eye on them until they all graduated from high school. Truth be told, they had started taking care of the boy's way before that. Their parents couldn't take care of themselves, much less three teenage boys. The Glasgow's were always there to lend a helping hand, but always from a distance.

Billy also had a half-filled bottle of wine, a Cabernet Sauvignon, in his left hand and a half-filled plastic cup in his right, but seemed in much better shape than his stepbrother, Buck.

"So, what's been going on? Why you all just standing here in front of Soul Mountain Restaurant while all of this excitement is going on all around us?" Billy asked.

292

"We're just talking about Mark and how maybe he'll be getting locked up," Buck blurted out, letting his wine do his talking.

Brady retorted quickly, in an agitated tone, "Buck is blowing things way out of proportion. They just came up here to check out a few things."

"Who are they," Billy asked, knowing the answer before he ever asked the question.

"The detectives from the Maryland State Police that we saw on the surveillance cameras at maw-maw and pa-paws house the other day."

"Ah, yeah, that's right. you two alright?" looking over at the Glasgow's with a genuine look of concern.

"Of course, we are, my dear, why wouldn't we be? Mark has done nothing wrong," maw-maw replied.

"Has anyone seen Mark?" pa-paw asked.

"No, I haven't, and I've been here all day," Billy replied.

"Same here," Buck said. "Look, my stand is right in front of Schewell's Furniture.

Jules has probably seen him," Billy said.

Walking up the street toward the court house behind the trio, Vladimir whispered to Victoria, "Did you notice Bucks hands? How shiny and glossy they were?"

"I hadn't noticed," but now she was looking intently at his hands and said, "It seems to be some type of residue. I've had something similar to that on my hands years ago. I just can't seem to place it."

"I was thinking the same thing, sweetheart, and I just can't place it, either."

As they approached the surveillance stand, there was not a single person inquiring about any of the equipment or devices being offered. On the other hand, the other vendors had tons of people interested in what they had to offer, from prints, to antiques, to simple cheap knick-knacks. Victoria watched Billy's body language and it told the story about how his business was doing. He went from a supremely confident man to looking like a scared dog cowling beneath a parked car.

"So, how has business been today, Julie?" Billy asked.

"I'm sorry to say this, but it's been terribly slow. A couple of people did come up and grab brochures, but that's been about it. I wish I could have gotten a couple of jobs or at least some estimates on the books for you but, I couldn't, and I feel bad, knowing how much you need the business. Maybe it was too serious to think about amid this party atmosphere."

Trying to obviously change the conversation and the suddenly somber mood, Brady quickly asked Julie, "Have you seen Mark"?

"No, I haven't. I thought he'd stop by, but he didn't. We are supposed to hook up later tonight. He told me he had a nice surprise for me, but I haven't seen him today.

Billy then spoke up and said, "Julie, why don't we just start boxing up all this stuff. It doesn't look like we're going to get any business out of this. It makes no sense keeping this stand open."

"Don't be foolish, my boy. There's still over two hours left to get some business out of this. It takes only one person to turn it into a big payday," Vladimir said.

"Pa-paw is right, and I don't mind keeping the stand open. I like it down here with all the people and activity," Julie replied.

"Are you sure?"

"I'm positive, Billy, it's really no problem."

As the group was about to disperse from in front of Schewell's, Mark came striding up from behind, looking very pleased with himself. He had the look of a confident man, walking tall, shoulders back, and head up, with a mischievous grin on his face. His body language said it all, but instead of carrying a glass or bottle of wine in his hand, he had a dozen long-stemmed roses. Upon seeing his grandmother standing there, he quickly pulled one of the roses from the bouquet. From behind her back without her noticing, he reached around her right shoulder and put the rose about twelve inches in front of her face. Then, in the same motion, he planted a soft kiss on her left cheek.

Maw-maw spun around and said, "My thoughtful, wonderful grandson. How I love you. You are such a kind and loving man. Now, why don't you give those roses to the one for whom they were truly meant." With that, she cupped both of her hands around his face, just like she had done a thousand times before. Mark bowed his head, just as he had always done, to accept the kiss of his loving grandmother on the top of his forehead. Mark looked over his grandmother's shoulder and saw a proud and adoring grandfather smiling his approval.

Then, Mark broke from the embrace and took two steps toward Julie. Jules came from behind the stand, her eyes welling up with tears. She thought to herself, *he is such a kind and loving man. Not the monster the police are trying to make him out to be,* as he presented her the roses. Before he could say a word, Jules took the roses and wrapped her arms around him, bouquet and all. She stood on her tip toes to kiss him passionately.

Mark could feel the warm tears on his face as he returned the kiss that he had so desperately wanted. He wrapped his huge arms around her and lifted her gently to meet him as he willingly returned the kiss.

Two of the onlookers were smiling proudly. The others had a different look, a look of disdain; certainly not a look of approval, even though they all were trying to force a smile. The woman they all desired and dreamed about was in the arms of another man. Try as they might to disguise their feelings for Julie, Victoria picked up on it right away.

"So, Mark, we were all wondering where you had been. I guess that we know now," Billy said, as he looked at the roses and again demonstrated that he had more class than his other two brothers combined. The conversation continued for another minute or two. Julie had a small radio set up behind the stand on a chair. As it blurted out the latest single of Staind new CD, it was suddenly interrupted.

"We pardon this interruption. 99.3, The Fox, has just learned there was a car bombing in nearby Frederick, Maryland, at Harry Grove Municipal Stadium, home of the Frederick Keys. It is feared that another ballplayer may have been murdered. There is no, I repeat no, official word yet, but we at Fox can confirm that there has been a bombing at the stadium. As soon as we have more details, we will interrupt this broadcast with further information.

Again, there is no official word yet, but we will keep you informed as this story continues to unfold."

Chapter 48

Guinea and I left the stadium and headed toward the outlet malls on I-70. The Jeep was eerily silent because I was in deep thought and Guinea knew it.

"So, what's got you in such a trance, pal?" Guinea asked.

"You know how I always tell the boy's family first, family always, family forever?"

"Yeah, it's kind of like your motto. I'm surprised you don't have a tattoo of it," Guinea said as we passed the mall, entering the I-70 ramp

"Well, actions speak louder than words; I talk a good game I just don't play one."

"BULLSHIT, you're on one of, if not the highest profile cases the state has ever had. And you still manage to spend time with your boys. Plus, I know that my sister would approve and would be proud of the way you raising your children," Guinea replied in a stern tone.

"That's part of the problem, Guinea, all of our cases are big. Add to that the school year, and my time with them is very limited. Then there's my mom. She'll be eighty-two the first of December, and yet the only time I see her is when I want or need something. I should be spending more time with her, too. Because of work, she doesn't get to see her grandchildren nearly enough. So much for that family first motto, Guinea."

"Welcome to adulthood, my friend. Where you been? I'm a single man with no responsibilities to anyone but myself. I'm thirty-five to forty pounds overweight. I can't find time to work out, and there's a great gym two floors down from our office in the state building. So go figure," Guinea said as we started to climb the mountain separating us from the city of Frederick. "Listen, everybody has the same juggling act, trying to balance time with work and time with family. You are not alone, my friend. Believe me, you do better than most, I assure you."

"Tell my boys and my mom that, will you? I constantly feel like I'm letting down those I care about the most. I'm afraid one day I will wake up and my mom will be gone, the boys will be grown and have moved out, and I'll have missed out on so much."

"I know what you need, Mike."

"What's that, Guinea, a shrink?

"You need to listen to some Neil Young." With that, he pulled out his iPod and the next thing I heard was Neil young singing the verse, *'old man take a look at my life, I'm a lot like you'.*

Chapter 49

We arrived at the stadium in what seemed like, no time flat. After my discussion with Guinea, I felt a new sense of urgency, almost invigorated, or energized. That is, until I caught a glimpse of the parking lot as we got off the ramp toward the stadium. There were a hundred emergency response units, maybe more. It appeared that there were just as many news outlets on the scene as well, which included some new players, like the BBC and stations from Japan and Austria. These murders had gone international now.

As we got out of the truck, Guinea and I couldn't even see the crime scene. The crowds of response personal, news people, and onlookers were a bit overwhelming. It reminded me of the boardwalk in Ocean City on the Fourth of July weekend. We saw a local Frederick County officer. As we approached him, we flashed our badges. He was very cordial and polite under the circumstances, or it could have been all the cameras on us as we spoke with him. He led us to the crime scene, through the roped off corridor of cameras and microphones pushing against us to the left and to the right. I personally had never experienced anything like it in my entire life. It reminded me of two heavy weight boxers being led to the ring, with hordes of people pushing and shoving against us. I could tell Guinea was really getting as agitated as me.

Then I saw someone who I thought could be a possible ally - Kelly O'Donnell from NBC Nightly News. I had always liked her on TV. She seemed to have integrity in her reporting. I stopped as she called my name, thinking to myself, *how cool is it that she knows my name? I hope I judged her correctly in my evaluation of her having integrity.* She called my name again, and I stopped and acknowledged her.

"Mike, is this bombing related to the other murders in the Orioles organization?"

"At this moment, I can't give you a definitive answer, but if I had to bet, I would say yes."

"Do you have any suspects on the other murders?"

"We have a few people of interest, but nothing I can, or will, elaborate on.

Her reply caught me by surprise and kind of pissed me off when she said, "From what we've been hearing, you and your team do not have a clue as to who could be behind this or even what the motive is."

Keeping my composure, I responded in an even tone, "Kelly, I assure you nothing could be farther from the truth. My team and I have been working around the clock on this, and we have made tremendous progress on this case. I, personally, resent the fact that anyone would speculate on how our case is going. Especially when they have no facts regarding what we've got and how we are doing our jobs. Furthermore", my voice growing a little more hostile, "Mrs. O'Donnell, contrary to popular belief, we don't, and can't, deal in speculation, hearsay or popular belief, unlike some other professions. We, and all other police forces, must deal in facts. We don't have the luxury or latitude to deal in anything but the facts!"

She started to ask another question, but I cut her off. "If you don't mind, I can't answer any more questions at this time. As you can see, I have a crime scene to investigate. I'll be making a statement as soon as it is warranted. Now, if you will excuse me."

With that, we briskly proceeded up the roped off corridor, past the throngs of people and reporters. I started to smell the charred remains of the vehicle, and then the smoldering smoke from the remains came into view. I spotted Bobby, and he saw us a couple seconds later.

"Hey, Mike, Guinea, over here," Bobby hollered as he waved his hand feverishly. "Have you ever seen such a cluster-fuck of a crime scene?"

"Come again?" Guinea said.

"All these onlookers and media types, not to mention this small army they call response teams around here. I pray to God that this crime scene isn't too contaminated from all these people."

"Why would you say that?" I asked.

"Well, it's better to show you. Come with me."

As we were walking in between and around emergency personnel, I noticed our local cop friend was still bird dogging us. I looked at his name tag and asked, "Officer Beatty, what's your first name?

He perked right up and said, "Jon."

"Jon, I want you to do me a favor. I want you to take a couple of your cohorts and get this fucking team gone - every emergency response team, media, onlookers, even the hookers, if there any here. You think you can handle that, Jon?"

"Yes sir. What about the fire personnel?"

"Good question. Get with the fire marshal and ask him to weed out who he doesn't need. All I want to see is you and your cohorts within eye sight, holding the perimeter. Understood?"

"Completely. How far back, Sir?"

"Your call, Jon."

"Okay, I'll give you plenty of real estate to work with, but my colleagues aren't going to be happy about this."

"We aren't in the 'making people happy' business, son."

"I know," he replied.

"Have you seen Freddie, I mean Officer Hunt?" I asked.

Jon paused, but Bobby was quick to answer, "I got Freddie taking some measurements for me."

Guinea, sensing what I was about to say, said, "Jon, you got any questions?"

"No sir."

"Well then, get to it. If anyone gives you any flack, you tell them to come see me, Special Agent Ginavan, okay?"

Jon nodded his head and continued walking.

The three of us were now overlooking the twisted, smoldering metal of, what I believed, was once a car. But it was hard to tell. It was a horrific sight, especially with the knowledge that someone was in it at the time of the explosion.

"So, what do you see?" Bobby asked Guinea and I.

"Not much. It looks like something you would see on CNN coming live from Israel or Pakistan," was Guinea's response.

"Not a bad analogy," Bobby replied. "First, look at the outer perimeter. What do you see?"

"Nothing, really. A few shards of metal. Why do you ask?"

"I'll tell you in a minute. Now pan in and tell me what you see. As you do, I'm going to try to teach you novices something."

"Bobby, we don't have time for a friggin' lesson. People are dying," Guinea responded harshly.

Bobby continued, "You've always got time to learn something, so bear with me big guy."

Looking in, we saw how the debris grew denser. Nothing unusual, I thought, but I knew Bobby was leading us somewhere. So, I played along and explained to him what I saw.

"Not bad, Mike. It clearly shows that our killer did not make a homemade bomb from one of a hundred sites on the internet. If he had, shit would be all over the place, so that tells us he certainly is no amateur. Now, let's take a closer look, shall we?"

"What are we exactly looking for, Bobby?" Guinea asked, now a lot more intrigued with what Bobby was explaining to us.

"I'll show you exactly what we're looking for." Then he paused, getting on his hands and knees at what had been the front of the car. He motioned to us with his left hand and said, "Guys, look here. Look at the frame right here." His words were coming at a furious and excited pitch now. "Look at the frame, right here, at the motor mounts - look how they're totally inverted. If the bomb had been homemade or made by a novice, it would more than likely been in the shape of a V. He put the charge right here, right under the steering column. I suspect it was a moving charge." I started to cut Bobby off to ask him a question, but he just put his hand up to stop me, then continued, "I'll explain later, now read the metal fragment. It tells us the bomb blew straight up, with a tremendous force. Look here, at the cuts on what is left of the engine block." He was pointing to multiple, large grooves, about an inch wide and four to six inches long, going straight up. "Now, where's the firewall?"

"There's a small piece over here, where the passenger door used to be," Guinea answered. It was hanging by a small piece of twisted metal, that was somehow still attached to the cage.

Like a teacher commending his star pupil, Bobby said, "Exactly, Guinea. Remember the scrapes on the engine block? Now, look at where the heads use to be. See the deep gashes right here?" again he pointed. "Look how they go up and back at a ten o'clock angle. Follow me." he said as he walked toward where the driver seat once was. "See these fragments lodged in the corner panel? Those fragments are from the firewall. My preliminary observations of the damage caused by the explosion tells me one thing. Either it was made by a professional, my best guess, someone Western European or someone with extensive knowledge of electronics and liquid explosives."

"Bobby, what exactly brought you to that conclusion?" I asked.

"Well, Mike, the bomb was designed for a specific purpose, besides the obvious, of course. It was designed to blow straight and back. In other words, the energy of the bomb was directed to just kill the intended victim, without too much, if any, collateral damage. The Irish Republican Army used this method often back in the day, and they perfected it."

"So, you're saying a novice couldn't pull this off?" Guinea asked.

"It's possible, but he'd have to be smart and really know something about car design to maximize the effect, and have an extensive knowledge of electronic components. As far as the explosives are concerned, unfortunately, you can get them anywhere. Since 9/11, though, trying to buy them raises a lot of red flags. It can still be done or you can just go on the internet and make it yourself."

"What do you mean, make it yourself?" I asked.

"All you need is some fertilizer and some household cleaners. It's that simple. Mike, you really need to get on the internet a little more often to see what people are capable of doing."

"You said European. Why?" Guinea asked.

"This bomb was designed to kill just the victim. Look at the bomb scene again. All the damage is in one, confined area, not spread out. The bomb blew straight up, not out. If bystanders would have been around, there would have been very little collateral damage, maybe just a couple of injuries and concussions. Again, it goes back to the design. Look at Al-Qaida, if this was their work, it would have been spread out, shrapnel all over the place, trying to do all the damage they could. Not this bomb. This bomb was built with an assassin's mentality. A single shot, single kill execution."

As Bobby was explaining his theory, I noticed Freddie approaching.

"Freddie, do we have a name for the victim yet?"

"I got who the car is registered to, Mike, but it will be a while before we can get any kind of positive ID. I'll have to defer back to Bobby on that. There is nothing left of him that I can see."

"Well, who's it registered to?" Guinea asked.

"A Tommy Burger, twenty-one years of age, and yes, he is a first baseman for the Keys. If he's our victim, the press is going to amp it up a couple notches."

"Why," I asked.

"Because he just got married two weeks ago, and his wife is three months pregnant. Her father is Congressman Anthony Tittle, from Texas. He's the one who has been spearheading all that border patrol stuff we've been seeing on TV." Freddie replied.

"Fuck me, it just keeps getting better and better. All these young kids getting killed, their dreams shattered, their parents and loved ones lives shattered, the heart break it causes them, their hopes and dreams for their children destroyed," Guinea said in a voice of disbelief and desperation.

"One more thing of interest, or at least I think so," said Freddie.

"What's that," I reluctantly asked, my voice an octave higher.

"Guys, he just bought this car two days ago, so how'd our boy get this Intel so fast? I mean, our main suspect is a ballplayer, not a cop, and he is supposed to be in Front Royal, isn't he?"

We just all looked at each other with blank stares for a moment.

"Bobby, when can you get me a positive ID?"

"I got a couple of guys from the local department canvassing the area looking for some DNA. I should have some results in six to twelve hours, if not sooner."

"Make it sooner, Bobby. The media will take notice of the roster for tomorrow's game right away. Freddie, get some local guys in their jurisdictions over to the homes of his wife and his parents. I don't want the media to inundate them until we get a positive ID. This is going to be tough enough on them. Let's try our best to ease their pressure during this whole ordeal. Ask them to keep the media and the onlookers at least two blocks away, and have the highest possible ranking officers go to their homes and explain to them that their loved one is missing, and then stay with the family. Also, give the Congressman's office a call. Tell them what has happened and that we will keep them in the loop. Until we close this case, we don't need the Congressman adding to the hype and pressure."

"No problem, Mike. I'll take care of it right away," Freddie replied.

"Freddie, what kind of car was it?"

"A brand-new Toyota Celica, at least that's what DMV says. Why do you ask, Guinea?"

"Thought it was the new style, can you get me the schematics?"

"Why do you want the schematics?" I asked.

"Mike, this is a brand-new car. How'd our perp get the intel on this? Also, they just came out. I've got a hunch Bobby was right when he said our guy would have to be mechanically inclined, but maybe he also knows body designs. Either way, the guy has some serious resources to know his victim got a new car and to get the schematics on the car which just came out. That's a lot to ask of our main suspect, considering he's a ballplayer, don't you think?"

"Mike, you've got that look. What are you thinking," Guinea asked?

"I'm doing just that, pal, I'm thinking. I hear what you guys are saying and I'm trying to digest it. I'm going to throw this out there and you are going to think I lost my mind, but maybe there are two killers, or we have a copycat. One thing I know for sure is this - if it's one guy, he sure is multi-talented, or a professional assassin. Bobby

312

says I'd be surprised with what I could learn on the internet. I suppose I should do some face time with that dusty old computer in the back of my truck. Bobby, I've got one question?"

"What's that, Mike?"

"You said the bomb was placed here?" pointing to the spot that he showed us earlier.

"Yeah, that's it."

"Can you tell me what that shiny liquid is?" I asked.

"That's the residue of the liquid accelerant. In itself, it's harmless…"

Cutting him off, I said, "What I need to know is, was it bought or was it made?"

"I can have that answer for you an hour after I analyze it, but I have a ton of work still to do here."

"I need to know asap. Can we send it to Sherry down at NCIS?"

"Yeah, I guess," was Bobby's halfhearted reply.

"Then do it, please. I need to know right away. I'll call Molly to set it up with Sherry. Freddie, get one of the locals to run it down to D.C. as soon as Bobby gets the sample."

"Consider it done, Mike," was Freddie's response.

Just then, an officer came up to Bobby and handed him an evidence bag. Bobby looked in the bag and began to shake his head. "They found a finger, and it has a wedding band on it."

Damn it, I thought to myself.

Chapter 50

Making our way back through the roped off corridor, Guinea said that he thought Bobby may have felt like I was stepping on his toes by sending a sample down to Sherry. I already had a million things running through my head, and now I had a million and one. *Bobby said the bomb could have been made. That's what I figured. What about the liquid charge? Guinea stated the killer must know something about mechanics and/or car design. Guinea saw a black truck in the body shop parking lot across from the Knotty Pine, then we saw one on our way here. The witnesses in Aberdeen and on the highway at the sniper shooting also saw a black truck. Shit, there's only a billion such trucks running around. On top of that, our killer is an electronics expert, and a marksman, to pull off the shot that killed our bonus baby. He also had to feel very confident in his hand-to-hand combat skills to go up against a man the size of Timmy Fallon, who was in excellent shape, even though he attacked him from behind. Plus, he has been getting Intel as fast as we have. How was that possible? How did he know Tommy Burger got a brand new car so fast? How'd he get the schematics and plan this out so fast? The Glasgow's had all these traits, plus a lot more, I imagined. But why would they purposely make us believe that their grandson, Mark, was responsible for these murders? Why would they do that? Why lead us to him? Perhaps trying the end around game? Make it appear to be him, only to have us, of all people, clear him of any wrong doing? But that would lead us straight to them. But they would have succeeded in their mission. they that arrogant to think they could still get away with it? Or do they figure that they're both old and their days on mother earth are short anyway? So why not sacrifice themselves to make Mark's dreams of being a big-league ballplayer come true? But hell, they'd have to know that no baseball organization in the country, or for that matter, the world, would want to take a flier out on him after this scandal. They're not dumb, this isn't their first rodeo. They've gotten it over on the K.G.B., mother Russia, and the C.I.A. So, how hard could it be to get it over on a couple local-yokel cops like us? We are small potatoes to them. Plus, they came to our office. Talk about cocky, what's with that?*

Guinea broke through my train of thought. "What are you thinking, Mike?"

"Guinea, I want a complete work-up on anyone and everyone who had a relationship with Mark or the Glasgow's, from junior high on. I want to focus on just the people who had relationships with the three of them, their inner circle. Also, red flag those who had a military background, tinker with cars, electronics, demolition, etc.… you know the drill. I'll get Molly to ask Sherry if she can find any of the Glasgow's old spook friends who are still active, and which ones may have a hard on for them and want some payback."

316

"I could tell your wheels were spinning, Mike."

"Yeah, they were. Just suppose we are looking at this from the wrong angle, Guinea."

"What do you mean, Mike?"

"Suppose Mark, or the Glasgow's, didn't have a thing to do with any of this. Suppose this is some sort of payback for a passed indiscretion of Mark or his grandparents. We can safely assume that the Glasgow's have skeletons in their closet."

"I'll do you one better, Mike, if we're talking hypothetical, suppose Mark is the last target, or the next target. Suppose this is not about any of them. Suppose this is all about the Oriole organization or ownership. If this is the case, I'm going to feel and look like shit, because I had Mark bagged for this from the get go. That is, until this bomb thing - way too sophisticated for him to be behind it, plus the timing thing in planning." Guinea paused, then added, "unless he had help."

"Good point. That's what I was thinking. Maybe we have more than one killer. I'm leaning hard on a set up on Mark. Like you said, the timing thing, the intel, the expertise of the hits - it's all going down too fast. Remember, only the Bowie attempt was a failure. Seems really odd, don't you think? How's a kid who's trying to hit 95 mph fastballs going to pull this all off? Guinea, did you happen to see a laptop in Mark's hotel room in Ocean city?"

"No, I didn't."

"Does that seem odd to you?"

"Yeah, it does, but that doesn't mean squat. Every hotel and motel has them now, or one of his buddies on the team has one, or it's in his truck."

"Possibly. I'll have Molly check for an email account. While I'm at it, I'll give Smitty a call and have him check out all the Orioles top brass to see if someone has any scores to settle with them. That way, all our bases are covered."

"Excellent idea, Mike. Now, what are you going to say to the press?" Guinea asked as we approached them.

"I haven't a clue. I thought I'd defer to you."

"To hell with that. You know how my Irish temper gets. Besides, I hear TV adds twenty pounds, and I'm already fifteen pounds overweight."

"Fifteen?" I said sarcastically. "You want to try again, pal?"

"Doesn't matter, pal, I'm not getting within fifty feet of you when you address the media. I'll just sit back. You dug your own grave when you told that lady, and I

318

quote, 'I'll be making a statement as soon as it is warranted.' For a semi-intelligent man, you sometimes make some asinine moves. And that little statement to Mrs. Kelly O'Donnell? - that ranks right up there, pal."

"Guinea, why don't you tell me how you really feel?" We both laughed, then I continued, "I'll make a short statement, answer a couple questions with vague answers, and get the hell out of there."

"Mike, let me know how that works out for you. Oh, I forgot, I'm going to see it up close and personal," he said, laughing so hard he could barely spit the words out.

Chapter 51

I stepped in front of the mass of media that had assembled, stopping some 15 feet away from where Mrs. O'Donnell was standing. As promised, Guinea kept walking, shaking his head as he exited, stage left.

"Ladies and gentleman, I'm prepared to make a brief statement and then I will answer a few of your questions. But I can assure you, this will be brief. We have a hell of a mess here, and a lot of work ahead of us that will need my team and my full attention, understood?" I didn't wait for a response. "After I make my statement and answer a couple of your questions, the local P.D. will be directing you to another part of the parking lot. If you would all now look towards the wreckage, you will see I have instructed the Frederick County sheriff's officers to move all nonessential personnel, including their own, away from the crime scene so that my team can more effectively do its job. That includes you. I want to thank you in advance for your cooperation. Now, as you know, at apparently 1:45 pm, there was an explosion involving a car. We also found what we believe to be a human body part. We are of the opinion that there is only one victim, but at this time, we do not have a positive ID on the victim. When we do, we will be notifying their next of kin. After notification, we will forward that information to you. We ask, at this time, when we do let you know, you respect the privacy of the victim's family." I purposely did not say he or her but victim so the press could not dig there claws in to bait me on. "Now, we have reason to believe that this crime is related to the previous crimes committed against players of the Baltimore Orioles organization. Before you ask, that reason is simply the location of the crimes. I said when we first spoke earlier today, we are not in the speculation business. With that in mind, I will now take a few questions."

The media started barking out questions like a bunch of wild dogs on a feeding frenzy. Out of the corner of my eye I saw a face I recognized - Joshua Michael from Baby Birdland, a local blogger who covers the Orioles. The boys and I always enjoyed reading his insightful articles. He was just standing there watching all the other reporters acting like wild dogs barking out questions, so I asked him.

"Joshua, do you have a question?"

"Yeah, I do, Mike. What's your gut feeling on this? Do you, or do you not think this is an attack on the Orioles organization? Or, is it serial killer? And if so, what do you believe the motive is?"

"Well, Joshua, that's really three questions. I can see that you're a real slick willie." That drew a couple of laughs from the reporters. "I will try to answer all three of them. My personal opinion, and the opinion of my team, is the same; this is not an attack on the Orioles organization. Because of the violent nature of the crimes, I also believe that these murders are some sort of personal vendetta. They've been planned, with near-perfect execution and with very deliberate targets. At this time, we believe we may be dealing with a serial killer, or killers. I must point out that we continue to explore every possible avenue. As far as motive, due to the nature of our investigation, we have numerous possibilities that cannot be elaborated on at the moment."

Kelly O'Donnell inched toward the front of the media members, but I purposely ignored her. I decided that next up was Peter Schmuck from the Baltimore Sun. I purposely chose sport reporters from the local area. I watched and read them, and I thought I knew them best.

"Mr. Schmuck?" I asked.

"Thank you. To follow up on your last comment, can you tell us why the killer or killers are targeting first baseman?"

"We have a couple theories, but again, I can't elaborate on that at this time."

As I answered Peter's question, he made his way up to me and handed me a small piece of paper. On it read, 'Detective, our resources have found all the Keys players have been accounted for except Tommy Burger who happens to be a first baseman.'

After reading Peter's note, I looked at him and asked, "Peter, do you have another question?" figuring that one class move by him deserved a return move by me.

"Yes, I do detective."

"Call me Mike," I replied."

"Alright, Mike, our sources have determined one player is unaccounted for from the current Keys' roster. Out of respect for the family, neither myself, nor the Baltimore Sun, will release the name of the said individual until your department does. But, could you tell me why the killer came back to Frederick to commit this murder? If, indeed, that's what has occurred here. I am by no means a detective, but it seems he, or they, have broken the pattern. There are still a couple of minor league teams in the area, not to mention the Orioles, to terrorize"

"Peter, first, I want to personally thank you and your paper for not divulging the name of the missing player, as does the department and the State of Maryland. I can only hope that your fellow reporters will show as much restraint and class as you and your paper have done." Peering at the crowd of reporters, they all seemed to be nodding their heads in agreement. Continuing, I said, "Peter, maybe you missed you're calling and should have been a detective, because my partner and I were discussing that exact same thing on the way here."

All eyes turned towards Guinea at that time. I spotted a familiar sight, the logo of the News 25 peacock. I also recognized a friend of my mothers who worked as an anchorwoman for them, Angelia Gonzales. I decided to take a chance and give the local news girl a chance.

Looking directly at her, I said, "Young lady."

"Angelia, Angelia Gonzales, detective."

"Do you have a question?"

"Yes, I do sir. As Mr. Schmuck, has pointed out about this being the second murder in the Frederick County area, do you and your task force think that the murder or murderers could be from, or reside in, this area? "

As I listened to her question, I surveyed the area, looking at where the smoldering wreckage was, all the bystanders and press, and the back drop of the stadium and the mountains - it all seemed so surreal.

"Due to the sensitivity of the case, I can't answer that question at this time. We should be able to answer it soon." As the words were coming out, I knew I was screwing up. Like a blur, I heard it, but couldn't believe it was coming out of my own mouth.

Standing there, getting hammered with a million questions at the same time, all white knuckled and nervous, I again found myself looking at the wreckage and the back

drop of the mountains in the distance. Then I looked at
Guinea and saw his look of disgust. Then seeing Joshua
Michael and Angelia Gonzales, it suddenly dawned on me;
the proverbial light bulb went off in my head. Ignoring all
the other reporters, I asked, "Angelia, do you have a
follow-up question?"

As she asked her next question, I got out my pad
and hurriedly began to write two short notes, one to Joshua
Michael and one to Angelia. The note to Joshua simply
read, 'Thank you for your professionalism. I've always
enjoyed your insight and expertise in covering the Orioles
minor league teams. I also was impressed to learn about
your playing career that began in Front Royal. How'd I
know you ask? I am a detective and a baseball fan, I made
the connection.

The other note to Angelia read, 'I just wanted to let
you know that I am the son of your friend, Charlotte
Carrier. When this case breaks, you and your station will
be the first to know. Thanks for your help.'

As I handed them both the notes, I mentally
prepared to answer the question I knew she was going to
ask.

"Detective, are we to assume you will be making an
arrest in the immediate future?"

Pausing a moment, I answered, "Yes." As I did, I
noticed, as I had fully expected, the pained expression on

325

my partner's face and a stirring of the crowd. I continued, "We should be issuing an arrest warrant within the next 48 to 72 hours. Now, if you will excuse me, that will be all for today."

As I started to walk away, the place was abuzz with reporters continuing to shout questions at me. I walked towards Guinea; the shock of it all still painted on his face.

"What the hell was that?" Guinea asked as I reached him and continued walking towards his jeep.

"Guinea, I was up there thinking about what Josh Michael and that local lady reporter was asking, and I started thinking about one of our random discussions we had some time ago, about love, and getting it, and keeping it at all costs. Suddenly, it all became so clear and a more heinous crime.

"Mike, you've got me baffled and confused."

"Guinea, I'll explain it to you later. If nothing else, when this hits the airways, it will at the very least make our killer blink, make a mistake, or at a minimum, make him nervous."

"Did you hear what Peter said about the pattern being broken? He asked why the killer or killers, would come back to Frederick."

Chapter 52

It didn't take long for the shit to hit the fan. As soon as I started the truck, the announcement was already in progress. On 98 Rock out of Baltimore, it stated that the Maryland State Police were planning to make an arrest in the next 48 to 72 hours, in what they were now calling 'The Birdland Murders'. I hit the pre-selection button over to 105.7, The Fan, another Baltimore station, to hear that they, too, had interrupted their broadcast to announce that an arrest was imminent. I again hit the pre-selection, but this time to a rock station that broadcast out of the Shenandoah Valley called the Fox 99.3, just in time to hear a special news bulletin.

We at Fox 99.3 are breaking for a special news bulletin coming out of Frederick, Maryland. Per our sources here at 99.3, the Maryland State Police will be issuing an arrest warrant for the murder or murderers of numerous baseball players in the Baltimore Orioles organization within the next 72 hours. We here at Fox 99.3 will keep you up-to-date as more information in this intriguing case develops.

"Mike, what the hell have you done? You've taken our asses out of the frying pan and put us in the fire."

"Listen to me, Guinea. These murders had absolutely nothing to do with the Orioles organization, its players, or baseball at all. The entire time, they have been used as pawns in a deadly love triangle. It's all about love, or perceived love, and getting it at all costs."

"I'm still listening, Mike," Guinea said as I got on I-70 heading north back toward Hagerstown to pick up the boys. I continued explaining my theory to Guinea.

"Did you hear what Peter said about the pattern being broken. Why come back to Frederick? He was right, the killer had other options. Why not Bowie, Baltimore, you name it. Then our little local reporter asked, 'Do you think these murders are being committed by someone local?'. I was looking at the mountains as she asked her question, and it clicked for me. I felt like saying, your damn right I do. Think about it, Guinea, Freddie said just about everyone from the tri-state areas taught to hunt and fish, like it's a religion. Hunting is killing. I was raised to fight for what I believe in, and to achieve it at all costs. I believe our killer thinks the same way. I believe the killer or killers has that same mentality. Our killer will do just about anything to achieve his goal." I said

"Ballplayers," Guinea mumbled. Then I continued "Mark Newman plays first base, Julie Wines, the waitress from that Knotty Pine place, is head over heels in love with him. We went right after him without looking around. We took the bait hook, line, and sinker, just like some poor rock fish under the damn Bay Bridge."

"I believe our killer is in love. What else could it be? He's is infatuated with Julie Wines, and he'll do anything to get her and keep her. In his warped little mind, he can justify these killings by taking out any perceived outside interest. He thinks he's found a way to take out his biggest competition without putting any motive or blood on his hands," I said. "You think the killer would have taken out all these ballplayers when he could have just as easily taken out Mark Newman"? Guinea asked

"Your damn right I do. I also think that he may have had help. Logistically, it's almost damn near impossible to pull all this off without help. Then, add the skill set involved; being an expert marksman and electronics whiz with extensive knowledge of car design and engineering, and let's not forget expert bomb designer and maker. It may be one killer, but he had to have some help. Think about all the Intel he, or they, gathered. That alone is a job in itself," I said. "We know a couple that's more than capable of doing that," Guinea said and then continued, "But that makes absolutely no sense to set up their only grandson."

"Exactly, my friend, but suppose our murderer knows their background, or bits and pieces of it. If you can't frame the grandson, framing the Glasgow could work just as well. Another major catastrophe in Mark's life and he is liable to go into a serious tailspin. Not a real great endorsement for a love interest. Tomorrow I have to get the boys to ball practice, Josh to South River High and

329

Shane right around the corner to Seahawk Park. After that, we will go to the office and focus our attention on Julie and all of her known associates. I guarantee we will find something that leads us right to where we need to be." I concluded

"Mike, I'm starving. After we pick up the boys, let's grab a bite to eat. I can't think anymore. All I want to do is fill this gut!!!"

"Guinea, mom said she'd feed the boys. I'll tell you what, I'll call her and tell her we're going to stop and get a bite to eat. We'll go to the Texas Roadhouse on Dual Highway. I'll treat you to a nice fat prime rib. And I think I'll get the rib eye. How's that sound?"

"Like a good plan," Guinea responded.

Chapter 53

We arrived at the restaurant and you could smell the steaks from the parking lot. I didn't realize how hungry I was until I caught a whiff of them. As I grabbed the brass handles of the large wooden doors and opened them, the first thing I noticed, besides the hostesses, were all the TVs.

On at least five of them, I was being shown doing the impromptu news conference. Suddenly, I thought this may have been a bad idea. As we were shown to our table, I couldn't help but notice all the glimpses and hushed whispers as we passed the patrons at the various tables. Guinea noticed, too, and commented as we sat down, "That is the price of fame." I didn't find his comment very amusing.

The TV directly in front of me was on the N.F.L. network. They were even reporting on the 'Birdland Murders', as it was now being called. Another TV showed an old file photo of me and it felt a bit overwhelming. The waitress approached, introduced herself, and asked us if we would care to have a drink.

I hastily replied, "I sure do. I'll take a 22 oz., Bud draft and a shot of Jagermeister, if you don't mind."

Guinea simple said, "ditto," and the waitress nodded her head and went to retrieve the order.

The waitress shortly returned with our drinks and then took our orders. As promised, I told Guinea to get the prime rib, which he did, along with a house salad and a baked potato. I ordered my rib eye, also with a house salad and a baked potato with sour cream and bacon bits. They used real bacon here. I told Guinea he was missing the boat. He then added that to his potato.

As soon as the waitress left, I took a big gulp of my beer and downed my shot. As I did, an older gentleman and his wife sat down adjacent to us. Ordering a drink for his wife and himself, I guess he noticed that I chugged what was left of my beer. He told the waitress to give us another round.

"Thank you, we appreciate it," I said.

"No need to thank me. After the day, you guys have had, I figured you could use it," and he gestured toward the TV.

"You thought right, sir. I think my friend here lost his mind today, and inadvertently just may have opened Pandora's box," Guinea replied.

"Son, what your friend did was the smart play, intentional or not. It has that bastard's attention, and in all probability, has got him running scared. Now, he is on the defense and you dictate the action, not the reaction. Pound him with 'we are getting close, we have a suspect, an arrest is imminent' type stuff to the press, and he'll blink. And then, gentleman, do us all a big favor and nail that bastard to the wall," he said before he turned his attention back towards his menu.

As the gentleman spoke, I noticed a Navy Seal insignia on his jacket, which was folded on the back of his chair. I asked him about it.

"I'm retired, but we have two sons that are, in fact, third generation seals. Why do you ask?"

"From the outside looking in, do you think this could be ex-military?"

"Absolutely, or a cop," he said without hesitation, and then continued. "Don't second guess your decision. I would have done it after the last murder. But, I'm a military man. I always believe in taking it to the opposition. That's what we are taught - put them in a defensive position, pin their backs to the wall until they either give up or die. And never, and I mean never, let the opposition dictate the action or movement. Never sit back and wait for something to happen - make it happen. But that's the military way. We don't have the same rules as you." Then without a second thought he said. "Being passive gets people dead!"

As I thought about what the gentleman was saying, I was nodding my head in agreement.

I happened to notice a tall, beautiful blond walking through the wooden doors. She was dressed for success, in a business suit and heels, with her long blond hair and wire rimmed glasses. She looked absolutely stunning, and very familiar to me. As I pushed my chair back and started to stand, I thanked the gentleman for the drink and his advice and input. Without saying a word to Guinea, I approached the lovely lady who was now sitting at the bar.

"Sharon Watson."

"Well if it isn't the now famous Detective Mike Carrier, how are you doing? It seems like it's been forever since I've seen you," she said as she stood up and put her arms around me to give me a friendly hug. Sharon and I saw each other on-and-off for about a year and a half after the death of my wife. We met at a ceremony on Capitol Hill a year after 9-11, but at the time, I thought it was too soon after the death of the boy's mom to pursue a serious relationship. I hadn't wanted to upset them any further, so I kind of just stopped seeing her.

We just stood there for a minute, exploring each other with our eyes, and all the while I was thinking to myself that I felt so much at home holding her. Finally, she broke the silence that had probably only lasted a second, but felt like forever.

"So, I see you have been a busy man," she said as she gestured at the TV over my shoulder.

"Yeah, you could say that. What brings you up here to the wonderful world of Hagerstown?" I really wanted to know if she was there to meet a date.

"I'm meeting a business associate about a possible merger."

"you still a branch manager at Congressional Federal Credit Union?"

"Oh, heavens no. A lot has happened since we last saw each other. I've had three jobs since then."

"Really," I responded.

"Yeah, I was offered, and accepted, a job in Virginia as a CEO at a credit union in Front Royal.

"Really," I said, thinking of the irony of the situation as she continued.

"The board wasn't as forward thinking or progressive as I would have liked, so I moved on, plus there were issues with the VP. Then, I went to a credit union in the W.S.S.C. building in Laurel, again as a CEO."

"I know that building. Looks just like a big glass condom. It's just off I-97."

Sharon laughed and said, "Yeah, it does, now that you mention it. I never saw it that way, but you're right, it does." Still laughing, she added, "Only you would come up with something like that. I see your mind is still never too far from the gutter."

"Yeah, some things never change, I guess. So, why'd you leave there, and what are you doing now?

"That board had real issues with me personally. I just rubbed a few of them the wrong way, even though I raised their assets by over five million and got two camel one ratings. So, I walked away and landed as a VP for the Federal Labor Board Credit Union. I thought it was a good way to stay in the loop, but as a VP, I didn't have to answer to the board, just the CEO. Then one morning I woke up and just decided to do consulting work for credit unions so I hung up a shingle and her I am"

"Well, good for you girl."

"Yeah, it's all good except for the hours with this merger. Speaking of which, my associate just walked through the door. I hate to be rude, but duty calls. Do you think we can get together when I finish my meeting later?"

"Absolutely, I 'd love to. I see my dinner has arrived, and my friend will eat his and then mine if I don't hurry and get over there to claim it."

She Glanced over at Guinea and smiled, and then added, "If we can't hook up later, my number is still the same."

"We'll hook up later. My friend wouldn't let us leave until he had a chance to meet you. And yes, I still have your number and I plan on using it."

"Good answer, detective," she said with a grin as she went to meet her business associate.

As I headed back to the table, I knew Guinea would have a million and one questions concerning Sharon, and for some unknown reason, I was looking forward to answering them. As I sat down, Guinea said nothing. He just sat there and continued eating his salad. So, I played coy and started on mine. I could sense that he was bursting at the seams, and I couldn't help but smirk as I began chewing, and then, all hell broke loose.

"What the hell's so funny?" Guinea began.

"You, big boy. You're dying to ask me who that woman is."

"Your damn right I am. Well, who is she?"

"Her name is Sharon Watson."

"Another Sharon," Guinea said.

"Yeah. What can I say? I met her about a year after your sister died at a ceremony on Capitol Hill for the victims' families. And before you ask, yes, we started seeing each other for a while after that. Any other questions?" I asked, already knowing the answer.

"What happened? Why you would stop seeing her? She is so sexy. What did she do, dump you?"

"No, Guinea, she didn't dump me. I just thought it was too close to your sister's death to be bringing another woman into the boys' lives. Then we just lost touch, that's all."

"What were you guys talking about for so long, or, should I say, what she was talking about? I just saw you nodding your head and making gestures, but I didn't see you saying much."

"Guinea, I shouldn't have to school you on how to have a conversation or pick up a woman at your age. But I guess I will. You just have to listen to what a woman has to say. They'll be more than happy to carry the conversation, even if you are not interested, which by the way, I was. You've got to listen, and, in my case, the more I listen, the better chance I have of not putting my foot in my mouth and saying something stupid. We're cops, listening comes naturally to us, so I use my strengths."

"Damn, Mike, you make it sound so easy. So, all I've got to do is say nothing?"

"Yep," I responded, as I took a bite of my melt-in-your-mouth ribeye.

"One more question, you planning on seeing her again?"

"Yeah, I am, and any other info you need you can ask her yourself, because she will be joining us for a drink after her meeting."

"Well, that's good. It seems like your personal life may be on the upswing, which is good, because if your little plan does not pan out your career maybe in the crapper," Guinea said as he gestured towards the TV replaying my comments on having an arrest with the next 72 to 84 hours.

Sharon joined us a short time later. I introduced her to Guinea. We both stood when she arrived, but Guinea beat me to the punch and pushed her chair in behind her as she sat down. I immediately ordered her a Robert Mondovi White Zinfandel, remembering that was her favorite wine.

After the introductions, we began to make small talk. Guinea took my advice and did a lot of listening as Sharon talked about this, that, and the other. Soon, the discussion turned to her time in Front Royal. Guinea and my interest peaked a little bit more as she talked about it. I felt a little uneasy about the subject, but at the end of the day, I was still a cop. If she could provide any information, it could be a big help in closing this case.

Guinea started the questioning with a simple, "Do you happen to know a Julie Wines?"

"Yeah, vaguely. She seemed to be a sweet girl. Why do you ask?

Ignoring her Question to Guinea, I asked," How do you know her?"

"She worked at the credit union part-time as an intern during her senior year of high school."

"You said she was an intern? We met her at the Knotty Pine and she was our waitress. Why would she turn down a chance at a career in the credit union to become a waitress," I wondered out loud.

Sharon interjected, "I had every intention of offering her a full-time position after she graduated, but there was an incident that I could not get passed that happened one Saturday morning. I felt that, in the best interest of the credit union, I had to pass on offering the job to her."

"What happened?" Guinea asked.

"Why so many questions about Julie?" Sharon again asked.

"Just answer the question," Guinea blurted out.

"Guinea, turn off the detective," I said, as I noticed Sharon was taken aback by his tone. "Sharon, when we first started the investigations of the murders everything pointed to a ballplayer from Front Royal, a young man named Mark Newman. At the time, we thought it was a slam-dunk and we had our guy. But, as this investigation has progressed, we started having our doubts. Mr. Newman insisted, during some intense interrogations, that he didn't do it and that he was being set up. So, to make a long story short, we are looking at someone possibly setting him up."

"You think Julie is involved?" Sharon asked.

"Hell no, but she might be the motive," Guinea responded. "Newman and Julie have become quite the item. Mike seems to think that someone maybe framing him to get to her."

"You can't be serious."

"Yeah, we are, Sharon. That's why anything you can tell us about her could be a big help," I said.

"I'm surprised, but not shocked, that they are seeing each other. Mark was a lady's man from what I heard, but Julie always had a thing for him. I guess she finally waited him out or wore him down. But Julie had her fair share of suitors, too. That's what caused the commotion at the credit union."

"Care to explain?" Guinea asked, as I shot him a stern look in response to his tone.

"I'll be glad to tell you, but one of you gentlemen are going to have to buy me another glass of wine. It's a long story, and my memory isn't quite what it used to be, so some more alcohol just might be needed to stimulate a couple of these old brain cells."

We all smiled and shared a laugh and then got the waitress's attention and ordered another round, like the lady asked.

Chapter 54

"I remember it was a Saturday morning. We had just opened the credit union. I was in my office when I heard a commotion in the lobby, so I went out to see what was going on. Two men were arguing at Julie's teller's window. As I approached, it turned into a shoving match. I instructed one of the other tellers to call the police. Fortunately for us, there happened to be an officer right across the street at the Shell station. He was there in a matter of minutes, before it got worse.

After the two men were escorted from the property, I asked Julie to close her window and come into my office. As soon as she came in, I asked her what had happened. She explained to me that two brothers named Billy and Brady had come into the credit union to ask her to the prom. Julie said something like, "are you kidding? I can't go with both of you." So, Billy said to Brady, "Fuck you, I want to take her." Then Brady said, "You don't understand, you need to choose between the two of us. We heard from Buck that you turned him down. So, we figured we'd give it a shot." I asked her who Buck was, and she told me he was the stepbrother of the two in the credit union. Sharon said, "Weird, right?" "Anyway, she said she had told them that she was flattered that they wanted to take her, but she was waiting for someone else to ask her. Julie said, at that point, Brady became very agitated and blurted out, "I guess you're waiting for fucking Mark Newman to ask you out." Then, Billy pushed Brady and told him he was way out of line and to watch his mouth. That was when I came out.

About five minutes later, the officer who had escorted the boys out returned and asked if I wanted to press charges against them. He explained that Brady would soon be leaving to join the Army to become a military police officer. He had been in the ride-along program to become an officer once his military obligation was up, and any type of record could derail his career. I knew the other kid, Billy, because he had applied for, and received, a student loan to go to some sort of electronic computer school. I decided at that point not to press charges. I knew that their guardians, who were very well respected, would raise a big stink over the whole thing, and that, in turn, could be detrimental to the credit union. At the same time, I knew from the rumblings of other staff members regarding Julie's personal life, that hiring Julie for a full-time position would not be one of my smartest moves. So, as soon as her internship was over, that would be the end of that."

"Sharon, I've never known you to shy away from people with clout. Why were you worried about them? Who are they?" I asked.

"I really wasn't worried. I guess I should have worded it differently. They really are good people who are very entwined in the community, and they have a super large account at the credit union. You should know that Billy, Brady and their step brother, Buck, came from a tough background."

"According to what I've been told, their parents were both addicted to drugs and alcohol. In fact, the mother died of a drug overdose, and soon after, their father just up and left them. That was one of the reasons that I approved the loan for Billy. That, and the fact, I knew that his guardians would be more than willing to pay off the loan if it went into default."

"Soon after their father bolted, their neighbors came right into the credit union and asked if they could pay off the mortgage on the home for the boys. They also set up a fund to cover all of the bills until they all turned twenty-one. It was a huge undertaking, but they managed to get it all done through the court system and the local and state government in no time flat."

"Sharon I'm going to take a shot in the dark. the guardians the Glasgow's?" I asked.

"Yeah, how'd you know?"

345

"Well, sweetheart, we are detectives," I said, looking to see her reaction to my use of the word sweetheart, which was met with obvious approval.

"Mike, do you see the irony here? The Glasgow's basically became the surrogate parents to those boys. Why on God's green earth would those boys want to set up Mark or hurt the Glasgows in the process?" Sharon asked.

"Think about it, Sharon," Guinea said. "Mark had a major catastrophe in his life and his grandparents stepped up to the plate, as you'd expect. From all accounts, we hear he was very good in the classroom, had a great social life, and was extremely popular. Plus, he is a sports star. Let's flip the script."

"These boys came from a very dysfunctional home. Again, the Glasgows step up to the plate and take care of the boy's. But this time, they don't invite the boys into their home with open arms, but keep them at a distance. Maybe a little animosity starts to build? Maybe these boys aren't as popular as Mark and they don't get the accolades Mark does. Then, after all that, the coup de gras hits. The girl of their dreams spurns all three of them. For him. To them, he's lead a charmed life and has everything they don't. We have seen people go off the deep end and murder people for a lot less," Guinea said.

I looked at Guinea as if he had just had an epiphany and figured it all out.

"Sweetheart, love and rejection can make men do some terrible things," I chimed in.

"Well, it seems as if you boys have it all figured out. So, who is the killer?" Sharon asked.

"We don't know, but we are getting close, and it won't be long until we do," I said with a matter of fact tone.

"Guys, I don't want to sound like Debbie Downer and burst your bubble, but if you've got this figured out, you can bet your lives that the Glasgows have this figured out, too. Back when they got all that red tape cut so fast to get those boys set up in a matter of days, I asked Victoria how they both got things done so fast. She told me they did it by being smart. When I asked how they got so smart, Vladimir said that, when they were very young, you either got smart or died trying. At the time, I laughed, but reflecting back on it, he seemed very serious."

Guinea responded, "You have no idea, Sharon, no idea at all."

Chapter 55

"Arrest imminent" the headline in the Northern Virginia Daily read. I saw it as I sat sipping my coffee in the Knotty Pine. The place was abuzz with the news, and everyone had an opinion on the police statement.

Personally, I knew they were on a fishing expedition. There was no way in hell they had me in their cross hairs for the murders of those young men. I had covered my tracks. There was no physical evidence left at any of the scenes. I was sure of it, and no witnesses either, and they would never be able to find a motive. *Could they? Stop with the self-doubt*, I told myself, and just as I was thinking that, up walked the motive.

"Can I get you another cup of coffee, sweetheart?" Julie asked.

"Yes, please, and can I also get a couple flapjacks with a double side of bacon, extra crispy please?"

"Will that be all?"

"Yeah, that will do it. I've got to try to eat my way out of this pounding headache"

"Too much wine yesterday?"

"Yeah, you might say that," I replied.

As Julie turned to walk away, I wondered how she would feel if she knew that the love I had for her was responsible for the death of the four ballplayers. I'm sure she would be flattered. Why wouldn't she be? Look at all the attention it has drawn. Maybe one day, years from now, I'll be able to tell her. *After we drop off our grandchildren,* I thought as a smile crept over my face.

I knew going in that this would draw national attention, and that was the purpose. I planned it that way. I planned to have all this attention directed to the person that stood in my way of love, and I would continue to do what was necessary to achieve my ultimate goal. To capture the love of Julie. If there was collateral damage, so be it. Family, friends, it didn't matter. To hell with them all. I'd gone this far, there was no turning back now. So, could all this attention really have turned from him to me? *It couldn't have, could it? No way. Did I cover my tracks? Of course, I did. The Knotty Pine customers talking about the murders and the impending arrest have got me jumpy and paranoid. Nobody knows that I'm the mastermind of one of the greatest mysteries of all time, and no one will ever know I'm sure of it.*

"Are you feeling okay, sweetheart?" Julie said, startling me and breaking the hold of paranoia that had engulfed me.

"Yeah, I'm cool."

"It looks like you've seen a ghost."

"No, it's the wine. It just got the best of me. I really tied one on yesterday," I said as Julie handed me my flapjacks, and what looked like a half-pound of bacon.

"So, what do you think about the impending arrest? It's so exciting. I just know in my heart that Mark will be cleared. Some people around here think he may be involved, which I thing is absurd."

"I'll be glad when they catch the son of a bitch. I'm tired of hearing about it. That's all everybody is talking about. I'll be so glad when we can put this all behind us." I said.

"Do you think it is someone in the Orioles organization?" Julie asked.

"I really don't give a shit. I couldn't care one way or another. But, if things don't go as you hope, Julie, I just want you to know that I'll be here for you. I promise, I will always be here for you," I said as passionately as I could, knowing that I had just planted the seed to our future life together.

At that very moment, the bell above the door jingled and I saw Buck coming through the entrance. He immediately saw me and grinned as he approached. I thought this was just what I needed, on top of everything else. Now I was going to have to deal with an overweight, overbearing, redneck asshole, to put a ribbon on this fucked up morning.

"Hey, guys, what's happening," Buck asked as he bumped the table. He caused some of my coffee to spill as he clumsily tried to pull out the chair.

"Watch what you're doing, fat ass," I responded, as I blotted up the coffee that had spilled on my newspaper.

"What's your problem this morning," Buck asked.

"He had too much wine yesterday, Buck. He's not feeling too good this morning."

"We all had too much wine, Jules," Buck said with a laugh. "Did y'all hear about the police report yet?"

"Yes, we have. The whole town has by now," I said in a deadpan tone.

"Do you want some coffee, Buck?"

"Yes, Jules, let me also have some French toast with eggs, hash browns with onions, and a side of bacon please."

"Is that it?"

"Yeah, Jules. I should start cutting back on my food intake. My pants are starting to get a little tight," Buck said with a chuckle.

"Why should that stop you? It never has before," I said as Julie headed for the kitchen.

"Not everyone has a high metabolism like you," Buck responded.

"True, but not everyone overeats like you, either, Buck," I said with a snicker.

Then Buck looked at me straight in the eye and said, "I've been meaning to ask you what in the hell that stuff was that you had me mix up for you. It ate right threw my jersey gloves and got on my hands and started to burn like hell. Later that day, the pilot light went out on the old stove at the house. I went to relight it, and when it lit, it also caught some of the residue of that stuff that was still on my shirt cuff. It immediately caught fire in a matter of seconds, scaring the shit out of me. Look at my wrist." Buck rolled up his sleeve to show a massive blister, then continued, "Thank God I was right beside the sink and was able to run water on it.

"It was an epoxy," I responded.

"What kind of glue is that flammable? And what the hell did you use it for?" Buck asked.

"It's an industrial epoxy. I use it for various things," I responded in an evasive way.

"Well, that will be the last time I do that for you. I could have gotten killed."

While Buck was crying the blues, I noticed Julie talking on her cell phone. She had a look of concern on her face. I could tell something wasn't quite right. She stared at our table as she talked. I continued to watch Julie as Buck mumbled about something or the other. Julie noticed I was watching her, and suddenly turned her back toward me. She continued talking for a few more minutes. After ending her call, she grabbed a pot of coffee and started making her rounds from table to table, before finally coming to ours.

"Buck, Mark's grandmother just called me. She wants you to meet her and pa-paw at their house this evening."

"Why didn't she call me?"

"Because she wants me to come, too, and they knew that you would be here," Julie replied.

"What do they want, and why at their house?"

"All she said was to meet them at the house.

I started to wonder why they didn't ask me to come. Could they possible have something on me? No way they could. Those old farts could never have figured this out. *Could they?* I could feel the paranoia beginning to overtake me. *This can't be happening. I know one thing, if I go down for this, I'm taking everybody with me. Then they'll all see just how smart I really am.*

Chapter 56

Sharon and I said our good-byes in the parking lot. We hugged and gave each other a peck on the lips, and I promised to get together with her later in the week. I met Guinea at his jeep and we followed Sharon to I-70. She headed east, toward Baltimore, and we proceeded west, towards I-81 and my mother's house.

"Guinea, start calling the team and tell them to sleep fast, because we're meeting first thing in the morning. And to make sure they bring everything they have on the case. Also, tell them we will be working through lunch and possibly dinner." As he did this, I called a good friend of mine, Bryan at Graul's Market, to see if his deli staff could whip us up something to eat just to get us through, and I'd pick it up after I drop off the boys in the morning.

As Guinea started making the calls, I thought about my remarks to the press. I knew that the pressure was on to end this case. We all had to ratchet it up now. I knew in my heart that it was one of six people, and I was almost certain I could possibly knock off two, maybe even three, in a matter of hours. But I wanted to be sure, so it would be advantageous to check every detail and not rush to judgment.

What I knew for sure was motive. It wasn't about playing time or moving up the minor league ladder. It was about love. About the love of a pretty, small town, country girl who held down two jobs and, by all accounts, fought hard to win the love of one man. As I contemplated what this would do to her, we were already turning on to Woodburn Drive in Fountain Head, my mother's house in sight.

We awoke early in the morning and left the house with my mother still fast asleep. I knew I would pay for that move at a later date, but I had no choice. Something told me this was going to be a make-or-break day. As soon as the boys fell back to sleep, I called Bryan Graul on his cell phone and asked about the food I had ordered, He said it was no problem, and he even offered to have it delivered if I promised to hook up with him soon to go fishing. I was more than happy to accept the deal, and I thanked him and said I'd see him soon. After getting the boys a quick bite to eat and dropping them of at their ball practices, Guinea and I pulled into the State House. It had been two hours and fifteen minutes since we left my mom's house. Not bad time from Hagerstown to Annapolis.

Making our way to the back entrance to avoid the press was an exercise in futility. There would be no escaping them today. After saying a couple, 'no comments' to the relatively small group of reporters gathered by the entrance, we made our way into the building and up to our office. Upon entering, we saw a flurry of activity. Bobby was on the phone. When he saw us, he waved us over?

We heard him say, "I'll see you in forty-five minutes," and then he hung up.

"Who are you going to see in forty-five minutes," I asked.

"Sherry, and she's coming here. She found something very interesting on that substance I sent her from the Fredrick bombing. She has some big boy toys over at NCIS. Mine are still running data and she has it analyzed already. Must be nice to have Navy funds," Bobby said. You could tell he was excited, and maybe even a little envious of all of Sherry's Fed bought toys.

"Alright, as soon as she gets here, we will all gather in the conference room. I've got to talk to Freddie. Has anyone seen Michael and Molly?"

"Freddie and Michael went downstairs, and I guess Molly hasn't made it in yet," Bobby replied.

"Have you tried calling her?" I responded.

"Yeah, she never answered. I guess she's in a dead area. It just kept going right to voice mail."

"Well, keep on trying. We are going to need her to get all the paperwork and time lines in order when we start pulling all of this together. Hopefully she'll get here soon."

"I will, Mike. I'll call her again right now."

"Thanks, Bobby"

"Guinea, do me a favor. I want you to get me all the info you can on that cop that stopped us at Mark's grandparents' house. I have a hunch it's going to be the same guy that Sharon told us about last night. What was his name?"

"It was Brady," Guinea responded.

"Great, while you're doing that, I'm going to focus on Julie's boss, the one that owns the security system company. I'm willing to bet the house that he's the other brother Sharon spoke of last night. You got his name, right?"

"Sure do Mike. His name Is Billy. Your memory sucks for a cop."

"Don't need one, pal, that's what I have you for," I said, chuckling.

Sherry arrived right on time. I called downstairs to summon Dewayne, Michael and Freddie. We were already in the conference room, with the rest of the team who were in front of their computers doing this and that. I still didn't see Molly. I went over to Bobby's desk and asked him if he had gotten a hold of her yet. He said he hadn't and that he tried both her cell and home phone with no response. I thought this was way out of character for her, but we couldn't wait for her any longer. Bobby said she probably would be walking through the door any minute, so I decided to start without her. But if she didn't show up soon, I had made up my mind to send a squad car to her house.

Dewayne arrived and everyone had their computers and stacks of files in front of them. I couldn't help but feel amazed and proud of how detailed and prepared our team was. It was why each one of them was chosen for this task force. They were the best of the best, and I was proud to be associated with them.

As we sat down, the buzz around the room had nothing to do with the case, but about what could be holding up Molly. I overheard Sherry telling Guinea that she came in on interstate 97 to route 50 and ran into no problems. Bobby had checked with the Anne Arundel County Police. They had no problems in the area to speak of. I, too, was starting to be a bit concerned. But we had a larger task at hand, so I sat down and addressed the team.

"Alright guys, I know you're all concerned and wondering about Molly's absence, as am I, but we have a case to solve. We know that takes precedent over everything else that's going on. I assure you, I am just as concerned as everyone else in this room about Molly, but we have a job to do, and by God, we're going to do it. If she hasn't shown up in a little while, I will send a trooper to her house to see what's up. Dewayne, I asked you to attend to get you up to speed on what we have and where we are."

"Thanks, Mike, from the minute your press conference aired, I've had the State House calling me nonstop, like I was a 911 operator. By the way, I thought you handled that well, considering that dealing with the press is not your forte."

"You think he handled it well? Then ladies and gentlemen, put your seats in the upright position and buckle your seat belts, because Mike Carrier is about to take you on one hell of a ride," Guinea said with a ton of sarcasm.

"Guys, I want everything you've got up to this point, and I'd like to start with you, Smitty."

"Well, Guinea asked me to work the alleged black truck that had been spotted at the crime scenes. I started with the paint that Bobby found, and after, a ton of phone calls, I can confirm it was a GMC model. We have two matches so far, and one is Mark Newman's. The other is Julie Wine's. Then I looked at the tire marks that we got off interstate 81, near the sniper nest, and I checked the Aberdeen hit-and-run. They both confirmed the Mickey Thompson after-market thirty eights, and again, both subject vehicles have them. I decided to concentrate on tire distributors in the Front Royal area, and, as luck would have it, I came up with a place called Duncan Brothers, located in the heart of town. They had sold thirty-eight pairs, dating back a month before the first murder, and, again two sets each were sold to Newman and Julie."

"Smitty, remember that picture I sent you from that auto body joint across the street from the Knotty Pine?"

"Yeah, Guinea, I was just thinking of that. From the picture, you sent, I ran the tag, and it belongs to a Kevin James, age twenty-four. He just happens to be employed at Royal Auto Body. If the name doesn't ring a bell yet, it will. After a background check on Mr. James, I found out that his nickname is Buck."

At that point, all of us except Dewayne, sat up.

Smitty continued, "He also has a GMC, but it's a Yukon Denali, not a Tahoe."

At that point Dewayne spoke up, "Aren't they pretty much the same, just a little higher price tag?"

"Yeah, Dwayne. Buck's truck also has the same Mickey's as the others, but his were bought just two weeks before the Brannon murder. After a little more digging, I found out that he and a coworker did a little after hour paint and repair on the right front of his truck late in the evening on the day after the hit-and-run. I was able to track down some receipts for a light lens and turn signal that had been shipped that day, with a little hacking help from Sherry."

Sherry grinned sheepishly, and Smitty continued.

"Dewayne, before you say we can't use it in court, it was just the end game to find the information. We can always call the coworker to testify to the night in question," he said before Dewayne could offer a rebuttal. "Also, in case you were wondering, the paint used on both the Tahoe and the Denali are the same. At this point, I'd love to get a cast of Buck's tires if we can."

"If this pans out, we will, you can bet on that," I said.

Guinea responded, "Michael Smith, you are the man. Great job."

"Guinea, wasn't James the name of that officer's that stopped us at the Glasgow's House?"

"Sure was. I thought it was his first name on the plate at the time, but now it makes sense."

Then Bobby spoke up. "Guys, judging from the cast taken at the Brannon sniper's nest, they were tires without a lot of miles on them. That should take Mark Newman's out of play. Remember, he's been driving around half the state of Maryland, from Frederick all the way to the eastern shore, and then going back to Front Royal, Virginia on numerous occasions.

Guinea then again spoke up, catching me a little off guard, when he said, "Smitty, try to dig up anything you can on our cop friend, Mr. James."

"I'm on it." With that, he flipped down his laptop and walked out of the conference room like a man possessed.

"Guinea, I thought you were looking into that."

"I was, Mike, but Smitty is on a roll. Besides, he's been on point throughout this whole investigation, so let's let him run with it. I'm better suited for the dirty work." With that, Guinea unholstered his service revolver and set it on the table, providing a little comic relief.

"Point taken, pal," I replied. "Alright, Bobby, talk to me. What else have you got?"

"Mike, Brannon's ballistics confirmed it was a TAC 50, what the military likes to call a big mac. It has a range of 2430 meters, which is about a mile and a half. As you know, we found no casings at the scene. It is my belief that the load of the shell was not factory packed."

"What makes you think that?"

"A 50 Cal weapon travels the first 1700 meters at super-sonic speed. Upon impact, at that range, it would have disintegrated his skull."

"Bobby, did you see the same body we saw?" Guinea replied.

"Sure did, only half of his head was blown off. At that range and speed, with a factory load it would have

363

shattered like a piece of fine china. The knife used at the Ocean City scene was, as I suspected, a standard sheath found commonly at any Army surplus store."

"Could you find one at a flea market?" Freddie asked.

"I can't see why not, why do you ask?"

"I know there's a big flea market on Commerce Street in Front Royal. I've been there a couple of times. We can ask around to see if it looks familiar to any of the vendors there."

"As far as the hit-and-run, it's cut and dried. Smitty covered that. I've got nothing more to add. As for the bombing in Frederick is concerned, I think it's in our best interest to defer to Sherry. She can run through it way faster than I can."

"Thanks, Bobby. As always, an outstanding job. Well, Sherry, I guess you're next, and again, we appreciate your help in all of this. We're glad that you could drive down here to join us. So, what can you add?"

"Bobby gave me his synopsis on what he thought of the fragments from the bombing, along with some shaved metal from the engine block, frame, and firewall. I hate to contradict Bobby, but…"

Bobby spoke up, "Sherry, if you found something that will steer us in the right direction, don't let my pride stand in the way."

"Well, you said in your e-mail that you thought it was a professional. I disagree with your assessment. I believe it was a person with a strong background in electronics, and perhaps even with a military background, but he was no pro. Unfortunately, I've seen far too many bombing attacks to classify this as a pro hit. I will say that he has an extensive background in electronics and chemical compounds, or knows someone that does. From my experience, trained assassins have one, maybe two ways in which they apply their craft. This person, or persons, has a lot of different skill sets; too many, I believe, to be a one-man-show. The bomb itself had a speed induced timer and a manual switch. I couldn't tell which one triggered the device because the accelerant burned so fast and hot that it destroyed much of it. My hunch is that he did it manually. Which brings me to the accelerate itself - this guy took a few chemistry classes. The accelerant served two functions. First, it was a heavy, compound glue that would adhere to anything. Second, and most importantly, it was an extremely fast and long burning compound. If it wasn't for the quick response of the emergency personnel, in another five minutes, we would have had absolutely nothing to work with. I mixed a small sample of it together and found it had the sticking and drying characteristics of an industrial strength crazy glue, with the texture of a cake batter. An amount the size of a tablespoon burned at 1700 degrees for forty-five minutes. The person who made this wanted it to burn for a long time, in hopes it would destroy the car completely. He didn't want to leave any traces that he was even there... but he did."

"What do you mean, Sherry?"

"Mike, as I stated earlier, he's an expert in electronics. Going through the fragments that Bobby sent me, I found a small piece of a circuit board. Granted, the piece was small, but the welds were meticulous. He certainly knew his way around a circuit board, and how to distribute electrical energy. Our guy seems to be highly intelligent. Unfortunately, that's all I've got."

"Sherry, excellent job. That gives us something really strong to go on."

"Mike, it's all about having better equipment. Time is always at a premium in cases of this nature." Sherry said, in an attempt to have Bobby's back.

"Sherry, we know that all too well, but on a local level we sometimes don't have the resources because of budget constraints."

"I know Mike, I'm just saying ...." was her reply.

"Alright, Freddie, you're up."

"Well, Mike, I've been working the weapon angle and I've been drawing a blank. I searched the tri-state area, considering the sales from every gun shop and every direct manufacturer sale to the Front Royal area. I found a few, but none that tie into any person of interest, which I found a bit odd."

"How so, Freddie?" I asked.

"When we took Mark's weapon in O.C., we ran it and found no results, so we were forced to give it back after seventy-two hours. After we released the weapon, we found out later that it was a procurement of the federal government."

Interrupting, Guinea said, "Anyone willing to bet it was the C.I.A.?"

Suddenly, Smitty burst into the room. "You're not going to believe what I just found out. Our cop, Brady James, has been with the Warren County Police Department for two years. Do any of you happen to know what one of his specialties is? He's on their Swat Team. And here's the kicker - he's their sniper, and he got his sniper training while serving in the Marines for four years, doing two tours in Iraq with seven confirmed kills."

"Well, that certainly levels the playing field," I said.

"Not so fast, Mike," Sherry replied as she pounded the keys on her lap top. "Mr. Robert Brady James made it into the corps, but he just passed his entrance exam by a hair."

"So, to put it bluntly, he doesn't have the beans to rig the bomb," Guinea responded.

"But his brother does, Guinea," I said as I punched my keyboard. "It seems Billy is the exact opposite of his sibling. He went to Virginia Tech and majored in computer engineering. Upon graduating, Billy went to work for Northrop Grumman, specializing in the development of high tech surveillance equipment. He left a little over a year and a half ago to start his own business, selling and installing the equipment."

Sherry interjected, "Mike, I'm running a program to find out the financials of his company right now. This opens up a whole new world of possibilities. He has the capability to manufacture any type of device he puts his mind to, if he has the schematics to do so, which is really only a click away."

"So you're saying he could have built this bomb, Sherry?" Guinea asked.

"Without question," she answered, as she continued hitting keys. "It looks like this guy is on real shaky ground financially. I can't see how he is even staying afloat."

"So, we are looking at a three-headed monster. Don't forget the step brother working at Royal Auto Body.

Someone had to be able to get the schematic for Tommy Burger's new car," Freddie chimed in.

"It's possible, but improbable. I can pull that info up in a matter of seconds. Besides, too many moving parts with three killers, and what's the motive for each one of them?" Sherry replied.

"I think you need to see this from my angle. Bear with me and look outside the box for a minute."

"Go ahead, Mike, tell them your crazy notion." Guinea said.

"I will, Guinea. This whole case is about misdirection. At first, everyone in this room thought it was a ballplayer trying to force his way up the ladder, or someone with a vendetta against the Orioles organization for some perceived wrong done to them. But, this case revolves around what so many other murder cases have since the beginning of time."

"Greed," Smitty blurted out, as if he was a contestant on a game show.

"Bzzzzz," Guinea voiced.

"Sorry, Smitty, its love. Julie had said to Guinea and I that Buck and her boss had a thing for her. Remember, Guinea?"

"Yeah, in the Knotty Pine, and she was creeped out about it."

"That's right. Then Guinea and I learned that there was an altercation at the local credit union involving both Billy and Brady - over Julie. So, there's two siblings fighting over Julie. Throw the stepbrother, Buck, into the mix we now have, as Freddie said, the three-headed monster. They all know that Julie is in love with our ballplayer, Mark Newman. They know nothing will deter her from him, not distance, long periods of time apart, and certainly not the advances of another man. She has tunnel vision, and the only man she sees is Mark. They also know that he is now committed to her."

"So why kill the ballplayers?" Dcwayne asked.

"That's easy to explain," Guinea responded, undoubtedly seeing where I was going with this. "If the killer, or killers, take out two or three ballplayers higher up on the food chain than Mark, it improves his chances of making it to the big-league level. He suddenly has notoriety, possibly wealth and stardom. With that comes scores of women hanging on to his every word. Just think of all those groupies following him around like a god. Hell, you don't even have to be good to have the attention, just be on a big-league roster. Your life changes in a heartbeat."

"Exactly, Guinea. He already had a reputation and track record as a lady's man in high school being a star athlete. If he made it in the big leagues, he'd never look back."

"So, what changed?" Sherry asked.

"I'll tell you," Smitty said, picking up where Guinea and I left off. "The murderer saw the relationship growing between Julie and Mark. She was no longer just a piece of ass to Mark. They started to become more seriously involved." Smitty glanced toward me, and as I nodded my head in approval, he continued. I could see that the whole team was now coming together. "When he realizes what is happening, and that time apart won't deter either of them, he, or they, decide that instead of just getting rid of Mark, it would be more beneficial to frame him for the murders."

"But why frame him? Wouldn't it just be easier to kill him?" asked Dewayne.

"If they kill Mark, Julie goes into mourning, loving and adoring him even more. They can't compete with him now, much less his ghost. So, they frame him, make him look like a nut job consumed with greed and fame. With him alive, the betrayal of their love is a dagger in her heart. Sick thinking, I know, but sick minds come up with sick shit!!!"

"Your right, Guinea. It was a brilliant Idea in his, or their, twisted minds. A win-win, however it shakes out.

Julie is left in Front Royal and they are left to pick up the pieces of Julie's broken heart."

"So who's the killer, Mike?" Dewayne asked with a look of bewilderment.

"That, my friend, is the million-dollar question. I can tell you who it isn't."

"Well, I guess that's a start," Dewayne replied.

"I know we can rule out Mark, even though he has plenty of motive, to move up the minor-league-ladder.

"You're right, Mike. After dealing with him in O.C., it doesn't seem feasible, unless he's as dumb as the day is long, and I don't get that vibe from him. Even though he looked really good at first. Now, I just don't see it anymore. I was following the path that the killer was laying." Guinea said

"We all were, Guinea," Smitty replied.

"I think we can take the Glasgow's out of the equation. They certainly have the experience and resources, but no motive to do it."

"I disagree, Mike. What an elaborate ruse, to make it appear that their grandson is behind it, only to paint the picture we are all looking at now. They throw the blame on one of the rivals for his girlfriend's affections, all the while clearing a path for him to achieve his dreams of playing major league baseball. It's high risk, but with that comes high reward," Sherry said.

"That's an interesting theory, and very elaborate, and I'm sure, over their careers, they've cooked up some doozies. But, I can't see them putting their only grandson in harm's way."

"You're probably right, Mike. I'm sure they both belong in a prison somewhere around the world for some crime, but not here for this one. I just wanted to explore all the angles and possibilities and not rush to judgment."

"Hey, Sherry, anything is possible, and those two are some real slick willies," Guinea responded.

"So, that leaves the three brothers. One's a cop and has the resources, plus he's a sniper, but he's not the brightest guy in the world. Brother number two has the brains and knows all about electronics, and from all reports, thinks he's all that and more. Then there is brother number three, who is a motor head, but little if no self-esteem. However, all three bring something to the table. Smitty, I want you to find out what they all drive, and what other vehicles they have access to. Also, check if any vehicles worked on at the body shop fit the description of those seen at the crime scenes. The rest of us will keep digging for as much information on our trio as we can. First thing tomorrow, Freddie, Guinea, and I will go to Front Royal and formally introduce ourselves to our boys and see who blinks first."

"Mike, do you think that all of the brothers could be involved?" Dewayne asked.

"Anything is possible, and at this point, it kind of looks that way to me. Not that I think it makes any sense. What is the end game - knock each other off in the end? If I had to bet, I'd put my money on the cop for the O.C. kill. He's a sniper with a military background and he also has Intel at his disposal. But we'll have most, if not all of the answers by this time tomorrow night."

"That's all I wanted to hear," Dewayne replied.

Chapter 57

We all were to meet at the Naval Bagel on Taylor Avenue at 5 am to get an early start and to beat the metro area traffic. I was surprised to see all the hustle and bustle that early in the morning as I waited for Freddie and Guinea at the plaza. Workers for Graul's Market were already arriving to work in preparation for their eight o'clock opening, and the Naval Bagel was already busy, with people shuffling in and out at a feverish pace. After Guinea and Freddie arrived a short time later, we went in, got our breakfast to go, and were on our way.

As we piled into my F-250, we all had the feeling that by the end of the day, we'd have a firm grip on which one of the three brothers was the killer. As we took the route 50 west on-ramp, we started to talk about how we were going to question the three suspects. We all had different ideas on how to proceed, and, after much debate, we decided that the best way to proceed was an all-out frontal attack. We were going to question the three brothers separately. Guinea and Freddie were going to take the lead, and then I would come in and mop it up. It was my responsibility to point the finger at the other two brothers, in hopes that the one we were questioning would roll on his siblings to save his own ass.

Guinea and Freddie were going to have to press hard and get right in their faces in order for the two that didn't do it believe that they were about to be charged with the murders. They were going to be made aware that Maryland had the death penalty, and that we were going to be seeking it. Basically, we're going to have to scare the living shit out of them.

We were just passing the Warrenton exit on route 66 when both my phone and Guinea's started ringing almost simultaneously. We both answered our phones. On the other end of mine was the Warren County Sheriff's Department, Sheriff Matt Lineweaver. He knew we had been considering Mark Newman for the murders of the ballplayers. When we first went to Front Royal, we paid a courtesy call to his office to let him know we were in the area, what we were doing there, and what our intentions were. At the time, he thought we were way off base on our thinking, but had offered to help in any way he or his department could. After a brief, one-sided conversation, I hung up and pressed down on the accelerator.

As Guinea hung up his phone, he gave me a grim grin and said, "Smitty just called and said there has been a night-long hostage situation…"

"… that resulted in a shooting at the Glasgow's home early this morning. Sheriff Lineweaver just called to inform me that his department and the Virginia State Police were on the scene as we spoke, and that one of his officers is there securing the area."

"Mike, why do you always interrupt and steal my thunder," Guinea deadpanned.

"So much for our best laid plans," I said, as I flicked on the emergency lights and pressed the pedal further to the metal.

We arrived at the Glasgow's home on Thunderbird Lane some thirty minutes later. As we approached the long lane that lead to their home, we saw a sea of police cruisers from both the Virginia State Police and the Warren County Sheriff's Department. We were instructed to pull over by a local sheriff. Upon doing so, the uniformed officer approached us and told us the road was closed, due to a police emergency. I handed him my credentials, as Guinea and Freddie flashed theirs in plain view for the officer to see. I proceeded to tell him that Sheriff Lineweaver had informed us of the situation, and that this might be tied to a case we were working in Maryland.

With that, he nodded and said, "We've been expecting you. If you will follow me, I'll take you to our command center to meet with Sheriff Lineweaver.

As he got in his patrol car, I phoned Angelia Gonzales direct and, as promised, told her to get down here with her film crew a.s.a.p. if she wanted to be the lead in perhaps the biggest ongoing murder case in the country.

After many thank you's from my newest ally in the press corps, we rounded the bend in the lane and came upon the house at the top of the Glasgow's driveway. As we approached, we noticed officers in crouched positions scurrying around. Closer, toward the house, we saw paramedics being escorted and shielded by officers as they made their way into a house that we soon learned was owned by the three brothers; the same house which Sharon had told us about earlier in the week that was paid for by the Glasgow's.

The officer who we followed in now stepped out of his cruiser and cautiously approached our vehicle. He told us to be careful as we exited the truck, and that the abductors had their sights on everyone.

As we made our way to the house and entered the foyer, there was a set of steps to our right that led upstairs. Further to the right of that was what seemed to be a large living room. As we walked past it, we couldn't help but notice that the paramedics were busy at work on someone. Continuing down the hallway, we entered the kitchen, where a group of officers sat and hovered over the kitchen table in the center of the room.

Upon entering the room, the officer who had been escorting us said, "Sheriff Lineweaver, the officers from Maryland are here."

"Gentlemen, we are glad you could make it to our little corner of hell. It seems we have a situation here that, in all honesty, I don't see ending well. Unfortunately for me, this came to a head in my jurisdiction. I know all the principals in this play, but you seem to have written the script. So, now I'll ask you, how is this going to play out?"

"Well, Sheriff, I don't think we've written any script. In fact, we just last night narrowed it down to three potential suspects, and were on our way up here to shake the trees for them when we received your call."

"You mean to tell me your news conference was a ruse?"

"So, you saw it?"

"Detective, the whole damn nation saw it."

"Well, sir, I meant what I said about having an arrest and it looks as if we will. It kind off played out the way I thought it might, with our suspect panicking into a mistake. But in a way you're right, I was banking on the murderer getting spooked by the announcement that an arrest was imminent. It was a calculated move I admit, but it seems to have paid off. But to call it a ruse," I paused, then said, "Well, maybe it was."

"You may have thought it was calculated, but you didn't consider two of my citizens putting the pieces together with the information you inadvertently gave them.

They then decided to use that information and confront the principals. Now, both of my upstanding, not to mention pillars in this community, are being held hostage, along with an innocent girl. Is this how you do police work in Maryland, by putting three innocents in harm's way, just to get an arrest?"

"Wait a fucking minute pal, you're way out of line. I bet your two outstanding citizens our the Glasgows, and I bet if you did a little homework you would be shocked to learn that they probably have more kills than the entire history of your police force," Guinea said as he muscled his way toward the sheriff.

I quickly tried to reduce the tension of the situation, "Guinea, it's alright. Look sheriff, you're right. I wanted to spook him, but I never foresaw this. The important thing now is, how do we defuse this situation without anybody else getting hurt?"

"I agree, detective. Let's start over, and please, call me Matt."

"Sounds good. I'm Mike, and this is my partner, Roger Ginavan, but we just call him Guinea for short, and that gentleman over there is Freddie Hunt."

With the pleasantries, over and the tension somewhat defused, I asked, "Well, Matt, where do we stand?"

"How about I let you hear it directly from the horse's mouth. Will you follow me, please?"

The sheriff led us back down the hallway to the room adjacent to the staircase, where we had earlier seen the paramedics.

As we entered the room, the sheriff asked the EMT how he was doing.

The EMT replied, "He has a serious concussion, with some fluid coming out of his left ear. The bullet wound to his left calf was clean; it went right through. He should be fine."

"Can we talk to him?"

"We were getting ready to transport him, but I can't see any harm in it."

The sheriff waved us over. Upon seeing him, I knew immediately who he was from the pictures that Smitty had shown us. It was Kevin James, a.k.a. Buck, our auto body man, lying on the gurney, looking as if he had one serious hangover.

"Buck, these gentlemen our detectives from Maryland. I want you to tell them everything you told me, and try to be specific. Don't leave anything out," the sheriff instructed.

"I recognize you. You're the cop that's been all over the TV. You come off like a real asshole, like you're a know it all."

"Well, that may be true, but this asshole may put you on death row for all these murders."

"I never killed anybody, mister," Buck responded in a defensive tone.

"At the very least, you'll do a lot of time for being an accessory after the fact, which should get you a minimum of twenty years, don't you think Guinea?"

"I'm thinking more like thirty-five, Mike," Guinea said.

We had started to put the fear of God in him.

"Wait a minute, mister, I just told you I had nothing to do with it."

"Doesn't matter, you're still going to go down for it. The State Prosecutor and the citizens of Maryland are going to want heads to roll, and yours my friend, is the first one on the chopping block. Unless, of course, you can possibly help us. In turn, I can go to my state's attorney and say that you're really not that bad of a guy and ask him to give you a break."

"I'll tell you all that I can," Buck said as his demeanor suddenly changed.

"Good, so why don't you start at the beginning. Take your time and just remember as much as you can. Even the slightest detail may be able to help us."

"That's exactly what the sheriff said to me earlier. Is that the first page of every cop's manual?"

"Buck, why don't you just tell us all you know. And for your own good, I'd stop with the smart remarks. My friends over there really don't appreciate your humor, and they are both real tight with the state's attorney."

Buck nodded, then started, "Well, just like every other morning, I got up, made a cup of coffee, and got dressed. I started to go to the Knotty Pine, but when I went outside, I noticed that Billy's truck was gone."

Guinea interrupted, "What kind of truck does he have?"

"it's a G.M.C. extended cab. It's dark blue, with four beautiful Mickey Thompsons on it. We all have them, why you ask?" He paused, then said, "It's out front, isn't it?"

Freddie took his cue and went to take a look.

I asked, "Is it odd that Billy would leave that early in the morning?"

"Hell, yeah, he doesn't open his store 'til 10 o'clock in the morning. He's never up that early! I already told the chief all of this."

"I know, but please go on."

Just then, Freddie came back in and said, "I see a black G.M.C. down by the Glasgow's."

Buck responded, "It's blue, what are you, color blind?"

"From this distance, it looks like its black to me, pal."

As Freddie said that, Guinea and I just looked at each other as if we werc reading each other's mind.

"Well, I get to the Knotty Pine and, low and behold, there's Billy's truck sitting right there in the parking lot. So, I pound what's left of my coffee and head on in. Once I get inside, I see Julie at his table, pouring him a cup of coffee. So, I go over and help myself to a seat. Billy must have gotten up on the wrong side of the bed, because he got really bent when I accidentally spilled a little bit of his coffee as I was sitting down. He was really agitated."

"What happened next?"

"I ordered my breakfast, and he made some smart-ass comments about my food intake, and then we just talked."

"About what?"

"About some glue that he had me mix up for him. It almost caught me and the whole house on fire."

Interrupting, the sheriff said, "You never mentioned that when we talked earlier."

"What did he say when you mentioned the glue?" I asked.

"Like I said, it was highly flammable and it almost caught me on fire. I was pissed, so I asked him what the hell it was, and what did he use it for. As always, he said he used it at work."

"What do you mean, as always?" Guinea asked.

"Well, for the past couple of months he's had me make up all kinds of concoctions."

Freddie asked, "When did you make up the glue?"

"I finished late Saturday night."

"What happened after you questioned him about the glue?" I asked.

"Well, Julie comes back to the table and tells me that maw-maw and pa-paw want us to meet them here this evening. But I couldn't wait, so I asked Julie why they wanted to meet, and she told me that they thought they knew who was committing the murders."

"Did they invite Billy to the meeting?" Freddie asked.

"Julie didn't ask him to come, so I guess not."

"Okay, what happened when you got here?"

"Maw-maw and pa-paw were here, then my brother Brady arrived about five minutes later."

"You mean your stepbrother the cop?"

"Whatever, Brady and Billy are my brothers. We've been through hell and back together."

"We know all about it, Buck. Was Brady invited? I don't know, I guess he was."

Buck looked at me puzzled, but continued, "Well, when I got here, Pa-paw started grilling me about the glue that was on my hands. I told him just what I had told you. I had never seen him like that before. He was a totally different person. Then he asked Brady about some work that he had done to his truck."

"And what did Brady say?"

"Brady said that he let Billy borrow his truck and that he hit a deer on Skyline Drive."

386

"Did you do the work on Brady's truck?" I asked.

"Yeah, it wasn't a whole lot of damage compared to most other vehicles that have hit deer. But Brady was adamant about getting it fixed right away. Pa-paw asked why Brady wanted the work done so fast. Billy said that Brady didn't want to ride around with his truck looking like shit." Then pa-paw asked if there was a lot of dear fur on the truck at the point of impact?" "Well, was it? Freddie asked. Honestly, I never gave it a second thought at the time, but no there wasn't, and there always is.

"Buck, you never mentioned this to me," the sheriff said.

"You never asked," Buck replied.

Interrupting, I said, "What else, Buck?" Then Brady knocked on the door. Maw-maw then started in on Brady, asking if Billy had honed his shooting skills? I knew where she was going with this, so I was quick to answer, before Brady had a chance, and I told her no."

"Care to explain?" Guinea asked.

"Sure, detective. I knew what this meeting was about, and I had read the papers and seen the TV. The shot that killed the kid in Frederick was almost 2000 meters away, and I now for a fact that Billy could never in a million years make that shot! I only know of five people in this area that would even attempt it, and four were in the room."

"So, Mark was there, also?" I asked.

"No, just maw-maw, pa-paw, Brady, Julie, and me.

The sheriff laughed and said, "Not in your wildest dreams, Buck, but I can confirm the other three. In fact, Brady's our designated shooter, if ever needed."

"Where's Mark now?" Freddie asked.

"Julie said he went to Baltimore to see a hitting instructor and would be back sometime today. He figured that once this mess was cleared up he'd be back with one of the minor-league teams."

"Good, that means at least he's out of harm's way. So, what did the Glasgow's do?" I asked.

"Pa-paw stood up and came right up to me and looked me straight in the eye, nose to nose, and said, 'You have the accelerant on your hands, you may even have been able to take the shot, you had access to the trucks, and to my surprise, you've got the guts to kill up close and personal.' I couldn't believe what I was hearing. Pa-paw was accusing me of these murders. I began to go postal. I told him that it wasn't me, and I was being set up. He said, "Sure you were, just like you were trying to set up my boy." Just then, Billy came through the door. I went right

388

at him and screamed, "You set me up after all I've done for you." I Tackling him, we rolled around, and I managed to get up and was going at him again when, suddenly, I felt a sharp burning sensation in my leg. I turned around and saw Brady with his service revolver in his hand. I didn't even hear the shot. I panicked and made my way to the door. Everything was going in slow motion. I made it outside, and remember stumbling as I was going down the steps. Then I awoke to see those two guys standing over me." Buck said, as he pointed two Warren County sheriffs standing in the door way.

"So, how were you notified, sheriff?"

"Two little girls were playing in the woods when they heard the shot. They ran toward the house and saw Buck stumbling out the door. Then they ran home and their mother called us. We called the paramedics, and when we got here, the officers and the paramedics were already here. Their station is just down 211, about a mile from here. When we arrived, we started to surround the house. I was walking down the lane when my cell rang. It was Brady on the other end. He told me that if I valued my officers' lives, as well as mine, we needed to pull back. So, that's exactly what I did!"

"Well, that pretty much explains the sniper kills and the killing in Ocean City. It seems our brothers are working together," Guinea said.

"If that's the case, what I can't figure is, were they planning on sharing the Wines girl?" the sheriff asked.

Buck suddenly spoke up and said, "We use to get drunk and watch Julie and Mark have sex. We use to joke that, if we could get Mark out of the way, we could all compete for her love."

"You sick," Guinea said.

"I'm not the sick one. I only fantasized about it, but those two seem to have acted on it. But thinking about it, this could really work out for me. I'm sure they're waiting for Mark to arrive, and when he does, they'll probably kill him. Then you guys will either lock them both up or take them out, and at the end of the day, it will just be me and Julie."

"You, my friend, have some serious issues that will be addressed. And yes, you are without a doubt sick," I responded. "Sheriff, have you been able to put eyes on them?"

"No, not yet. I'm a little apprehensive to get my men too close. But, we do have the perimeter surrounded. And everybody is trying to see what's going on."

"Buck, where did you and your brothers go to watch Julie and Mark when they were intimate?"

"Here."

"Where were they?"

"Maw-maw and pa-paws."

"Okay, smart ass, you want to tell how and where?" Guinea demanded, putting a hard squeeze on his wounded leg.

"Shit, man, you're hurting me. I'll tell you. Just go up the stairs, down the hall, and when you're almost at the end, look up. You'll see a trap door that's latched. Unlatch it and pull it down and go up the fucking steps, asshole."

Guinea, Freddie, the sheriff, and I headed up the steps. The sheriff asked the paramedics to stay there with Buck and continue to care for him, in case we needed them or him. In the back of my mind, I was wondering why he got so little information from Buck, especially how to get eyes on the Glasgow's house.

We got to the end of the hallway, pulled down the door, and climbed up the steps. I was the first one up, and it kind of reminded me of a teenager's club house, with either Playboy or Penthouse posters on the walls and skin magazines scattered about. At the end of the room was a table with three chairs. On top of the table were a couple candles, three sets of field glasses, and assorted empty beer cans. Behind the table was a large, wood- framed window that over looked the Glasgow's home. We picked up the glasses and looked. I spotted the Glasgow's and the Wines girl sitting on the couch, tied up, facing the window. There was a figure to their left facing them.

Suddenly, Guinea shouted, "Gun - second floor at 11 o'clock."

It was to the right, above the bay window that gave us the view of the Glasgow's. We noticed the second figure was looking through the gun's scope as we took cover.

"How did you spot him, Guinea?" the sheriff asked.

"From the reflection of the sun on the scope."

"Good, we can use that to our advantage for a couple more hours, but we will lose the sun early due to the tall pines surrounding their home. Plus, the sun is in their eyes. It will be difficult for them to see us for the time being. We will be able to see them far better than they can see us for a while," the sheriff said.

Freddie grabbed Guinea's binoculars and carefully took a peak.

As he did, I asked the obvious question. "Gentlemen. what our options?"

"Whatever we decide, we have maybe three hours max, to do it. Two hours with the sun in their eyes. Once the sun goes down, then they will have the advantage. The sight lines will change, plus, under darkness, they may be able to escape via the river. Right now, I have my men all along the river banks and around the woods. But those boys have lived here all their lives and they know these woods far better than my men or I," the sheriff stated.

Chapter 58

... *Enlightenment*

"So, what's this all about?" Julie asked as she and Buck where greeted at the door by the Glasgow, "Please come in and we will try to explain and get to the bottom of this mess and make sense of it all." Victoria said as both she and her husband, Vladimir, ushered them through the door. "I guess you're going to try to convince us that Mark didn't commit all those murders", Buck said.

"We are going to do more then convince you, we are going to prove to you that our grandson didn't do what some simple-minded people, like yourself, think he has done," Vladimir said in response to Bucks comment. "Gentleman I want you both to just calm down, this will be a civil discussion." Victoria responded.

"Buck, have you noticed anything unusual in the way your brothers have been acting or behaving? Victoria asked. "No mam, they both seem to be the same ass holes to me. Why do you ask?" Well we heard you did some repair work on one of your brother's trucks. Something about hitting a dear is that correct Buck?" Victoria asked. "Yes mam, Billy hit a deer with Brady's truck and came to the shop and had it repaired. So, what's the big deal we get at least one a week, triple that during rut season" Buck said, just then there was a frantic knock on the door. Vladimir went to answer it.

"Well Brady what brings you down here?" Vladimir asked, as he noticed a shadow further down the driveway. "I saw both Buck's and Julie's trucks and I wanted to see what was going on. "Look who stopped by my dear." Blinking twice as he informed his wife that they had another guest. She, in turn, placed two fingers on her lips before she spoke.

"Well Brady, we're glad you could make it" Victoria said, catching the uninvited guest of guard. And immediately continuing, "So have you been helping your brother Billy hone his shooting skills?" "Hell, no Billy couldn't hit the broad side of a barn with all the practice in the world." Buck shouted. Immediately Vladimir said, "Buck I guess that leaves just you, what kind of epoxy is that all over your hands and what did you use it for?" Before either could answer, Victoria asked Brady, "Why wasn't there any deer fur on the bumper or fender of your truck?" Again, Vladimir followed suit almost as soon as Victoria had finished her question. "Buck I believe you know a lot more then you are letting on. As he said this, Victoria glanced at her cell phone and noticed that the other person that her husband had warned her about minutes ago, was now on the front porch ease dropping and looking in the front door window, all thanks to the high tech surveillance that was installed by their next uninvited guest. Placing two fingers on her lips again as if she was in deep thought, she began tapping one finger gently against her lips. Her husband immediately took notice.

As all this was going on, Julie sat still completely dumb founded as the two young men were being overwhelmed by all of this. Vladimir stood straight up and approached Buck knowing he had no hand in the murders, but doing his best to bait him and said "Buck that's an accelerant on your hands, used in conjunction with bombs. Plus, you brag you're a great shot. You might have even been able to make the shot that killed that young man in Fredrick. You had access to the trucks and, to my surprise, maybe the guts to kill someone up close and personal"

Buck took the bait just as the Glasgow knew he would and lashed out at his accuser. I had nothing to do with any of these murders, Pa-paw you know I can't make a shot like that at that kind of distance. And I have a hard time skinning animals that are dead much less slicing a living man's throat." Buck said in a fit of hysteria. He started to sob like a child pleading to his parents and continued, "...and the stuff on my hands, Billy made me make that shit up for him." Just then the uninvited guest came barging threw the door. Buck sprang to his feet. Racing toward the door, screaming at Billy that he had set him up, he lowered his shoulder and tackled him driving both to the ground. Buck sprang to his feet like a man possessed. As Billy tried to get up, Buck hit him with a series of left-right combinations that would have made Sugar Ray Leonard proud. Suddenly a shot rang out. Buck collapsed to one knee, screaming in pain. He turned and saw that his brother, Brady, was holding a gun. He managed to get to his feet and go the three feet to the front door expecting to feel another sharp pain that never came, as he exited the house.

Meanwhile Julie was hysterical, screaming at what had just transpired, as the Glasgow just sat and watched the whole episode unfold as they had planned. Billy staggered to his feet screaming at Brady to finish the job. "He's our fucking brother!" Brady yelled. Billy shouted back. "He's not blood, kill him…, you're signing our death warrant… you're ruining my plan."

Vladimir then spoke up. "Billy, your plan was doomed from the beginning."

"Shut the fuck up old man, you don't know shit. I had this scenario all figured out till Brady let Buck walk out the door," Billy said.

"If this was part of your plan then you're really not as smart as you think Billy," Victoria said, then continued, "Why don't you tell us your grand plan Billy."

"You two think you know everything, well your right we committed the murders to set up Mark. We wanted him out of the way, he had everything in life that we wanted and needed. He had everything handed to him on a silver platter. Never a struggle in his life."

397

"He lost his parents," Victoria said. Brady countered, "All we had were two pieces of shit and then we had nothing." At least he had parents then he had you.

"We helped you boys out, we purchased your home, we made sure you had clothes on your backs and food in your bellies. We even bought that expensive surveillance package that we had no use for just to help you get your business off the ground."

Looking at Billy as he spoke before continuing. "We also taught you both how to hunt and fish and fend for yourselves and to become men. We did everything we could for you," Vladimir said.

"You didn't love us, you didn't invite us into your home when mom died and dad walked out. You just went through the motions. To this day, you give us strange looks when we call you pa-paw. Like it disgusts you. You didn't want us to be part of your family," Brady said before Billy abruptly interrupted.

"Fuck this shit, you're as guilty for what's been happening as we are," Billy said as he looked at Julie and then the Glasgow. After Mark got drafted the three of you continued to look at us as second class citizens. Julie, you continued to refuse are advances and you two just never accepted us period. So, we hatched this plan to nudge you in the right direction. With Mark in jail or dead, he'd be out of the way."

"You both are sick. What where you planning to do, both share me?" Julie asked.

"No, we knew you'd decide that fate. The loser would get the wealth. It was a win- win for us," Billy said.

"What on earth are you talking about?" Julie asked.

"With Mark out of the way, they thought we'd leave them our money when we died. Americans' lust and greed," Victoria said, sadly shaking her head. Then she continued, "The last part is a bit of a surprise. But you both should know that you would have been looked after when we were gone.

"It doesn't matter now," Billy said, as the faint sounds of a siren screaming could be heard in the background drawing closer.

"When this started going south, I thought we could pin all of this on you two, if numb nuts over there would have killed Buck. But now we'll play the hand that we've been dealt, said Billy.

"Brady call your boss and tell him we have an arsenal in here and hostages. If he values his life and the other officers' lives, he should stay far away. Tell him we want a plane or some outlandish bullshit. We will make our escape tonight under the cover of darkness," Billy stated.

"How are we going to do that?" Brady asked.

"We live in the canoeing capital of Virginia dumb ass. We know the surroundings better then anybody. We make our way down to the river and float quietly away, "Billy replied.

"That's right the canoes are still tied up on the shore line," Brady said, as a smile crept across his face.

"What about us?" Julie asked.

"Well that's up to you. You do as we say and you live, if you don't ….", was Billy's reply.

"You two will never make it out of here alive," Vladimir said. "If we don't you won't either so I suggest you get with the program old man," Billy countered.

"I've seen this happen many times before Billy. You should listen to Vladimir," Victoria said.

"Sure you have, just shut up maw-maw was Billy replied.

If you only knew, Victoria thought.

Chapter 59

Suddenly we heard a large commotion downstairs. One of the deputies peeked his head up from the steps.

"Sheriff, we have a problem. Mark Newman is downstairs, and, when he saw Buck, he went on him like bees to a hive. We got them separated and they are in separate rooms. What do you want us to do with them?"

Before he could answer, I suggested, "Sheriff, why don't you go ahead and send Buck to the hospital and get some other paramedics here, or at least on standby, in case something goes awry."

"You heard the man, deputy. Get on it."

"Will do, Sheriff."

Then I asked, "Sheriff, have they tried to contact you?"

"No, not at all."

"Well, we should try to open up a line of communication."

"I anticipated that; there should be a command truck outside by now."

"Good, let's get down there and see if we can figure out what their intentions. Can you get two of your officers up here with detective Hunt to keep an eye on the house?" I asked.

"No problem."

"Freddie, give us a heads up if anything out of the ordinary happens."

"Will do."

"Sheriff, I also would like to have a word with Mr. Newman."

"Yeah, I'd like to hear what he has to say myself."

"Hopefully, he may be able to give us some info we can use before we make the call," Guinea chimed in.

When we entered the kitchen, we saw a man who had, just minutes earlier, lost his composure. Now he seemed focused and in control, no doubt a trait he picked up by playing ball or perhaps from his grandparents. Probably the latter.

"Detective Carrier, Jules and my grandparents alright?" Mark asked.

"At the moment, they are. Detective Hunt is watching them as we speak. We are going to try to contact them now to find out their intentions."

"That's a waste of daylight, detective. Billy is no dummy. He knows Maryland has the death penalty, and Brady wants no parts of being a cop in the penitentiary. I'd bet my life they're trying to get my grandparents to tell them where all their money is so they can get out of the country. They're desperate, and they have nothing to lose at this point, and everything to gain. They will wait you out until it gets dark."

"Mark, we've thought of that. I've got deputies all around the house a safe distance back in the woods. Plus, I also have them all up and down the Shenandoah. We're going to do our best to keep them in check."

"Sheriff, you've got to get them out of there right now. Pa-paw had Billy put in all kinds of surveillance equipment to help out his business. There is equipment a mile deep in every direction around the house, plus up and down both banks of the river. Motion detectors, cameras, infrared, you name it, it's out there. Those guys are sitting ducks," Mark pleaded.

"That must have cost your grandparents a small fortune," Guinea said.

"Yeah, about three hundred thousand wasted, because they really didn't need it. Even at their age, they're still both as sharp as tacks and can take care of themselves pretty well."

"If that's the case, how'd they get in the situation they're in now?" Guinea countered.

"You don't know too much about my grandparents, do you? Everything they do is calculated. Don't take their generosity as a sign of weakness."

I interrupted and said, "We know more than you think, Mark."

"How's that detective?"

"We know all about their past, and we know that they have been receiving large payments throughout the years from the C.I.A. for services rendered."

As I was speaking, I looked at the sheriff and watched his jaw drop until he had the look of a basset hound.

"So, I guess you know they bugged your office, and, in all likelihood, got loads of information from you and your team to set this all up?"

Guinea and I just looked at each other knowing we had been screwed.

"You guys leaned on me so hard, I guess they felt they had no choice but to go on the offensive and bring the killers to you. They knew by doing this, it wouldn't make it to the American justice system. And trust me, I know they weren't going to let those that they helped so much get away with trying stab me in the back. My grandparents may have a shady background, but believe me, they're all about family. They defected and left everything they knew in Russia because of my mother."

"I've got one question everyone has forgotten to ask? Why in the world didn't Billy and Brady just grab some cash and leave after Brady shot Buck?" the sheriff asked.

"That's easy – greed. They want it all. They know maw-maw and pa-paw have cash stashed all over the house, and probably buried on the property, as well. Hell, it wouldn't surprise me if they have more cash on hand than the Front Royal Credit Union."

"You got to be kidding," Guinea responded.

"I wish I was. They're not big fans of the American banking system."

"You mean the I.R.S," I deadpanned. "Gentlemen, we are running out of daylight. We need to talk to those boys, and talk to them now. Mark, you wait right here. We'll be back in a few minutes." Leaving the room, I asked the sheriff to put a deputy with him.

As we entered the mobile command, the sheriff immediately got on the phone and called the Glasgow's home. They answered on the first ring, a sure sign of anxiety.

"This is Sheriff Lineweaver. To whom am I speaking?"

"It's your deputy, Brady, sir."

"Brady, you've got yourself into quite a little pickle here, son. How do you suggest we get you and all those in the house out safely?"

"I seriously doubt that's going to happen, sir, unless you pull everyone far back from the perimeter, and I mean far away."

"We can do that, Brady."

"Sheriff, this is what you're going to do - move everybody back right now, at least two miles from the house. Once that is done, I want a State Police chopper to take us to Dulles Airport, where a 727plane full of fuel is running and waiting," said Brady.

"I don't know if I can do that. It's going to take some time, Brady."

"Well, if you can't, you better start getting a lot of body bags together, because we are prepared to take as many of you with us as we can, starting with the three in here. And believe me, pa-paw has a large arsenal in here. We will pick you off one by one, if need be. The clock is ticking. You have until 10 pm. It's your call. Oh, one more thing, why don't you send that son of a bitch Mark

406

down here and I'll be a sport and give you Julie in return. I just hope the superstar is man enough."

"Brady, don't do anything to make the situation any worse than it already is. We can work this out. Give me some time to get back to you with some answers. I will also speak with Mark about a swap, but please give us some time."

"You've got until 10 o'clock", Brady said. With that, the line went dead.

"There is no way we can meet those demands."

"Sheriff, he knows that. He's stalling for time. That's why they never tried to contact you. They're planning on escaping under the cover of darkness. Now we know who the mastermind was behind all those lost lives. Billy is the snake's head. He's calling all the shots. I could tell Brady wasn't speaking freely. He was told what to say. So let's go over our options."

"Obviously, it's best if we keep them in the house with eyes on them. Problem is, we can't get close enough to try and breach the house, and if we could, the loss of the hostages is almost certain. Guinea and I can confirm that they have enough fire power in there to inflict a ton of damage. So, sheriff, do you have a sniper ready?"

"My best sniper is down there, and he's playing for the other team. I have others who say they can make the shot, but if they miss, it's the start of a blood bath."

"Mike, we have no time to call one in. Maybe Freddie could take the shot?"

"Guinea, it's one thing to shoot a deer at that range, but a man is a whole different animal, no pun intended. But, we are short on options. Sheriff, if they make it to the river, where do you think they will come out?"

"My best guess is they'll come out at the River Road entrance, off Kerfoot. But, that may be too obvious. In all honesty, Mark would probably have a better idea than me. This is his neck of the woods. He and the boys have been playing in this area all their lives. Plus, he'd know what kind of toys Vladimir and Victoria have in and around the property."

"Well let's get back to the house and talk to Mark and see what our friends are doing at the bottom of the hill."

As we walked toward the house, I remembered seeing a squad of helicopters flying over Front Royal on one of our previous visits. I asked the sheriff about it and he told me that there is a base in Martinsburg, WV. I knew from our travels that it was about a forty-five minute drive from here, so I figured that it was about twenty minutes' flight here, if we needed them.

Here we ran into a little bit of luck. Sheriff Lineweaver was a Reservist at the base and had the ear of the Company Commander. My thought process was, maybe we could get a sniper and a helicopter to use as a diversion.

As we entered the house, Freddie was coming down the steps to meet us.

Guinea immediately asked him, "Freddie, if need be, could you take a shot at those boys from this distance?"

With hesitation in his voice, Freddie responded, "If I had to."

The way he answered and his body language told me all I needed to know. If he didn't get both of them, then all would be lost and a bloodbath would ensue. He wouldn't be asked to take the shot.

Just then, a voice said, "I definitely can."

As I turned around and saw Mark moving toward us, I had a knee-jerk response, "Hell no."

"Who else have you got, detective? I'm your best option. I've been trained by two world class snipers, and now they need me. And, quite frankly, I'm your only option, detective. I'm a good ballplayer, but I was born for this. There's nobody better. Detective, you're only going to have about five seconds to kill two men. At one second, the bullet will travel eight hundred meters. It will have more impact than a 357 magnum at close range. The shots that need to be taken are roughly 1500 yards, a little over ¾ of a mile. Plus, you must figure in the wind and the humidity, not to mention locating the second target as the first bullet is hitting target number one. There are only a handful of people who can do that, and I assure you, I'm one of them!"

"He has me convinced," Guinea said.

"That's all well and good, but let's see what the sheriff comes up with. Besides, he's too involved. And how will this play out in the court of law, not to mention the press and the court of public opinion?"

"Mike, how's it going to play out if those three hostages in that house die, or a couple of these deputies up here lose their lives and we had the resources to stop it?" Guinea argued.

"I reluctantly agreed with Guinea. We don't have much of a choice, or a lot of time to debate this. I've heard and read a lot about how well this boy can shoot," Freddie chimed in.

The sheriff was listening while he was on the phone. When he ended his conversation, he said, "The good news is, we've got a chopper. But it's a tactical unit, and they have no snipers."

After talking it over with the sheriff, we agreed our hands were tied, and we had no choice but to go with Mark. The final decision was the sheriff's, and he made the call.

We formulated a plan to give us what we hoped was a greater chance of success. We decided to bring in the helicopter and have it hover above the Glasgow's home. I would switch clothes with Mark, add a Kevlar vest to the wardrobe, and start walking down the lane. If all went as planned, they would release Julie.

Their attention would be diverted in four different fronts - the helicopter above them, Julie's release, me walking towards them, and guarding the Glasgow's in the home. It was our hope that, with all that going on, we would gain an advantage. It at least sounded good in theory.

"Detective, where is your truck?" Mark asked.

"Why?" I responded.

"I have to get my rifle."

"What does getting your rifle have to do with my truck?"

"My grandfather hid it above your spare tire back in Ocean City. He knew that you would be in the thick of anything that would happen. He didn't know when or where, but he wanted to cover every scenario. I told you he was smart. He kind of choreographed this whole thing."

I just sat there dumbfounded, and I wasn't alone as I looked at the expressions of all my colleagues in the room. Now we knew what they picked up at the post office when we had a tail on them. I had the feeling they had played us like a fiddle again, and I didn't like the sound of the tone.

The sheriff immediately sent one of his deputies out to my truck to retrieve the rifle. Mark didn't want anybody handling his weapon, but we were fearful that Billy or Brady would see him. They may decide to take a shot the minute he showed his face.

The deputy soon returned with Mark's weapon. Mark reacted like a star struck boy on Christmas morning. As he opened up the duffel bag, he announced its presence as if he was a game show host talking about a brand-new car.

"Gentlemen, this is the Mk 11, the Navy Seals' sniper weapon of choice. She weighs a mere 15.3 pounds, with a caliber of 7.62, firing a whopping 750 rounds per minute with a muzzle velocity of 2,951 feet per second. And, she was made to cover the distance like a hot knife going through a stick of warm butter. She is also nicely equipped with infrared and night vision. I always wanted one of these babies, and maw-maw and pa-paw delivered again. If Oswald would have had this, there would have been no reason for the second shooter on the grassy knoll."

Within seconds, he had the rifle assembled and said, "Just show me where you would like me to take the shots. Anywhere is good, because we have the advantage of shooting down into the valley."

We headed back up to the attic. This was Mark's first time there. He noticed the naked pin-ups, empty beer cans and trash scattered about. Then he saw the table and chairs, along with the binoculars. It became all too clear what this place had been used for, and his response was justified.

"Those sick, perverted bastards! They sat up here and watched us? That's an invasion of not only mine, but my loved one's privacy. And, all the while, they were getting their rocks off. What kind of sick son of a bitch does that?"

"Mark, what they did should be the least of your worries right now. Your loved ones our being held hostage by two men that have no regard for life. You say your grandparents choreographed all of this, so undoubtedly, they are counting on you to stay focused and do the job. Now, can you still do that?"

"Yes sir, I can, and will, detective."

"Good, then let's get to work and go over the plan. As I was putting on the Kevlar vest, I laid out the plan. "Sheriff, get on the horn and have the helicopter on standby. Then call Billy and tell him Mark has agreed to the swap. Tell him we'll send Mark down as soon as we see Julie step out the door. The minute she steps out the door, we'll have the helicopter hover directly over the Glasgow's house. The noise alone should be very distracting to them." As Guinea adjusted my ear piece and microphone, I continued to go through it, step by step. "Now, at that point, I'll start walking down as Julie is walking up. With their eyes on the both of us, plus the helicopter overhead, I would think that would be the most opportune time to take your shots, Mark. What, if anything, can we do to make it easier on you?"

"Keep that helicopter high in the sky. Maw-maw has those wind chimes all over the house, so judging the wind and distance shouldn't be an issue. Plus, it's a dry and high sky. All that is left to do is contact pa-paw to tell him it's a go."

"What do you mean, contact your grandfather?" Guinea asked.

"As soon as I get set up, I'll dot his eye with the infrared. He'll know it's me, and we will be able to communicate."

"How?"

"Simply by the blink of an eye. When they were both in the war, that's how the snipers were trained to communicate with one another. We use to do it all the time when we went hunting. I'll find a fixed object that only he or maw-maw can see, and I'll blink it with Morse Code. Pa-paw will respond with the blink or two of his eyes."

"You got to be friggin' kidding me. Morse Code?" Guinea said in awe.

"That's fantastic. When the sheriff calls, Billy will take his eyes off Mark's grandparent's, then Mark can notify his grandfather and let him know what we're up to. Maybe he can get some more inside intel, as well. Freddie, do you still have eyes on our targets?"

"Sure do, Mike. The shooter is still upstairs, second window to the right. The hostages are still on the couch in the living room and the perp is now looking out the bay window with his back to the hostages."

"All right, let's do this. Sheriff, get the chopper in here. Then call Billy and tell him to release Julie, and that you're sending Mark down. Try to drag the conversion out. Mark, get in contact with your grandfather as the sheriff is talking."

Mark nodded his head as he adjusted his sights and checked the wind and down angle. He turned his ragged maroon ball cap with the white F.R. logo bill backwards.

415

Guinea suggested that he give me the hat to make me look more like him.

"I'm sorry. I can't do that, detective. I've been wearing this cap since I made varsity my freshman year of high school. It's my good luck charm."

"You don't wear it when you play now," Guinea argued.

"But I always have a piece of it in my back pocket, or under the bill of my playing hat. Besides, I've never taken a shot without it on."

"Guinea, let him wear the hat. I don't want him to be worried and miss. I know all about ballplayers and their superstitions. I don't want to be the cause of him losing his mojo and me losing my life."

"Detective, I've got one in my cruiser. It's not as beat up as Mark's, and it has the wildcat logo instead of the F.R., but I seriously doubt they'll notice the difference," a young deputy about Mark's age said.

"Great, problem solved, thank you deputy."

With that settled, I asked the sheriff to make the call. He told me the helicopter was already inbound and would be here on cue. He then dialed the Glasgow's home. As we kept our eyes glued to the house, we listened intently. As soon as the sheriff started talking, we spotted

416

Mark's red dot, first it was on Vladimir's knee, then his chest. Victoria was the first to notice it on her husband's knee. By the smile and nod of her head as she gestured to her husband, she knew it was Mark. Billy, as luck would have it, had his back to his hostages. Then the light hit Vladimir's right eye. We had made contact - *thank God, I thought to myself.*

We watched Vladimir slightly tilt his head as he started blinking in rapid succession. Mark responded by blinking the light on Victoria's left foot. It was amazing to watch them work in perfect harmony, like two well-oiled machines.

Meanwhile, the sheriff was explaining the process to Billy as I had presented it, but more importantly, he was keeping Billy occupied while Mark conversed with his grandfather. Billy agreed to the plan, with one slight difference. Mark, or should I say I, had to appear first before he would release Julie. With that agreed upon, the sheriff told Billy the helicopter was en-route and would be here shortly. All that was left to do was execute the plan.

As if on cue, the deputy returned with the ball cap. Putting it on, I pulled it down to shield as much of my face as possible. Guinea did the sound check. I said good luck to Mark as Freddie patted me on the back and Guinea gave me the thumbs up.

We heard the helicopter approaching as I headed down the attic steps. As soon as it was hovering above us, I opened the door and walked out onto the porch. I knew I was a sitting duck. I held my head down low as we waited for Julie to emerge from the Glasgow's home. It seemed as if I waited forever. *Has the shooter realized I wasn't Mark? Am I about to die?* A million thoughts ran through my mind. I grew more apprehensive by the second.

Finally, Guinea's voice came through my ear piece. What he said wasn't what I wanted to hear, but it didn't surprise me at all.

"Mike they're moving the hostages and we don't have eyes on them."

"Find them, Guinea. Do you have eyes on the shooter?"

"We've got nothing...wait."

A pause for what seemed like an eternity, then suddenly, "They're upstairs in the window that the shooter vacated," I heard Freddie say in the background.

"Do you see the shooter? Do you see the shooter? Guinea!" I all but screamed.

"No, Mike, we haven't located him yet."

"Screw this, Guinea, I'm going to draw him out." My adrenaline was pumping so fast, but I felt strangely at ease as I stepped off the porch and started heading down the lane. With the noise of the helicopter above, everything seemed so surreal to me.

"Mike, get back in the house! Mike, you fucking idiot, get back in the fucking house now, goddamn you," Guinea screamed in vain. "Freddie, find that fucking shooter or Mike's a dead man."

"I've got nothing, Guinea, I've got nothing," yelled Freddie.

Then Mark said, calmly, "I've acquired his scope and barrel. Look for the sun's glare off his scope. Third window from the right, bottom right side corner."

"All I see is Julie," Sheriff Lineweaver screamed.

"I know."

It was all Mark said as he squeezed the trigger. The next chain of events happened so fast that it was all over in a matter of seconds. Mark had taken his shot, but it arrived a second too late. Brady had his target in his sights and started to squeeze the trigger. When he saw a flash of red light, he got off his shot, but the red light would be the last thing he would ever see. The bullet that Mark had fired pierced the scope lens and entered his left eye socket. The back of his head exploded, chunks of his skull and brain matter spewed all over Julie as she stood up and screamed.

Mike, walking down the lane, heard the volley of the shots being fired. He felt pain as one shot blew him back into the brush along the side off the road.

Guinea, seeing that his best friend was hit, pulled his service revolver and raced down the attic steps in an attempt to help his partner. As he reached the door that lead to the porch, he began firing wildly at the Glasgow's home racing to save his friend, not knowing that the threat had already been eliminated in a matter of seconds.

Mark took the second shot just as the first one hit its target. That shot hit Billy in the left shoulder as he turned to help his mortally wounded brother. Vladimir rose to his feet, his hands still bound together, hitting Billy with such force that it pinned him straight up against the window.

Vladimir's bound hands seemed to be holding Billy's neck up, as his own face was just inches away from Billy's left ear. Vladimir could be seen whispering something to Billy as Mark again fired. The bullet struck Billy at the base of his brain, spraying blood and bone fragments everywhere. It looked, at first, that Vladimir may have been hit. He had blood all over him. But as he let Billy's limp body go, we could see that he was all right.

"Did you see that shit? Did you see that shit? That was fucking unbelievable, totally unbelievable. I've never seen shooting like that," Freddie screamed, as he jumped up and down.

Mark rose to his feet and wiped the sweat off his forehead with his ball cap and asked, "Where are detectives Carrier and Ginavan?

Freddie began yelling out the window for us. The bullet that Brady got off had missed my head, but glanced off the breast plate of my vest, knocking me back and out. When I awoke, I saw Guinea hovering over me, screaming my name and trying to find an entry wound. I finally convinced him that, besides a couple bruised or broken ribs, I was fine. I asked Guinea to acknowledge Freddie and help me to the house. As we entered the house, we were greeted by the sheriff, Freddie, Mark, and a slew of deputies.

Guinea turned to Mark and said, "I owe you an apology, and I want to thank you for saving my friend's life. If you wouldn't have fired when you did, that round would have killed him."

"I knew I was in a precarious position. There was a lot to compute, with Julie behind Brady, Billy and my family to his left, and the detective walking down the lane trying to be a super hero," Mark said.

I interrupted and said, "You did good kid, you did really good. Would you like to go see your family?"

"I sure would, detective."

"Well, let's go see them. I have a few questions I'd like to ask them."

"I bet you do, detective."

Just then two men approached seemingly out of nowhere. "You won't be asking the Glasgow anything!" The man wearing a plaid shirt, jeans and cowboy boots said.

"Who the fuck are you?" Guinea asked as the other man wearing a suit and tie reached into his jacket and pulled out his ID, flashing F.B.I. credentials. "Well who's the cowboy barking orders?" Guinea asked, "He's a special liaison," the F.B.I. agent responded. "You mean C.I.A. don't you," I said. "Yeah, something like that" The cowboy said, "Well pal, you have absolutely no authority inside the continental United States so what you say really doesn't mean a hill of beans," I responded to the C.I.A. agent.

"Yeah, you're right but he does," jestering toward the F.B.I. agent before continuing. "The American Government is full of loop holes and he is mine! So here is how this is going to play out gentleman. You can ask the Glasgows about what happened in the house but that's it, period. Anything else is a matter of national security.

"You've got to be kidding," I said.

"No I'm not, unless you want Homeland, the F.B.I. not to mention our friends on the hill, crawling up your ass.

Hell, they may even have the IRS poking around your personal finances if you don't play ball."

"So, I strongly suggest you just sit back and take all the credit and accolades and be grateful that these guys are off the street."

We didn't like it, but the cowboy got his point across. However, I had to vent so I asked the F.B.I. agent, "Tell me, what does it feel like to be a puppet on a string."

"Fuck you," was all he said.

Almost as an afterthought, Guinea said, "Mark if that baseball thing doesn't work out, you can always team up with us. I'm sure we can find a place for you."

"It's a good thought detective, but if my baseball thing doesn't work out, I think my grandparent's friends at Langley may have dibs on me. But, you never know.

Just then, Freddie caught up to us and said, "I just got off the phone with Bobby. It looks like we're going to have to leave right away. We've got a problem. I got word that they found Molly's car. Preliminary reports from the officers at the scene seem to suggest foul play. They say it looks like she's been abducted. The scene seems to suggest there was some sort of a struggle. The door was open and the keys were still in the ignition."

"You've got to be kidding me," I said. "How could this happen and why?" We all looked at each other in stunned silence. Guinea started walking away, shaking his head and staring at the ground, as he mumbled ...

"God, damn it".

Made in the USA
Middletown, DE
08 November 2017